CW01460803

Sitting Tenant

Sitting Tenant

Rosie Radcliffe

The
Book
Guild

First published in Great Britain in 2025 by
The Book Guild Ltd
Unit E2 Airfield Business Park,
Harrison Road, Market Harborough,
Leicestershire. LE16 7UL
Tel: 0116 2792299
www.bookguild.co.uk
Email: info@bookguild.co.uk

Copyright © 2025 Rosie Radcliffe

The right of Rosie Radcliffe to be identified as the author of this
work has been asserted by them in accordance with the
Copyright, Design and Patents Act 1988.

All rights reserved. No part of this publication may be
reproduced, transmitted, or stored in a retrieval system, in any form or by any means,
without permission in writing from the publisher, nor be otherwise circulated in
any form of binding or cover other than that in which it is published and without
a similar condition being imposed on the subsequent purchaser.

The manufacturer's authorised representative in the EU
for product safety is Authorised Rep Compliance Ltd,
71 Lower Baggot Street, Dublin D02 P593 Ireland (www.arccompliance.com)

This work is entirely fictitious and bears no resemblance to any persons living or dead.

Typeset in 10.5pt Adobe Garamond Pro

Printed and bound in Great Britain by 4edge Limited

ISBN 978 1835743 287

British Library Cataloguing in Publication Data.
A catalogue record for this book is available from the British Library.

For my wonderful daughters - Kate, Hannah and Jessica.

ONE

Discharge Assessment (redacted summary copy for patient)
Thornbank Psychiatric Unit
York Teaching Hospitals NHS Trust

Patient: Mattea Francesca Lombardi (prefers to be known as Mattie)
Age: Thirty-one
Occupation: Maths lecturer
Patient History:

Admitted from York General Hospital during a severe depressive episode beyond the scope of A & E Crisis Resolution Team.

On admission, patient acutely distressed and experiencing auditory hallucinations despite compliance with treatment regime. Following a reassessment of medication and implementation of a new drug programme, in recent weeks Mattea has shown significant improvement and from being withdrawn and agitated, has become engaged and social, speaks calmly and makes consistent eye contact.

In partnership with her named nurse, she has developed coping strategies for integration back into community living. She demonstrates insight into her condition and has not repeated

1

her earlier claim that the voices she hears are real. She now appears to accept them as part of her diagnosed condition and has reported no further episodes.

Mattea has agreed to cooperate with newly appointed key community worker, Georgina Frost, from Mental Health Services, Blackpool and Fylde, who will be contacting the patient when she moves to her new home. There is some concern about the psychological and emotional impact of her relocation plans but with appropriate supervision, she seems strong enough to negotiate this major life change.

Conclusion: Recommended for supported discharge.

I kept my expression appropriately solemn as this form was handed to me along with a paper bag of medication, and some final words of wisdom on coping outside in the big bad world. Inside me, a bubble of excitement and happiness at finally being let out waited to explode. I wanted to jump up and down shouting "free at last", but it wouldn't have gone down well with the staff.

It wasn't altogether their fault that I'd been bored out of my tree on the unit, and the nurses had (mostly) been kind and supportive. The truth is that being cooped up in the hospital, with no autonomy and too much daytime TV, made me crazy to the point of wanting to beat the doors down with my head. Full disclosure: the me who was admitted to hospital back in January desperately needed to be there. I'd been existing in shades of grey, couldn't stop crying, and was so overwhelmed as to see no point in even trying to get better. With time and patience, a medication adjustment had done the business, and I was functioning almost normally again. Yes, the edges of sensory experience and thinking were somewhat dulled, like a knife with a blunted edge, but that seemed to go with the territory whatever pills they gave me.

The letter about inheriting the house arrived while I was still an inpatient, and it was as if a fairy had waved a magic wand. Everything changed, and I went from half empty to half full, as my imagination exploded with the possibilities the unexpected legacy offered. I could begin again on the other side of the country, in a small coastal town, and make an anonymous fresh start. Best of all, outside the hospital I could organise the days to suit myself and not be woken up at stupid o'clock to take tablets.

'Lucky you, inheriting a property,' said Reuben, the nurse who was with me when I opened the solicitor's letter. 'I can't even afford a deposit, not round here. Were you close to your aunt?'

My unalloyed delight at the news must have suggested that I wasn't grief-stricken with loss.

'Didn't even know she existed,' I told him. 'It's so weird that Mamma never mentioned having a sister, let alone one who would leave me a house.'

Visions of life by the sea carried associations of ice cream, sand in your knickers and the tang of seaweed. The prospect brought with it the same fizzing excitement as childhood holidays at Whitby and Scarborough, though maybe a bucket and spade wouldn't be required in my new home.

Reuben looked at my ecstatic face and said, 'I went to Lytham St Annes on holiday once. It's on the upmarket side, kind of "gin and Jaguar belt".'

No seaside rock then, and my preference for living in tracksuits and trainers might not meet with approval either.

'What are you saying? You think I'm not an appropriate class of resident? Well, that won't be a problem because I'm planning to live a quiet life and not engage much with the wider world; it's safer that way. I've never understood why it's frowned upon to be antisocial and prefer your own company.'

Reuben gave me a sideways look. 'Mattie, you're not antisocial, but you are scared of being rejected because of your depression, and that can make you a bit defensive.'

He was right, of course. People didn't know what to say or how to help when they understood that I had mental health issues, so mostly they dealt with the issue by not engaging or outright avoiding me. They never think it might happen to them too, as it does to one in four of us. The very few people who stuck around anyway were the real thing, genuine friends.

A few days earlier, as part of the discharge process, I'd had a formal interview with one of the unit doctors, mainly a box-ticking exercise.

'Will you need help to claim benefits?' she enquired.

'Officially, I'm on sick leave from the university for the remainder of the summer term, so my salary is still coming in for now.'

I didn't tell her that the mathematics faculty had let it be known my fixed-term contract would not be renewed from September. They can do that when you aren't a permanent member of staff. Even in these supposedly "enlightened" times, employers tend to be unforgiving about stuff like a severe depressive episode. Such discrimination isn't supposed to happen, but it does. There's no point blaming people for not trusting you when you aren't even sure you can trust yourself.

I left my tiny, rented flat in York a few days later with no regrets. Looking with newly liberated eyes at the featureless modern box in a block thrown up in the 1970s made me wonder why I'd ever chosen to live there. The only positive things about it were the location on a bus route for the university, and the fact that it came fully equipped and furnished. Moving in with only a suitcase at the start of my master's degree, I'd added almost nothing in the years since, so had pretty much zero attachment to the place.

I'd never learnt to drive, so had persuaded my friend Polly to bring a hired van across with my books and remaining clothes at the weekend. I may have strong-armed her just a teensy bit, but she's dead nosy and was desperate to see my new home.

The cross-country rail journey was grim, with smelly toilets, crap coffee and too many of my fellow humans. I don't like crowds so kept my head down in a book. No point in letting anxiety get its claws into me when my new life had barely begun.

Things looked up when Lytham turned out to be a little jewel of a Victorian seaside town, with not a kiss-me-quick hat or a stick of rock in sight. Making my way to the lawyers' office in the April sunshine, there was a hint of ozone in the air, and the sound of gulls calling overhead. I hate those bastards; they're way bigger than you'd think and will crap on you or pinch your chips any day of the week.

The "village" of Lytham isn't historic or interesting enough to attract the massed coachloads of tourists who made life in the ancient city of York hideous. Still, the sheer variety of cafés and fancy eateries lining the square and main street suggested my new home must be a popular place to visit. There was even a branch of my favourite coffee chain. Some of the shops were distinctly high-end, but I couldn't even afford to look in the windows of those. Small trophy dogs were much in evidence, being carried or wheeled about in those dog pram things. It all struck me as unexpectedly cosmopolitan for the north of England. I'm an inveterate people-watcher, so the vibe of the place appealed to me, providing plenty of opportunities for free entertainment while I figured out what to do with my life.

The man on the desk at the offices of Haltwhistle & Brown was grumpy and harassed, disinclined to bother being courteous to a brown-skinned person wearing travel-stained sportswear (unfortunate coffee spill down my white T-shirt when the train lurched). Perhaps I didn't give the impression of someone able to afford their services, because he barely glanced up from the reception desk. Such rudeness makes me bristle like a cat with its fur on end, especially the horrible way some people are with waiters and shop assistants. I soon put him right.

'My name is Mattea Lombardi, and I'm here to collect the keys to 47 Lodge Road.'

That got his attention. 'Oh, I didn't think… My apologies, Miss Lombardi. I'm Douglas Brown. My partner Mr Haltwhistle has been dealing with the Lombard estate, but he's not here at the moment. My girls are both off work; one's gone down with a tummy bug, and Carol is in Tenerife. It's all very inconvenient, and such a struggle to find anything.'

'Then the sooner you lay your hands on those keys, the faster I'll be out of your hair.'

After a long day, I was disinclined to be nice to him. Inside I'm a big softie, honest, but don't let people see my vulnerabilities very often. Plus, feeling like an alien in a new environment didn't help.

'Yes… well, of course. They're here somewhere. Probate estate, wasn't it?'

'My aunt. She died last year.'

'I'm sorry for your loss.' His insincerity was at least genuine. 'Ah, yes, here they are.' He produced a bulky manila envelope. 'There's a letter from my partner enclosed; I believe it explains everything.'

'Good. Is it far to the house?'

'Heavens no, walking distance; everything around here is, as I'm sure you'll discover. Well, if you plan to stay, that is. If you should decide to sell, we'd be delighted to act for you; lovely property in a very desirable location, likely to be snapped up if it came on the market.'

'I'll let you know.'

Lodge Road was two blocks from the main shopping area, a tree-lined street of upmarket terraced Victorian properties. The small front gardens were all beautifully kept, featuring shrubs in elegant planters and an abundance of gravel or slate chips. Box topiary may be fashionable as a front-door accessory, but it smells like cat pee. The houses at Aunt Emilie's end of the street were larger, and number 47 was bloody gorgeous, one half of a pair of imposing semis, with a gothic porch over the side entrance to each house. The exterior was all very tasteful, polished brass shining against the glossy, black front door, and a fancy cast-iron boot scraper. Original sash windows too; you can tell by the downward-facing horns.

The letter from the solicitors had only included a photo of the house exterior and a written description of the main rooms. There'd been no sales particulars or online information I could look at because Auntie's house had never been on the market.

A stained-glass porch with an encaustic tiled floor opened onto a hall like nothing I'd ever seen – think Aladdin's cave on speed. The immediate impression was of a classic Victorian interior, the walls painted a deep green below the dado rail, and above a wallpaper of swirling ferns that I vaguely recognised as a William Morris design. There was gold everywhere – in the elaborate overmantel mirror, the heavy gilt frames of many pictures lining the walls, and a glittering antique chandelier dangling from the high ceiling. The deep, opulent carpet in a subtle green-and-gold pattern continued up the stairs to a half landing sporting an upholstered armchair and a potted fern, before disappearing out of view.

Standing there, mouth open in amazement, I began to notice eccentric details which suggested Auntie had been quite a gal. An enormous stuffed moose head wore a plastic tiara, alongside a framed sign which said "Drink More Gin", with a life-size pink plastic flamingo and two gold cherubs in a distinctly intimate embrace. It was a joyfully bizarre mishmash, and I loved it, unexpectedly feeling right at home.

The first door off the hall opened onto a living room at the front of the house. The deep-turquoise walls were covered in art, where framed Moorish tiles rubbed shoulders with some dark oil portraits and a poster of the London tube map. A huge sofa stood against one wall, upholstered in a cream-and-black steampunk print. This was weighed down by a selection of cushions which encompassed furry pink, several cat designs and a suffragette slogan print. An assortment of Middle Eastern brass lanterns and inlaid side tables finished the look. And books, thousands of them, housed in floor-to-ceiling mahogany bookcases which must have been custom made for the space. Auntie's taste in interior décor blew my mind.

Exploring further, a huge living kitchen at the rear was decorated in a similar style, with an elegant conservatory beyond, providing dining space and French doors into the garden. Retracing my steps, I made grateful use of the toilet tucked under the stairs, with time to appreciate its impressive grandeur. A throne-like loo of blue floral porcelain had an opulent mahogany seat, the whole surrounded by flocked wallpaper, gilt mirrors and a wild assortment of pictures, including framed cartoons, some of which were very rude indeed. A particular favourite sign said "Friends Welcome, Relatives by Appointment". To describe Aunt Emilie's style as eclectic would have been an understatement, going much further than the eccentric and into the territory of gloriously bonkers.

For someone whose only additions to the beige interior of my York flat had been one brown rug and a functional lamp (both left behind), this was a revelation. I'd previously aspired to simple, modern lines, imagining them to be balm for the troubled soul, but this house was *mine* from the outset, a muddled disorder of objects which nonetheless made a kind of sense. I wouldn't be changing a thing.

To my relief, the power was on, and the house clean and dust-free. Aunt Emilie had died six months earlier, so someone must have had keys and been looking after the place. This was confirmed in the big living kitchen, where I found milk in the fridge, along with butter, eggs and bacon. The cupboards above contained some basic groceries: ground coffee in a foil pack, a box of muesli and a selection of tins. I made immediate use of the fancy bean-to-cup coffee machine, which was a close cousin to the one Polly owned. Auntie must have shared our preference for top-quality coffee because rich flavours exploded on my tongue, but this small fact and the wild interior were the only clues to the personality of a woman I'd never known.

Sitting at the kitchen island, I decided to read the letter from the lawyers, before exploring the potential delights of the upper floors.

Dear Miss Lombardi,

In accordance with our instructions from the late Ms Emilie Lombard-Harper, please find enclosed the keys to 47 Lodge Road, left to you under the provisions of her will. With the completion of probate, we can now provide you with the deeds or hold them securely if you prefer. You should also be informed of the details of the trust set up by our client prior to her death.

Perhaps you would be kind enough to arrange an appointment at our Lowther Street Chambers to discuss these matters at your earliest convenience.

Yours sincerely,
Edward E Haltwhistle
Senior Partner

Not quite the promised explanation of Auntie's bequest, generating more questions than answers, and it was the first time I'd heard mention of a trust. Come to that, why had I never known about this mysterious aunt, whose surname was plain Lombard and mine Lombardi? Perhaps Emilie had anglicised it, and my mamma might be able to explain, but since we hadn't spoken in two years, I wasn't going to ask. It would have been like poking a wasp's nest with a stick.

My stomach rumbled in protest; the only things I'd put in it all day were coffee and a sickly chocolate bar bought at the station. I had the ingredients for bacon and eggs but couldn't be arsed to cook. Finding a Chinese takeaway leaflet pinned to the fridge, I rang the Orient Queen to order duck chow mein with a side order of crispy seaweed. Having investigated the drawers for crockery and cutlery, I then wandered out into a modest courtyard garden enclosed by a wall of mellow, old brick. The design was strictly low maintenance, with shrubs, gravel paths, and plants in pots. Further down, a couple of mature trees provided a shady spot to sit, and since everything appeared to be alive and well, once again someone must have been taking care of it in recent months.

From the big squashy pink sofa in the kitchen, I watched the news on Auntie's plasma-screen TV while munching my takeaway with enthusiasm. It was fantastic, a massive improvement on the place I'd used in York, where the food was never quite hot enough by the time it was delivered. The news programme was less good, the whole country going downhill fast and basically fucked, as usual, telling me nothing I wanted to know. Fortified by more caffeine, I lugged my suitcase upstairs and explored the rest of the house.

The bathroom off the first-floor landing had a central claw-footed tub, black-and-white floor tiles, thick purple towels, and a walk-in shower of the sort most of us aspire to but can't afford.

The front bedroom overlooked Lodge Road, but I preferred the one at the back of the house, with a view of the neighbouring rear gardens. I suspected this might have been Emilie's room as it had a small en-suite and a gorgeous cast-iron bedstead with an antique quilt and lace drapes on each side. The bed had been made up with fresh linen and was luxuriously springy when I bounced on it. The only other furniture was a huge Victorian armoire and tallboy which provided more storage than my modest collection of clothing could ever require.

All of Emilie's possessions were of a quality to suggest affluence but despite the collection of pictures and funky objets d'art, all other traces of the former occupant had been removed with ruthless efficiency; nothing personal in the drawers, no clothes or paperwork. Perhaps Auntie had given instructions for this, but it left me no nearer to understanding who she was or why she'd chosen to leave her fabulous house to me.

On the top floor, I found another small bedroom at the front, an ultra-modern shower room and behind these, the custom-fitted study lined with shelves and books. A matching large desk held the latest in computer technology and two screens, further evidence of Auntie's comfortable financial status. A narrow dormer window looked out onto rooftops, trees and gardens, but the desk was placed away from this view, presumably as an aid to concentration. The titles on the bookshelves were in considerable contrast to the more highbrow collection downstairs. Auntie appeared to have had a penchant for popular female fiction, with one author a clear favourite – what some might dismiss as "chick lit". Fair enough, personally I don't do gruesome crime or murder (mostly female victims and handsome, rugged detectives); happy endings all round are my preference. It was also the first real clue to my benefactor's personal life.

Standing up there in the attic, reality came up and hit me with a giant thud – I'd been so blithely dismissive when the hospital staff had worried about it being too soon to put myself through the stress of moving. With the new drugs working so well, I'd been confident about escaping my past, and, if I'm honest, my diagnosis too. Now a little voice was whispering that it might have been a bit ambitious, reckless even, to leave everything familiar behind and begin again alone in a strange place.

It was all a bit more than my overtired brain could deal with, and after the full-on assault to the senses from exploring the house, Auntie's comfortable bed beckoned. Grabbing a title from her shelves at random, I gave up on day one of my new life and decided to call Polly with a full technicolour description of my glorious new surroundings, after which I planned to read myself to sleep. Unpacking could wait until the morning, so I slept in my undies and didn't bother brushing my teeth, something I regretted in the middle of the night when my mouth tasted disgusting.

TWO

Without the hospital's early morning medication round to jolt me awake, I slept luxuriously late until 7.30am. This having a lie-in business was going to take work. Yesterday's tracksuit stank of trains, so I headed for the shower and washed the smell out of my hair and body too. There was even a hairdryer in the bedroom, an accessory I don't often bother with. My short, dark curls are usually towelled dry and then left to their own devices. Having never been what you might call "high maintenance", the only reason for using the dryer that morning was my eagerness to get dressed and ready for the day. How long had it been since I felt like that?

Unpacking my case took all of ten minutes, and in my clean tracksuit I took the stairs two at a time. My first job was to dispose of the remains of last night's takeaway, before taking a cup of coffee into the garden. After my panic of the night before, the fact that I didn't know anyone in Lytham didn't feel quite so daunting; being a natural loner, I even preferred it. OK, maybe that part about being a loner isn't true, but at school I'd learnt through bitter experience to manage without a host of friends.

As my mental health problems emerged in adolescence, the other kids called me "weird" and "spooky". University had been a much better experience, but even then I'd only been close to a small group of people, and most of them were maths nerds, such as myself and Polly. Numbers have always been a lot less complicated than people, and their exquisite orderliness made sense when life and relationships often didn't.

Deciding to go out for an exploratory walk, I discovered a note had been pushed through my door.

Hi Mattie,

I'm Georgina Frost your new CPN and wanted to touch base with you as soon as possible. I'll be in the area around 4.00pm and will hope to catch you then, but otherwise please call this number to arrange something.

G.

CPN stands for community psychiatric nurse. It would have been preferable to start my new life with a clean slate and no labels, but that was never going to happen. I hoped Georgina would be an improvement on the person who'd been my CPN in York; he'd been fond of dishing out homespun advice from the pages of his tabloid newspaper. Not helpful.

But I'd promised full compliance with the new medication and agreed to my care being transferred to the local mental health team, so this Georgina person was only doing her job. The doctors were probably right – moving to a new area was undoubtedly taking chances with my new-found stability. All I wanted was a fresh start and the sort of normal, easy existence other people seem to take for granted; a modest goal as life ambitions went, but, so far, my success index results weren't high. It was surely reasonable to hope for a life in full colour instead of the shades of grey imposed by depression.

So, what to do on your first morning in a seaside town? Go and look at the beach, of course. It wasn't hard to find, I could smell the tang of ozone on the air, so followed the gulls, dog walkers and keen running types to the coastal road. A black-and-white windmill decorated a wide stretch of grass with an uphill slope. Only when you crested this did the shore itself come into view – estuary rather than beach – with humps of seagrass, a bit of sand, driftwood reduced to matchsticks, scraps of orange fishing net, and a lot of shingle. A promenade walkway ran the length of the shoreline, and under the wide, grey sky my mind was free and empty, as if the sea breeze could blow away all the detritus of the past.

Speeding up my pace to look like a jogger, which saves talking to people, I first explored the shoreline and then more slowly made my way back into the central area of shops and restaurants. As I'd seen the previous day, most of the architecture was Victorian/Edwardian, and the main street had a cosmopolitan feel with high-end stores mixed in with more homely ones, such as a hardware emporium and the ubiquitous charity shops. My phone was at home on charge, but a nice older lady in a turban with one of those old-fashioned wooden walking sticks directed me to the supermarket. I grabbed a few basics, but it was clear I wouldn't be shopping there often. Their produce was gorgeous and local, but a cheaper establishment would be required if I was going to eke out the last of my teaching salary.

It wasn't the kind of establishment where plastic carriers were available either. Under the stern eye of the woman operating the till, and to avoid future embarrassment, I obediently purchased a cloth shopping bag. Back at the house, I found a kitchen drawer full of the damn things – how had I managed to miss seeing them? The pills were making me dopey, meaning joined-up thinking couldn't be guaranteed.

Auntie's German range cooker was all brass knobs and shiny black enamel. It had a griddle section which made it easy to put together a full English breakfast – one of the few things I could cook. Locally made sausages and black pudding from the supermarket augmented the beans, eggs and bacon which came with the house. I munched this feast watching the rolling bad news on the TV before wandering outside to the courtyard garden with tracksuit pants straining at my now-distended belly. Naming plants isn't my strong suit, but even an amateur like me could tell that the garden had been designed by someone who knew what they were doing. Height and colour were carefully balanced, with bright daffodils flowering in urns and pots. Sitting outside on the bench among the scented herbs, I savoured every glorious moment of precious freedom.

This being the north of England, it didn't take long for the already grey sky to turn a leaden shade of pewter. The threatened rain sent me indoors for further exploration and a fuller appreciation of my new home's interior decoration. Drawn back to the study on the top floor, I sat at the desk and switched on the PC, which promptly demanded a password. Dammit. Polly might be able to work out how to get into it when she came over with my stuff; she was the computer whizz, I was just someone who used them. My laptop was two years old, elderly in terms of technology, so access to Auntie's top-of-the-range hardware would be a major improvement.

The books up there intrigued me; in particular, the collection of hardback titles by Emma Leigh, a name I'd vaguely heard of or perhaps seen in shop displays. Auntie appeared to have been a superfan of this prolific author, but although I'd chosen one of the titles as bedtime reading, sleep had overtaken me before I'd even opened it.

One of the hardback volumes fell off a higher shelf and made me jump, breaking the deep silence of the empty house. I wasn't even standing anywhere near it. The cover showed distant hills under a threatening sky and in the foreground a woman in historical dress whose hair blew back in the wind. It might have been an illustration for *Wuthering Heights* except for the title, *Eye of the Storm*. The blurb on the back promised "dark family secrets and a betrayal of trust", and since the book had fallen at my feet, I took it back downstairs with me. Lying on the kitchen sofa, I was onto chapter four when the doorbell rang. The chiming sound reminded me of Big Ben; not so much a ding as a deep dong.

The man on the doorstep was early forties, blond and balding, but trying to conceal this fact with artful combing and a lot of spray or mousse.

'Hi there, I'm Nigel Layton, your joined-on neighbour. Saw you arrive yesterday and thought I'd come by and say welcome.' He proffered a bottle of champagne, but I don't drink much because of the tablets.

'I'm Mattea Lombardi, and that's so nice of you,' I said automatically. His smile didn't reach the pale-blue eyes that were too close together. Then again, friendly neighbours weren't to be sniffed at when you didn't know anybody, so a greater effort to be sociable was called for.

'Would you like coffee?'

'That'd be super, thanks.' As he came through the hall into the kitchen, his expression was not necessarily appreciative. 'You haven't made any changes yet then?'

'I've been here less than twenty-four hours, so there's hardly been time.'

'And is all this… your sort of thing?'

'Are you asking if I admire the décor? I love it, everything about Emilie's style makes me wish I'd known her.'

Uninvited, he plonked himself on the kitchen sofa. By an unfortunate coincidence, the sign above it read "Better to remain silent and be thought a fool than to speak and remove all doubt". I'd taken an unreasonable dislike to him from the outset.

'We prefer a modern look; chrome and leather are more

our thing,' he said, looking around as if he found it all in dubious taste. 'You were related to Miss Lombard?'

'Yes, she was my aunt, although we'd never met. I was amazed to find out she'd left the house to me. How do you like your coffee?'

'Cappuccino, please… Well, if you can manage that?'

'This machine can do anything.' I set it going while he studied me with evident interest.

'A runner, are you, Mattea?' It must have been the tracksuit.

'Call me Mattie, and no, not in any serious way. You might say I trot a bit.'

He flashed me a smile showing over-whitened improbably perfect teeth.

'We've got a gym on our top floor, rowing machine, weights, that sort of thing. The wife uses it more than I do.' This was evident from the paunch bulging over the top of his trousers. 'Davina says you must come to dinner, once you're settled in. Of course, you might be more of a city type and not planning to stay long-term. This place would fetch a lot of money.'

'It's nice round here, maybe it's time I settled down.'

Nigel didn't blink and surveyed me unashamedly. 'From your colouring, we took you for Indian or something but since Emilie was white…'

That was just bloody rude, but it happened all the time; my skin isn't that dark, just more olive than most, and my almost-black hair only adds to the overall impression. Coming from a university faculty, I was used to people who were fully aware that race was a non-PC subject to ask questions about. It was a fair guess Nigel would turn out to be someone who wouldn't have welcomed Asian neighbours, whereas mine in York had been fabulous, and I was going to miss Jaya's amazing samosas.

'My father was Italian,' I said, despite owing him no explanation of my heritage.

'Ah, *la dolce vita*, the sweet life. We adore Italy.' He seemed reassured.

'I've never been.'

'You should, the people are so friendly, and Davina is just wild about the Amalfi coast. Are you married or still looking?'

'Happily single.'

Nigel was asking a lot of intrusive questions, so, handing over his frothy coffee, I got in an enquiry of my own. 'And what do you do for a living?'

He was more than willing to talk about himself. 'I'm in property development. Self-made man. Scored some flats in Manchester last week; once I've spruced them up, there should be a tasty profit in the project. Got quite a few irons in the fire. And yourself?'

'I've been lecturing in pure mathematics, but maybe it's time to start over. My master's degree was in data science and analytics, but I'll wait and see what's out there.'

That wiped the smirk off his face.

'So you're a *clever* girl,' he said, with raised eyebrows and a hint of acid.

'Always have been, yes. It's a gift, don't you think?' I gave him my brightest smile.

Nigel reddened. 'Well, you must come and see what Davina and I have done with next door, it's quite a contrast to this place, but we like it.'

'Have you been there long?'

'Almost ten years. Davina won't move away, her friends and family are all here. We've made a lot of improvements to the property. Of course, no exterior changes are permitted; it's a conservation area, did you know?'

'I didn't, but that's good news; it's all so charming exactly as it is.'

There was an awkward silence in which I fiddled with the

coffee machine, still uncertain about some of the controls. When I glanced back over my shoulder, I caught him staring appreciatively at my bum.

Like a pebble dropped into the smooth surface of a pond, into my head came the clearly spoken words, '*Mattie, do not trust this man.*'

It might as well have been an electric shock which left me rooted to the spot. The voices were back already? For God's sake, the new medication was supposed to fix that. The mug of black coffee I'd made slipped from my grasp and shattered on the tiled floor.

'Such a shame,' said Nigel, 'and one of your aunt's lovely Emma Bridgewater cups too.'

I was standing frozen, fighting a rising sense of fear and dread as the puddle of black liquid spread around my feet.

'It'll clean up as soon as I discover where the mop is.' My voice came out ever so slightly strangled.

'*In the tall cupboard by the conservatory door,*' said the voice.

Crap, this was seriously crazy, having auditory hallucinations telling me where to find stuff. I so didn't want to believe it was happening. My mind protested that I was not depressed, the medication had fixed me, and I'd been feeling happy and excited about the move.

'I'd better leave you to it,' said Nigel, draining his coffee with a slurping noise. He stood up but made no effort to help, just gave me another wide smile, all neighbourly and beneficent.

'Now don't forget about dinner, as soon as you're settled. Davina and I will look forward to it so much. I'll see myself out. *A presto*, see you soon, *ciao.*'

'Tosser,' I muttered, hearing the front door close.

The mop and bucket were exactly where the voice had told me they would be.

'*Oh good, you can hear me then?*'

I pretended not to be aware, and on autopilot began to pick up the shards of crockery with shaking hands. Inside, my brain was shrieking, *no! Not again, please.*

Remembering the coping strategies taught in the hospital, I tried to relax and breathe slowly but ended up slumped in a puddle of coffee gazing at the wall, numb with shock and despair. So much for a new life and a clean slate. Mad as a box of frogs, as Polly had so creatively put it.

'*I'm sorry, don't be upset. I'll go away.*' The husky voice could have been male or female.

'Just fuck off and leave me alone!' I shouted into the empty kitchen, but only silence bounced back off the walls.

It took some time to calm down; a struggle, but the breathing techniques did help. *No need to get in a state*, I kept telling myself, going upstairs to change my wet trousers. A clean top wasn't necessary as all my tracksuits were pretty much identical – navy with white stripes – and a selection of plain, white T-shirts; it kept life simple.

Mopping up the coffee, it was blindingly obvious that I'd been bonkers to imagine that a move across the country would make anything better. It was undoubtedly a strange kind of denial, as if I could somehow outrun the voices by putting physical distance between us. Bloody idiot. Hearing voices was part of my depression and came with the hot mess that was my disordered brain. The shrinks had repeatedly said it was important to acknowledge that they weren't real, even if they seemed to be, but something to learn to live with and ignore, like having tinnitus. I'd done it before, too many times.

By the time the CPN arrived at 4.00pm, my heart was no longer pounding in my chest and, while I hate to admit it, a part of me was even reassured by having a mental health professional around. The system had a protective arm around me, which, for once, didn't make me feel hemmed in.

'Georgina Frost, but everyone calls me George, and you must be Mattie?'

I guessed she was about my age, with short ginger hair and loads of freckles. Following me into the kitchen, George was wide-eyed with amazement. 'This place is just wild! You inherited it, right?'

'Yep, exactly as you see it, furniture and everything. The style is all my aunt's.'

'But do you like it?' George was studying a wicked cartoon of the previous prime minister.

'It surprises me, but yes. I used to think simple, modern interiors were my thing until I came here, but I'm already a convert. Can I offer you coffee or anything?'

'Yes, please, strong with just a little milk. Sorry to land on you when you've only just arrived, but I wanted to at least introduce myself.' She gave me another smile, a genuine one, unlike nasty Nigel's. 'Moving house sucks, I know, but you do look to be amazingly well organised.'

I grinned back. 'That's because it was dead easy; all I had to do was arrive with my case, nothing else to unpack. A friend from York is bringing over some boxes at the weekend, and that's about it.'

George frowned. 'That certainly sounds like minimum stress but relocating is still a major life event. Your records were sent over from York, so I'm up to speed with your history and medication. The immediate concern is how difficult it must be for you, in a new area where you don't know anyone, so I figured you might need support, or at least some help finding your way about at first. Our office is north of here, in Blackpool, but I know Lytham well because I live up the road in a village called Freckleton.'

It was a struggle not to giggle at the irony of this but, seeing my reaction, George only laughed. 'Yeah, everybody thinks that when I tell them.'

'Did you get teased at school?'

'Did I ever; sometimes it was awful, but I took refuge in being clever and stuck with the other swots.'

'Me too,' I said, remembering. 'Everyone called me a Paki, but some of my closest friends were of Indian ethnic origin, so why would that worry me. The bullies never listened anyway when I explained about being Italian; you'd think my name would have made it clear. Mum sent me to a private school to do my A-levels; things were much better there.'

'Kids can be bloody rotten.'

'They were,' I said.

'So, what next? Another lecturing job?'

'No immediate plans and I'm on sick leave until June. I can afford to look around and get a feel for the area first.'

'Sounds good, Mattie. No extra pressure, keep everything calm while you adjust. Have you found the shops yet?'

When I explained about the morning's supermarket visit, George nodded. 'Yeah, it's a gorgeous place, they pride themselves on stocking local produce, and their artisan cheese and bread are seriously good, but maybe not the obvious choice if you're on a tight budget. Do you drive?'

'No, in York I used my bike.'

'I'm only asking because the cheaper shops are on the Preston road just out of town, or in St Annes down the coast, only a short bus ride away. Another nice place, but a different vibe.'

'Google Maps has been very informative; it'll be fun to explore.'

'Don't forget to take a look at Blackpool, which is in a class all of its own and pretty much defies description except that it's very diverse. The central area is touristy and can be fun, but once you get out into the suburbs there's a huge amount of social deprivation. Loads of rented housing that once served the market for bed and breakfast, or holiday flats.'

'*It's a bloody dump,*' said the voice.

It was a severe struggle not to let panic overwhelm me again, or let George see what was happening. I wanted her support but wasn't yet ready to confide.

Another more distant voice added, '*Yeah, but some of the rides at the Pleasure Beach are a blast and you gotta love candy floss.*'

I closed my eyes for a moment, desperate to shut them out.

'Are you OK?' asked George.

'Headache. And I've run out of paracetamol.' I gave her a weak smile, desperate to silence the voices in my head.

'Ah, I can help you there.' George produced a strip of tablets from her enormous tote bag; I could see several files in there, one of which had to be mine.

'Look, I'll leave you to it, but can I come again next week, same time and day if it suits, see how you're getting on? In the meantime, here are the numbers you need for my office. Ring us if you experience any worrying symptoms, you're only a week out of hospital.' She gave me an expert, assessing look and I responded with my best innocent and guileless face. 'You won't have registered with a doctor yet – the health centre on the corner of the main road is good. Maybe give that priority, before your current prescriptions run out? I'd recommend some walks now the weather is improving, and it's a good way to explore the area.'

Seeing her out, I reflected how much more relaxed and empathic George was than her counterpart in York. Every instinct said I could trust her, and she didn't make me feel too defensive, so I figured we'd get on well. I didn't tell her about the voices being back, but that was partly my reluctance to believe it was happening again. Only a few people with depression have such symptoms and I was hoping their reappearance could be put down to the temporary stress of moving.

'Thanks for coming,' I said, 'it was kind of you. When Polly brings the rest of my stuff this weekend, I can maybe get further afield while she's here with the van.'

'Take it steady, learning your way around a new place takes time. Look after yourself.'

Returning to the kitchen sofa, I picked up the book again, in search of distraction.

'*She was nice*,' said the original voice. '*What's a CPN?*'

'Fuck off,' I told him.

THREE

By the time Polly arrived, I'd got my arse in gear and ticked some boxes on the Things to Do spreadsheet, even catching the bus to St Annes to stock up with food for her visit. I should have known not to bother – Polly (being all too familiar with my limited culinary skills) arrived laden with goodies from our favourite York delicatessen.

'Hey, you mad cow, it's so good to see you!' she squealed, jumping down from the cab of the hired van. Not many people are allowed to make jokes about mental illness around me, but she's an exception.

'Bloody cheek, who are you calling mad? I've got a piece of paper to say I'm better and safe to let out.'

My friend was beautiful as ever with her almond eyes and inky-black straight hair.

She wrapped me in a hug, saying, 'God, what a relief to stretch my legs, vans are *not* built for comfort. My spine has protested at every jolt and bump in the road.'

'Your sufferings are duly noted, but all for a good cause, right?'

Polly held me by the elbows, eyes searching mine. 'Are you OK, I mean really? Not too stressed out with all this sudden change?'

After we'd bonded at university over our mutual "weirdness", Polly always made me feel safe enough to tell her the truth. I heard voices and she had a form of synaesthesia in which her mind translated numbers into music. Her description of computer programming language as "like a symphony" was something I could identify with, even if I didn't share it. For both of us, mathematics was beautiful.

'Honestly, after a slight wobble on day one, it's been good for me; maybe I needed digging out of my rut. Are you sure you brought a big enough vehicle?'

'The smaller vans were all taken, so this was what they had. Anyway, there were a lot of books, not to mention that antique sewing machine. You don't even use it, and the bloody thing weighs an absolute ton. I dropped off the flat keys, and the landlord says the deposit will be returned to your bank account next week. He sends his thanks for being an exemplary tenant.'

Taking a proper look at the house behind me, her eyes widened. 'Wow, somebody landed on their feet; this place is fabulous.'

'Wait till you see inside,' I told her. 'Auntie turned out to be kind of bonkers, but in a good way.'

Polly's home was a flat in a converted Victorian house, and her taste ran to vintage furniture, so I had a feeling she'd like the house. Her expression when we stepped into the hall was everything I'd hoped.

'This is freakin' awesome,' she said, gazing around the hall in wonder. 'Listen, I'm desperate for the loo, so where is it?' While making use of the under-stairs facilities, she shouted through the door, 'I am so going to redo mine like this, it's brilliant.'

'The upstairs bathroom is pretty cool too.'

Once she'd had coffee and stretched her legs with a walk around the garden, we embarked on the full guided tour, which left even the articulate Polly running out of adjectives. At the top of the house, she was intrigued by the study and its very different style.

'There's a password on the computer, and I was hoping you might have a go at getting into it later. You're a genius at stuff like that,' I said.

'Most people's choice of passwords are a joke, they're so easy to figure out.'

I waved a hand at the shelves. 'Auntie seems to have been a secret fan of chick lit. The grown-up books are downstairs.'

'Don't be so dismissive,' said Polly, with a mock frown. 'Emma Leigh's books are *good*, beautiful writing and wonderful locations; she's a top fiction seller.'

I blushed at my own snobbery. 'Yeah, OK. I admit it, the one I started yesterday is well written, not at all what I was expecting.'

'That's why they're so popular, you don't always want heavyweight literature. I've read a few of hers myself and enjoyed them. She knows how to tell a good story, writes multi-ethnic characters, and includes gay people, which, from where I'm standing, makes a refreshing change.'

I'm straight but Polly was always "out and proud" from freshers week onwards. Both of us were single and we'd shared many late-night conversations about whether our being clever might intimidate potential partners within the general population. This could explain why our occasional relationships had tended to be within the university faculties.

Back downstairs, we unpacked the van and dumped the boxes in the "front parlour" as Polly christened it, along with the sewing machine, which she insisted I carry. My talents in the sewing department were on a level with my culinary skills, but the vintage machine had belonged to my granny. I kept it partly for sentimental reasons, but also because it was a beautiful object in its own right: shiny black with scrolling gold decoration and a polished wooden case.

I peered into the brown paper carrier bags from the deli as we took them through to the kitchen. 'You didn't need to bring all this; I've already been food shopping.'

Polly rolled her eyes with one of those "oh really" looks. 'I wanted to get you a housewarming gift and, knowing you don't cook much, decided to stock your larder with goodies. It was easy because I had the van, though the smell of garlic has haunted every mile.'

Once I'd spotted the unpasteurised brie and sourdough bread, I stopped protesting. Polly knew what I liked.

'Right then, lunch,' she said, grabbing a pan from the hanging rack over the island, and emptying cartons of carrot-and-coriander soup into it. 'What a fabulous kitchen, such a shame it's wasted on you, Mattie.'

'I might learn to cook while there's nothing else to do; it's only science, isn't it?'

'Seriously? It's about time; your diet is crap, you should probably have scurvy by now. I can suggest a great basic recipe website, and if you do get into it, I'll come and visit again at the end of term.' She gave me a wistful smile and another hug. 'I miss you already and you've only been gone a week.'

'It's not like we haven't texted every day,' I protested.

'Us crazy people have to stick together.' She looked around again. 'Seriously, this is such a wonderful house; the only thing I ever inherited was my father's Chinese looks. Looking at the glorious miscellany of your aunt's stuff, I bet you wish you'd known her?'

I smiled, putting bowls and spoons out. 'As I get to know the house, it's like opening a memoir of her life in the middle pages; revealing all sorts of details, but with the main facts missing. She's set me something of a puzzle to discover who she was, but there's no doubt about her sense of humour.'

'I get the impression there was no shortage of cash either.

How odd that you didn't know she existed – perhaps she and your mum had fallen out?' Polly stirred the soup, which was already scenting the room with the fresh coriander she'd added.

I nodded. 'It has to be something like that. If they were in touch even occasionally, I was never aware of it, which brings me back to the question of why I didn't know about her. Maybe she was the black sheep of the family, and cast into outer darkness, although that doesn't sound like Mamma at all.'

'I guess it would depend on what happened… You could ask? Even if you and Sofie aren't speaking, there's always email as an olive branch. She needs to know your new address, so that might be a place to start?' Polly always had a soft spot for my mamma, and they'd got on well. I had a suspicion that my friend might have let her know how I was doing now and then, but had chosen not to enquire.

'I'm conflicted, mainly because of a real reluctance to stir things up again,' I said. 'You know how Mamma feels about my depression; she could never get her head around it. Anyway, some harsh words were said in that last big row we had.'

Polly gave me a straight, unflinching look. 'Hey, I know she doesn't understand your illness, I could see that for myself, but it's not like she never tried. Anyway, she loves you very much; at your master's graduation she was so proud – remember the awesome hat she wore?'

I did. Mamma was a fashion addict, something she'd failed to pass on to me. Once I'd begun to buy my own clothes, I'd got into sportswear and become stuck there. She'd given me a wonderful childhood, but my teenage years had been troubled, and our relationship became something of a shit show as a result, especially when the voices began. I'd been unable to explain or make her understand, so instead channelled my energies into making Mamma proud of my academic achievements.

But Polly was right, Mamma's happiness had lit up that graduation day. Maybe I'd been too hard on her, insisting she should understand my state of mind when nobody else did. Some of my anger had its roots in the loneliness of that experience.

Polly handed me a fragrant bowl of soup, and we sat at the island on high stools, demolishing the bread and cheese, a huge improvement on the bland white rolls and tinned cream of tomato I'd been planning to give her. Lamb chops waited in the fridge for dinner, and I was counting on Polly to know a way to cook them beyond the simple grilling which was the best I could manage. Maybe I could watch and learn while she did it.

After lunch, we walked into Lytham, which Polly instantly loved. 'It's like an urban village, and so tiny and compact after York, but it's great. I know someone who grew up here – one reason I was interested in coming; not just you, obviously.' She grinned.

We stopped for coffee on Clifton Street, and then I took her to see the shoreline and the windmill. Polly's long hair blew everywhere in the gusty, fresh wind, but she put her face up to the sky with obvious enjoyment. We even went down the long wooden jetty by the lifeboat station to the muddy sea water itself, before heading back towards town.

'Google says this promenade goes almost as far as St Annes, via a place called Granny's Bay,' I told her.

'What a great name,' said Polly. 'Maybe you should get a dog if you're going to do a lot of walking, they do appear to be pretty much compulsory around here?'

'I have enough trouble looking after myself, let alone some poor animal I might forget to feed.'

Polly laughed. 'But opening tins is your particular talent. So, no bullshit, please, how have things been since you talked your way to freedom?'

As we meandered back towards home, I opted for the truth. 'It's only been a week, but such a huge relief to get away from the strict routine of the hospital. You know I was bored witless in there; too much time to fret, and I do *not* enjoy daytime TV, but was too drugged up to read at first. Exploring somewhere new has been stimulating, and there hasn't been time yet for my mood to take another nosedive.'

Polly had seen me on some of the worst days, so she got it. 'Do you think it will?'

'How can I know? I've never understood what sets it off except that it has something to do with brain chemistry. I do know from experience that stress and pressure often make it worse, so I keep taking the tablets, stick to a routine and live a boring, predictable life because it feels safer that way. The thought of having to go back into a psychiatric unit, somewhere unfamiliar over here where I don't know the staff, is seriously scary.'

Polly peered into the window of a fascinating hardware store.

'Look,' she said. 'I worry about you, and don't want to intrude, but you've uprooted yourself from a settled life. In a couple of months, you won't have an income or a job anymore. I know how much you enjoy teaching, and you're good at it. Won't you find it dull here, not to mention being broke?'

I'd asked myself the same questions. 'Perhaps. I'm not looking too far ahead and can claim benefits, if necessary. It would be preferable to do something to pay the bills, even if I'm not sure what that might be. I've considered taking on some school students for maths coaching, though it's unclear whether there is a market or if it would earn me enough. There's also some kind of trust Auntie set up; not sure what it means, but the lawyer will explain – I've got an appointment to see him next week.'

Back at the house, I produced the lamb chops from the fridge while Polly did a scan of Auntie's small shelf of cookbooks, many of which she identified as classics.

'Easy peasy,' she said, choosing one. 'Look, instructions here for marinading the meat. Didn't I see fresh rosemary in the garden? Even you can manage this, so set to work while I go upstairs and try my hand at hacking into the computer.'

I was aghast. 'You're leaving me to cook by myself? What if I mess it up?'

More eye-rolling. 'Just follow the instructions and you can't go wrong. Before I go, what was Auntie's date of birth and full name?'

'Not sure about her birthday, but she was sixty-five when she died last autumn, so must have been born around 1959. Her full name was Emilie Alice Lombard-Harper.'

Polly frowned. 'Not Lombardi like you? That's odd. And you're a year younger than me so your birthday is the 9th of February 1991, right?'

'Yes, but why do you want to know?'

'People often use that kind of stuff as passwords, stupidly easy to hack, and it's somewhere to make a start.'

As she disappeared upstairs, I had another look at the recipe, studying the helpful picture of the required herb before heading to the garden in search of it.

'*You'll need scissors; in the cutlery drawer,*' said the voice, which had been silent since Polly's arrival.

'Will you please get lost and stop being so helpful,' I snapped. It was odd how readily I was getting used to his presence in my head, but most of the past voices had made a lot less sense. He was right about needing scissors to snip the herbs. Polly was also right; it was no great challenge to chop rosemary and garlic and mix it with olive oil. Auntie's fancy salt and pepper mills provided the freshly ground seasoning the recipe called for, and when I rubbed the result into the lamb, the smell was incredible. I put the dish into the wardrobe-sized fridge, where the marinade could work its magic.

'*Well, that wasn't so hard, was it?*'

'I told you to get lost. Not listening, la la la…'

There was a snort of disgust, but he said nothing more. For some reason, this voice no longer produced the visceral fear reaction it had at first or scared me as much as some of the others had done. I hadn't been taking the new medication very long and had counted on it making things different. Very few drugs had ever banished the voices completely, only dampened them into the background. They were the most difficult thing about my diagnosis of depression, a label I instinctively resisted. It was ridiculous to resent my mother's inability to accept my illness when I still struggled to come to terms with it myself.

Polly was calling from upstairs, so I went and stood in the hall.

'I've tried your aunt's name but it's not working. I'm going to change tactics, so have you got a middle name?'

'Francesca,' I shouted back.

'*Matteafrancesca9291*,' said the voice. Why was my subconscious mind supplying information I already knew? Stretched out on the kitchen sofa again with *Eye of the Storm*, I carried on reading. The language was rich and descriptive, and the historical details well researched, adding atmosphere to where I could almost smell the main character's much-loved Yorkshire moorland. Half an hour went by before I realised Polly was still slogging away upstairs on my behalf, and I hadn't even taken her a coffee. Carefully carrying two of Auntie's surviving mugs, I arrived at the study just as Polly announced, 'And I'm in! Oh coffee, brilliant, thanks.'

'You've cracked it already?' The computer screen now showed a photograph of a cobbled street with a quaint-looking old bookshop, the kind where you'd discover all manner of hidden treasures. Against this backdrop were very few icons, not like the home screen of my laptop, which was cluttered with them.

'Got there in the end.' Polly was triumphant. 'At first, I was spelling your middle name with an "h" but after that it was easy.'

'Let me make a note of it,' I said, grabbing a pen from the desk.

'You do know that passwords should never be written down?'

'Cut me some slack here; medication makes my brain too foggy to remember them.'

'Right, all lower case, matteafrancesca9291.'

'*Told you*,' said the voice.

It was like being drenched with cold water. How could a voice invented by my brain guess a computer password?

'Mattie, are you OK? Here, sit down,' commanded Polly.

An involuntary shiver left me feeling even colder. 'I'm all right,' I lied, 'but it feels kind of wrong to be breaking into Auntie's computer.'

'Well, you did ask me to, and sorry to disappoint but I don't think you're going to find anything revelatory here. It must have been reset, only the basics left now.'

She was right. There was the usual suite of office apps for email, word processing and spreadsheets, but nothing else. Once again, any clues to Emilie's personality had been stripped away.

'Never mind then, perhaps it's for the best. It might feel as if I were spying.'

'You're entitled to be curious,' said Polly. 'A virtual stranger leaves you her home and all its contents; anyone would want to find out more.'

35

It struck me again that the study had a special quality of peace; I liked the way the light slanted through the skylight windows. 'Now I've got computer access, it might be nice to work up here. I'd feel closer to Emilie too, using her room. I hope she wouldn't mind.'

'You'll need to clear space on the shelves for your books, there's not nearly enough for the ones I lugged over,' said Polly, going across to look. 'How odd; some of these seem to be foreign editions of the same titles – look, Spanish, German, French, and what might be Dutch.'

I peered over her shoulder. 'How odd to have her favourite books in other languages, and they all look brand new. If we cleared the foreign titles, it would make shelf space.'

Getting my boxes of books up to the top floor took several trips but provided useful aerobic exercise. My heart got a real workout, and I was embarrassed to end up so out of breath. Time to take walking and running more seriously. Polly fared no better, despite being a keen squash player.

'Climbing stairs uses different muscles, and I live on the ground floor,' she said. 'I'm promising myself a long soak in your posh bathtub after this.'

We put my extensive collection of maths textbooks on the shelves and repacked the boxes with Auntie's foreign titles. 'Not sure what to do with these,' I said. 'The local charity shop won't want them.'

'Don't be so sure,' said Polly, 'they might pass them on to city branches with a more multicultural population. It can't hurt to ask. Your fiction collection is in these two boxes, do you want them up here or downstairs?'

'Those are all particular favourites; some have been with me most of my life. For now, they can go in the bedroom where I'll see them every day.' They'd be comforting, so many old friends among them. We dropped the books off on our way downstairs, and Polly eyed the antique storage with envy. 'This armoire is to die for, but why is it almost empty? That's downright criminal.'

Guilty as charged; all it contained were the few simple outfits which had been my lecturer uniform, items Polly would recognise; short black skirts with a variety of tops and blouses and opaque tights in the winter. I wasn't going to need them now. All my everyday tracksuits were in the tallboy drawers, along with winter sweaters.

'Mattie, you don't think it might be time to buy yourself some decent clothes. You can't live your entire life dressed as a PE teacher.'

I gazed at her in horror. 'Please don't say that's what I look like! Bloody hockey at school was torture, I hated every damn minute, and the sadist who taught us.'

'Well, it's not like there isn't a choice, Lytham has some great shops, so for God's sake why not branch out a bit, even if it's only into trousers and tops. Any colour but navy or black.'

'*She's so right*,' said the voice, but I ignored it. His opinion was not required.

*

We opened Nigel's bottle of champagne to have with our dinner, and Polly's eyes widened at the label. 'Nice. Generous neighbours you've got.' I stuck to one large glass, but it was gorgeous, with a delicate hint of pear. Later, we had the chops with buttered new potatoes and French beans, followed by what remained of the brie.

'The lamb was delicious and unbelievably easy to do,' I told Polly.

'Here endeth the first lesson.' Her grin was wicked. 'I'll leave this book out and mark a few other things you might try.'

37

I'd been planning to eat up the cans of soup bought for her visit but kept that to myself.

'I don't bother much when it's just me.'

'Hey, I know you appreciate good food. Like you're not worth the effort beyond fry-ups and tins,' said Polly. 'Why can't we enjoy nice things even when we're alone? I do. While you're building a new life, do some work on self-care too.'

Since this was almost exactly what the psychiatrist had advised, I bristled. 'I'll think about it,' was my grudging response. We took our coffee through to the parlour, as Polly now insisted on calling it, where the sofa was even deeper and more luxurious than the pink one in the kitchen. The room's contents included a phone dock and speakers, so I was able to play my favourite music in the background. Polly was, as ever, such easy company, and we laughed and talked about our university days while she polished off the rest of the champagne. By the time we headed upstairs to bed, a bit tiddly in her case, she'd told me about meeting "someone" who might be special.

'It's early days, but it feels like a promising beginning,' she said. 'Her name is Harriet, and I'm not saying any more for fear of jinxing it.'

I waved her goodbye the next morning with real regret and promises on both sides to visit, but Polly had lectures and tutorials to prepare for and the van was due back by 4.00pm. After she'd gone, the weight of being alone in a new place descended on me again.

'OK, so now what?' I said aloud.

'*Go for a walk,*' offered the voice, '*it'll do you good.*'

'For fuck's sake,' I said, sudden cold drenching my skin. 'Who the hell are you to tell me what to do?'

'*My name is Lee,*' came the reply.

My voice had a name? This had never happened before, and the shadow of the hospital loomed large. Heading out of the house, I broke into a run in my eagerness to get to the shore and clear my head. On reflection, even I had to admit that the idea of somehow outrunning my inner voices was pretty damn crazy.

FOUR

Assorted clouds striped the wide sky as I ran along the seafront – OK, maybe actual running was a goal to aim for and build up to. Watching the gulls pick their way through the detritus on the tideline, sorting and discarding what they found, the understanding grew that I needed to do the same thing. It was more than time for a mental clear-out of the leftover baggage from my previous existence, and to make positive plans for any future life I hoped to build.

Before I got home, a plan was forming in my head to attract clients for maths tutoring. A card on the community noticeboard at the supermarket, another in the paper shop window, and maybe an advert in the local weekly newspaper which had come through my door. Once the summer was over, it would be clear whether I could make a go of it or have to look for a job instead. No voices troubled me while I was out, boosting my confidence and sense of control. I could do this. Lots of people lived with severe depression and I'd done it for years, with varying degrees of success. Perhaps this time it was all going to be OK.

Making my way back along Clifton Street, I glanced at the reflection in the window of a clothes store and recognised, with horror, the games teacher Polly had described. There was even a bloody lanyard around my neck, even if it held the front door key rather than a whistle. All that was needed to complete the look was a hockey stick over my shoulder. Polly might have a point, and maybe Mamma was right to despair at my lack of fashion sense.

The very idea of resembling Miss Collins, our much-detested hockey teacher, was enough to stiffen my resolve, even though I hate shopping. The "uniform" I'd worn to lecture in would do for tutoring sessions (if I got any clients), but my everyday look required a revolution. The early May weather was soft and warm, and I'd ended up tying the tracksuit top around my waist, so some alternative summer things would be needed too. Hovering outside the shop, I almost made it inside before chickening out and running for home. A new look might have to wait until Polly came to visit again; probably not a procedure to be undertaken alone. Left to my own devices, I'd panic and grab any old stuff off the rails.

Heating a can of oxtail soup, I ate it with a couple of the white rolls which needed to be used up, along with some fabulous pâté which had been part of Polly's food parcel. Stilton and Guinness had she said?

Out of nowhere, Lee was back in my head. '*You could make that yourself; it's not complicated.*' I didn't want him in there – it felt too much like going backwards just when I'd resolved to forge ahead.

I was close to hyperventilating and a tightness rose in my chest, prickling right down to the ends of my fingers. 'Look, please, just bloody stop!' Trying not to allow it to take over, I remembered to breathe slowly as I'd been taught, and added in a firm voice, 'Go away. You are not real; you're from my subconscious brain.'

'*No I'm not.*'

'Of course you are, don't argue.'

'*I have to because you're talking bollocks,*' said Lee.

'What? Get out of my head, you're an auditory hallucination.'

'*Nope, I already told you that.*'

I admit to feeling very frightened at that point, threatened and unstable, my heart pounding in my ears. Bloody hell, if I told George about this, I'd be put back on tranquilisers sharpish, and that would plunge me back into that dazed and confused state where my brain would be too fogged to function sensibly and allow me to earn a living.

'*Mattie, don't be scared of me. I don't mean you any harm. I can help you.*'

In a sudden flashback to my teens, I remembered telling the child psychiatrist how the voices in my head were real people that I heard distinctly. It had been drummed into me over many years by any number of doctors that, however real they seemed, what I was experiencing wasn't external but came from my subconscious. And now one of them was claiming he could help me?

'Prove it,' I said.

'*I told you the computer password.*' Lee's voice was triumphant.

He sort of had a point. 'Insufficient evidence – Polly worked it out on her own anyway,' I said after a pause. 'A mathematical proof must proceed logically from the axioms to its conclusion using agreed definitions.' I was falling back on the pure logic I'd lived my life by, but on the other hand, this was a conversation with a hallucination.

'*I've got no idea what you're talking about,*' said Lee. '*But I can tell you things about your Aunt Emilie.*'

'What kind of things?'

'*For a start, Sofie and Emilie were very close. You didn't know that did you?*'

'You're making it up. Mamma never even mentioned having a sister.'

'*There were reasons.*'

'I don't believe you. Who's talking bollocks now?'

The book I'd been reading was on the arm of the sofa. '*Look in the back at the author's picture,*' instructed Lee. '*Who do you see?*'

The woman in the photograph did resemble my mother, but some twenty years younger, with stylish glasses and a short grey crop rather than Mamma's chin-length blonde bob. Studying the features, I could see there were strong similarities.

'But the writer's name is Emma Leigh,' I said, struggling with the implications.

'*Haven't you ever heard of a pseudonym? Emma Leigh – Emilie. For a bright girl, you're being a bit dense.*'

'Auntie wrote these?'

'*They sold well and made a lot of money.*'

'So the foreign language editions…'

'*Are author copies. The publishers always sent one. Do you believe me now? Is that enough proof for the mathematician?*'

My brain was reeling, leaving me oddly nauseous. 'Stop. I can't take this in.'

Taking the stairs two at a time, I ran away from him, desperate to look at the other books again. The same picture was replicated in several editions, but there was an earlier photo of someone with an even stronger resemblance to my mother. The chin-length bob was very similar and if I'd seen the image anywhere else, I might have thought it *was* my mother. The sisters must have been in their thirties then, and I remembered a picture on the mantelpiece at home where a young dark-haired baby was cradled in the arms of a woman looking very like this, but surely that had been my mamma. Or had she displayed a picture of her sister, hidden in plain sight?

A more recently published volume showed a woman in her sixties, thinner in the face than my mother, slim and stylish where Mamma had become plump and matronly.

'*Still think I'm making it up?*' Lee's voice was caustic.

'All right, yes, my Aunt Emilie wrote the books. Mamma wouldn't have had time to write anyway, teaching full-time and raising me.'

'*Geography. Such a pedestrian subject,*' said Lee.

My brain was close to exploding. 'This is too much,' I told the empty room. 'Please just go away, you're frightening me.' Visions of being put back in hospital rose before my eyes. When you've both seen and experienced the zombie state heavy-duty sedatives can produce… let's just say that the prospect scared me more than the voices did.

There was silence, suggesting the demon tormenting me had fled. Standing by the dormer window, gazing over the grey slate rooftops, the sky had changed, and the clouds promised rain. I did my slow breathing and began to calm down. Nothing weird was happening, it was all only a coincidence. Seeing the author's picture in the book I'd picked up to read must have set off some subconscious train of thought, connecting two similar-looking women.

It was clear that I needed to talk to my mother, Emilie's sister, who could answer all my questions, except that we hadn't spoken in two years. Polly was right again, an olive branch was well overdue, and email – communication at one remove – could be a good place to start. I logged in from the desktop, added my email icon, and watched as a few commercial messages bounced into my inbox. I'd barely bothered with email since leaving York, and it appeared I wasn't missing anything, or anyone missing me. It also looked as if I'd been struck off the mathematics faculty mailing list. Nice.

I did *try* to write Mamma a message, but several painfully composed drafts later, the words still wouldn't come, leaving me stressed and anxious. I gave up and deleted everything; it would have to wait for another time.

The doorbell donged and I went down to answer it, grateful for the distraction, and more than willing to think about something else. On the doorstep stood a tall man half hidden by the size of the glorious bouquet he was holding. Behind the foliage, he had silver hair and the nicest smile, a proper one which reached his eyes.

'I'm Lucas Fallon, your next-door neighbour at number 45. I've come to say welcome.'

He held out the flowers, which were fabulous and very much to my taste. Not the usual bog-standard arrangement of carnations, roses and gypsophila, done up in cellophane. These were loose and lovely, with sprays of blue-green eucalyptus and a selection of blooms I couldn't even name, all tied together with jute ribbon.

'They're beautiful, amazing.'

'Local shop called Floribunda. Original and different, aren't they? I'd have come at the weekend but saw the van outside and guessed you had someone visiting, so didn't wish to intrude.' That made him a big improvement on my other neighbour.

Lucas was good-looking in that way older men can be, with a beard the same silver-grey as his hair and sharp blue eyes against his tan; he came with a faint whiff of cigarettes overlaid with mints.

'Come in, it's lovely to meet you.'

As we went through to the kitchen, Lucas's expression changed, grief and loss written in every line of his face.

'This place is so redolent with her presence; Emilie, I mean. I do miss her; we were great friends over many years.'

'Oh wow, it's wonderful to meet someone who knew her; I didn't but I'd love to learn more.'

While I was trying to remember if Auntie had any vases, an item not so far required, Lucas walked straight to a cupboard and opened it. Turning back holding a plain glass column, his expression was stricken and guilty.

'I'm so sorry, Mattea, I did that without thinking. Used to have the run of the place, so it was automatic. Forgive me. Here are the keys. I was asked to keep an eye on everything until probate was granted. You'll think me foolish, but I used to sit in the front room sometimes, and pretend Emilie was still here.'

'Call me Mattie, and why not keep the keys?' I trusted this man at first sight, unlike Nigel. 'It's never a bad thing to have a spare set somewhere safe. Beats hiding them under a plant pot.'

'Mattie, are you sure? I don't want to intrude, but I've enjoyed keeping the garden tidy and my cleaner, Ruth, has taken care of the house. Did she leave you some basic groceries?'

'Oh, that was your doing. Thank you, Lucas, for everything, including the food supplies. Do I owe you for those or the cleaning?'

He was almost absent-mindedly producing an expert flower arrangement.

'Not at all, Emilie left provision in her will, including a small fund to look after the house until probate was complete, and to tide you over in the short-term. The council tax is paid in full for this year and there's a substantial credit with the utility supplier. She wasn't sure if you'd want to stay or sell, but I promised to offer whatever help might be needed.'

'I never met Emilie, yet she went to all this trouble to make the house welcoming for me. I don't understand what made her do that?'

'We knew you'd have questions, and I'm happy to answer them if I can,' said Lucas. 'Shall I make us some coffee while we talk?' His hand was on the machine but then he stopped.

'Oh, Lord, I'm doing it again. So sorry, it might take me a while to get it into my head that this is your house now not Emilie's.'

'You could show me the finer points of the coffee machine? I do mostly know how to use it because a friend has something similar.'

Another smile lit up the tanned face. 'I bought this for Emilie one Christmas. She used to call it "The Beast" because it's so big. I weaned her off the dreadful instant stuff, introducing her to good coffee and the niceties of making it.' His expression was wistful at the memory.

'I'm fussy about my coffee too – strong and black is my preference. Rocket fuel. Caffeine helps counter the foggy side effects of medication.'

He seemed unsurprised by this information and nodded. 'Emilie told me about your illness. She worried that it made life hard for you.'

'It does,' I said shortly, thinking Emilie had known a lot about me so she and Mamma must have been in some kind of regular contact.

'Yet you've still managed to have a successful academic career?'

'Only up to a point. Fixed-term contracts, regular work but no tenure so somewhat precarious. After a recent episode put me in hospital, the university decided to dispense with my services. Presumably, I now carry the label "unreliable".'

'That's rotten; is it even legal?'

'They can get away with anything if you aren't permanent staff. At least it made for an easy decision to relocate here when I inherited the house. I can live rent-free while working out what to do next.'

'Do you like it?' Lucas waved a hand to indicate the eccentric décor.

'Yes! I have from day one. If all this is anything to go by, Emilie must have been quite a character.'

His face lit up. 'She was. Fierce, feisty, bloody-minded and very independent. Always lived life on her own terms. Talented as well.'

Picking up the volume I'd been reading, I said, 'I've only just discovered that she wrote these books and confess to being surprised how good this is. I was expecting it to be a bit, um, lightweight.'

'A lot of people made that assumption; Emilie never cared, as long as her readers enjoyed them.'

'She could have been a serious literary author.'

'Yes, undoubtedly,' said Lucas, 'but it wasn't what she wanted. Emilie always said her books were the kind she enjoyed herself. For her, popular and commercial didn't have to mean lightweight or fluffy, and she always enjoyed writing an unexpected plot twist and keeping readers guessing.'

One question was uppermost in my mind. 'But why me? This house is beautiful and, I'm told, very desirable. The solicitors have mentioned a trust, and I just don't understand.'

Warring emotions crossed Lucas's face, as he struggled for the right words. 'Over the years there were some… tensions between Emilie and your mother, which meant she was kept at arm's length from her only niece. But she followed all your doings from childhood; it was obvious to me that she cared about you very much.' He hesitated, then reached into his jacket pocket and produced a photograph. It had been taken at my master's graduation and showed Mamma and myself arm in arm, wreathed in happy, excited smiles. Off to one side was a figure I now recognised as Lucas, holding a cigarette, and with him the handsome woman with short grey hair, whose image was on the most recent book jackets.

'You were there? Both of you?' I was even more confused.

'Sofie – your mum – can explain. I think it belongs to her rather than me to do so. But I thought you might like to have this picture and to understand how much Emilie loved you, even if from a distance.'

'She never married?'

'Once, briefly, as I did. Not a success in either case. That's where the Harper part of her surname came from. She told me very firmly she couldn't share her home with anybody and much preferred her own company. I used to tease her about Queen Elizabeth I, who famously said, "I will bow to no man; I will have but one mistress here and no master." Emilie was the same.'

'She sounds formidable.'

'She was, but don't go imagining some kind of reclusive author up in her attic; she adored a party and the two of us travelled together and had a lot of fun times.'

I was trying to process this, and all the new information Lucas had provided.

'She must have known she was dying then, to set everything up this way?'

'Yes, she did. Emilie was as brave and practical about it as everything else in her life. She had a brain aneurism, inoperable because of the location, nothing to be done. She named me as a trustee of the estate, so when she died I followed her instructions to remove everything personal from the house. She wanted you to have a clean start here, without too many complications, and never took it for granted you'd want to stay, understanding that if you were settled in York it might be your choice to sell.'

'Here is as good as anywhere since I'm jobless with no immediate prospects, but I have been wondering about doing some maths tutoring. Lucas, thank you for telling me all this, but I don't want to hear any more, for now at least. It's all quite a lot to process.'

'Mattie, I'm sorry, I was trying to help.' Lucas's face was full of remorse.

'You have, but it feels as if an avalanche fell on me. I need to talk to Mamma, but we haven't been in touch for some time.'

'She struggled with your depression.' A statement, not a question.

'And I was angry with her. Didn't she think it was hard for me? I felt different and isolated all my adult life, and her pretending it wasn't happening didn't help. After a huge row I shut her out, which hasn't improved a damn thing.'

'Time to build a bridge?' asked Lucas, his voice gentle.

I nodded. 'I'm planning to at least try.'

Lucas got up to go, then said, 'Mattie, would you like to come to dinner? I'd so enjoy having someone to cook for; my nephew hasn't been around much lately. Next week perhaps, when you've had time to come to terms with some of this? I'm so sorry if I've overwhelmed you.'

'I'd like that. Dinner would be great.'

'And should Ruth keep cleaning every week? The cost is all covered to the end of the year, or until you sell the house.'

'Might as well then,' I said. 'I'm tidy and organised, but not a massive fan of housework.'

We exchanged mobile numbers, and he added, 'No need to fear my bachelor cookery. Emilie taught me, so I'm a dab hand, but it's dull when there's only me. Is there anything you don't eat?'

'I'm omnivorous but need to learn to cook real food before I end up with a vitamin deficiency. Thank you so much for introducing yourself, and for the gorgeous flowers.'

When he'd gone, I couldn't help thinking that my to-do list was getting longer. Discover how I might earn a living, buy some clothes and not get mistaken for a PE teacher, master the skills of making decent food and looking after a garden: it was clear I had a lot to learn.

FIVE

George was on my doorstep again, this time by appointment. I took her into the kitchen, and almost before she sat down, demanded, 'My friend says I dress like a PE teacher. Is she right?'

George took the cautious approach. 'Well, I wouldn't be quite that brutal…'

We both studied my outfit – navy tracksuit bottoms, with a white T-shirt and coordinating trainers, an identical outfit to the clothes I'd been wearing at her last visit – and burst out laughing in unison.

'Fair enough.' I held my hands up in mock surrender. 'She's probably right. But now I've been invited next door for dinner and haven't got a thing to wear beyond this or the skirts and blouses which used to be my teaching uniform. The current state of my social life isn't exactly sparkling enough to require anything fancy.'

'You must have some going-out clothes?' protested George.

'I had two dresses; the same style but one red and one black, both of them impulse buys, and they went to the charity shop when I moved. I'm nursing the last of my salary so daren't spend a lot on something I don't expect to wear much.'

'Look,' said George, with the blithe confidence of someone for whom fashion isn't the mystery it is for me. 'No need to buy a new outfit because you can smarten up anything with the right jewellery. OK, well maybe not a tracksuit. Show me the "uniform" and we'll take it from there. I can lend you a necklace once I know what we've got to work with.'

George made a heroic effort not to look dismayed at the limited options in my wardrobe and picked out a short black skirt and a white blouse with decorative buttons.

'Good so far,' she said. 'Black tights and shoes?'

'Standard accessories of the uniform.'

'You can't go wrong with black and white. Any jewellery of your own?'

'These silver studs are all I've worn in my ears since I was thirteen, and later Mamma bought me a plain bracelet to go with them. But that's it,' I told her with a rueful grimace. 'I'm not exactly a high-maintenance sort of person.'

George was effortlessly stylish, and I studied her working clothes properly for the first time. The basic black she always wore set off her red hair and colouring, and all she had to do was vary the jacket or top. I made a mental note of this as step one in learning how to dress, realising for the first time that I'd used my "uniform" in a similar way.

Back in the kitchen, George studied me as I made coffee.

'You look well, Mattie. Are you getting out for regular walks as we discussed?'

'I've been trotting a bit – more than walking but not sure it would count as actual running.' I handed her one of Emilie's mugs, which said, "Today is not your day, and tomorrow's not looking good either".

'Are you enjoying it, or do you have to make a big effort to go out?'

'No, I like it and try to get a bit further every day. Being on the seafront clears my head.' I was keen to demonstrate how obediently the instructions were being followed.

'Good. Does it help to lift your mood?'

The CPN was probing my state of mind, and a familiar resentment crept over me. The feeling of being supervised or checked up on makes me irritable, and I start kicking against it like a grumpy pony.

'Yes,' I said curtly, focusing on my coffee to avoid her gaze. 'I never actually *want* to go but always feel better when I do. And no, I'm not sliding down the bloody plughole again, if that's what you're asking?'

'Mattie, please don't be prickly,' she said with a sigh. 'It's my job to make sure you stay well. I'm only concerned about someone isolated in a new place with no local friends. Meeting the neighbours is a good start, but it's hardly a full social life. Don't look like that, I'm on your side, remember? And we both want the same thing – to keep you in a stable condition and out of hospital.'

Being hostile was unfair, and I knew it. Accustomed to my own company, I really hadn't been lonely except for a brief slump after Polly's visit. It had been fun getting to know Auntie's weird and wonderful house, and I'd been out exploring the area. But I didn't want to be reminded of the realities which had dominated my entire adult existence. George was bringing me back down to earth, and I minded. A lot.

'You don't know what it's like,' I told her, from a deep well of bitterness born of years spent fighting for a foothold on quicksand. 'I'm constrained by my depression, monitored, labelled, not free to make my own choices, always having to plot a safe, cautious path in case something tips me off balance. I fight for control, take the medication, do what I'm told, but you'd feel the same resentment in my position; anyone would.'

'The system isn't meant to make you feel controlled, it's a framework in place to support and help you, Mattie, to keep you safe.'

I groaned in frustration; how many times had that been said to me?

'Ignore me, I'm just being cranky,' I admitted, because it was all true. 'Nigel next door has invited me for a meal as well. A formal notecard pushed through the door.'

'Great.' George smiled encouragement. 'It's important to know your neighbours; are they nice?'

'Lucas is – he turns out to have been a long-term close friend of my aunt and shared some information about her. It's fascinating to understand more about who she was.'

We got onto safer ground when I told George about Emilie's career as an author and the books I'd found upstairs. There was no need to mention where the information had come from.

'Wow. I've heard the name, of course, who hasn't?' She turned my book over and looked at the back cover. 'But my taste runs to juicy crime and thrillers.'

'What, even with having to listen to people's dark thoughts every day? I'd have expected you to want something lighter?' This was me making a conscious effort to be less spiky; didn't want that on my "report".

George grinned. 'Nah, I love a gruesome murder, spies, or suspense. It keeps me sane.'

I had to smile. 'Each to their own. Not many people enjoy books about maths, but I read them for pleasure. And you'll be pleased to hear that I also have a plan to secure my long-term future.' I explained about looking for pupils in the area and George was delighted; I'd been hoping she'd approve of the effort I was making.

'It all sounds good, and I'd be glad to put some postcards around further afield for you. My appointments mean I get about the area a fair bit.'

'Would you really? I've already printed some out and can repay any costs if you're willing to do that.'

'Course I am, and it sounds a great way for you to gradually get back into doing something you enjoy.'

She gave me another of those long, considering looks, her freckled face serious.

'Mattie, please don't go all hostile on me again, but there is another question I have to ask. Are you hearing any voices? I need to know if that's a problem.'

It was tempting to lie, but George was so kind I couldn't bring myself to do it. Also, my hesitation must have been a dead giveaway.

'Yes. It has happened, but I put it down to the stress of moving and starting over. There were a few days when it was troublesome, and I was able to deal with it. It wasn't one of the nasty voices, telling me to piss off and die, but relatively benign. Anyhow, it's gone away now.'

Completely true; Lee hadn't spoken since I'd told him to get lost days ago.

'*I'm here…*' said the other, distant voice. He was easy to ignore.

George had brought me leaflets about the benefits system and tried to be encouraging about my employment prospects.

'Once your salary stops coming in at the end of the summer term, you should be able to claim financial support if your tutoring ideas don't come to anything, so no pressure there. One look at your health records and the GP is sure to sign you off.'

'Yeah, thanks for pointing that out.'

George caught my sideways look and blushed, but continued calmly, 'When or if you're ready to look for work, you do not have to disclose your mental health history to potential employers.'

All my sick notes for the university had carefully mentioned "stress", which everyone in the maths department had known as a polite euphemism. It was theoretically possible to start somewhere new with a clean slate, always assuming my former employer would provide a reference that didn't mention large chunks of sick leave. But was another lecturing job even what I wanted?

'You know, it's hard to explain but, for no identifiable reason, I'm longing for change – something more and better than the dull, contented life I'd settled for, even though I have no idea what it might look like.'

'Good,' George affirmed. 'Look, Mattie, I genuinely understand that it isn't easy, even if I haven't experienced it for myself. You're doing so well considering it's not long since you came out of hospital, and all the changes you've been through since. Remember, you can always ring me or the on-call helpline if you experience any kind of crisis.'

I nodded and smiled but knew it wouldn't happen. Not unless there was no other choice, and maybe not even then.

'Same time next week then,' said George. 'It works well if you're my last call of the day because then I can go straight home. I'll drop a necklace through your letterbox when I'm passing; there's bound to be something in my extensive collection. I have drawers full of stuff.'

*

The morning of my dinner date with Lucas, I was in the office under the eaves. It was cosy up there, a place to work which, for unfathomable reasons, gave me a feeling of safety. From the first few postcards I'd put up in Lytham, two enquiries about maths tutoring had come in. They were both A-level students needing support, and since I'd lectured at a much higher level, the syllabus wasn't even challenging, even with the medication blunting my brainpower. I'd decided to work with the students at the conservatory table. The kitchen was my living space and the study upstairs had become a special private retreat; I hadn't used the parlour since Polly's visit.

She'd sent me an encouraging email which pinged into my inbox.

Hey Mattie,

Much grumblement here from the maths department. Your former workmates say they miss you and are indignant on your behalf about the faculty not renewing your contract. Evidence that your colleagues appreciated you, even if the powers that be didn't.

I mentioned a "someone" who is turning out to be special. Very. Isn't it just amazing that she's from Lytham – maybe the stars were aligned? I'll bring her to meet you one of these days – she loved the description of Auntie's house and the parlour.

Take care of yourself. I know you're bloody-mindedly independent, but let people help and even get close. None of us is an island, remember, and not everyone's out to get you even if you are effing paranoid.

Polly xx

I laughed out loud at that. Mental illness isn't exactly a funny subject, but Polly could always tease me about it and, with her, it was somehow OK. The same black humour had existed among patients in the psychiatric unit, where we'd had a running joke about digging a tunnel to get out. The unit was on the third floor of a modern block, but for some reason the staff didn't find our silliness funny.

Wandering back downstairs, instead of opening a tin, I began work on an omelette for lunch. Polly would be proud of me. Lucas had donated a cookery book aimed at beginners, and I was working my way through the first chapter which dealt with eggs. Who knew they were so versatile or delicious, especially with chopped, fresh chives from the garden? Well, everyone but me, apparently; all I'd ever done was fry or boil them. One of my exploratory forays led me to the discovery of an awesome deli in Lytham, which almost rivalled the one on Gillygate in York. The local one stocked gorgeous, local, free-range eggs which had deep-yellow mounded yolks, so different from the supermarket kind. I'd also bought some hot-smoked salmon to put in my omelette and a sourdough loaf. Might as well push the boat out a bit while my university sick pay was still coming in.

I got ready for dinner next door by putting on the black-and-white outfit plus George's chunky silver necklace and earrings. The latter were quite large (for me anyway) and had caused some hesitation, but looking in the armoire mirror, I had to admit they didn't look bad dangling below my short, curly hair.

Lee had been silent for days, but now he said, '*You look nice.*'

'Shut up and leave me alone,' I told him, determined to win the battle going on in my head.

Lucas answered his door wearing a soft-blue linen shirt, and at his knee was a small, scruffy, black terrier, evidently of mixed parentage.

'This is Mutt; I'm trying to teach him some manners, but it's a work in progress.' He hauled on the dog's collar in a vain attempt to stop him from launching at me.

As I bent to fondle his soft ears, Mutt was delighted to greet a visitor and licked my face with enthusiasm. Good job I don't wear make-up as it would have been washed off.

'Mind your tights,' said Lucas. 'I have clipped his claws but not yet managed to persuade him that jumping up is ungentlemanly.'

'He's adorable; only a puppy?'

'Nine months old now; got him from the rescue after Emilie died. I was so lonely without her, and he helps a lot now I'm retired. Company in the long days.'

By now the little creature was snuggled in my arms. 'I absolutely love dogs, and terriers are my favourite, but I've never had one of my own because of always living in rented flats.'

'Emilie was a fan of dogs too but didn't want to be tied down by a pet. She liked being free to go off to Mexico or whatever at a moment's notice. She'd have loved this fella though. Now *sit*, you disgraceful creature!'

Lucas led me through to the back of the house into the kitchen, and beyond lay the dining room extension I'd glimpsed from my bedroom window. Like the rest of the street, his house was Victorian but smaller than mine and the end of a terrace, furnished in a much simpler style than Emilie's. The interior was classic Scandinavian; blonde wood and heavy cream textiles: the black dog hairs were going to be murder on those. The kitchen wasn't big but fitted out with pale birch ply units and a table was beautifully laid for dinner.

'I can't tell you what a pleasure it is to welcome you here,' said Lucas, handing me a glass of chilled Chablis (he'd enquired about my preferences). 'My nephew Tom came to stay at Easter, but you're my first guest since.'

'It's so nice of you to invite me. I've even changed out of my tracksuit in honour of the occasion.'

Lucas grinned. 'I'm flattered you made a special effort just for me.'

Every instinct warmed to this man, who'd so obviously been head over heels in love with my aunt.

Over roasted duck breasts with green beans and boulangère potatoes, our conversation was light. Perhaps Lucas was afraid of overwhelming me again? We got onto the subject of travel, and his particular love for Italy.

'Mamma always promised she'd take me to Venice one day,' I told him. 'But then, when I was reaching an age to appreciate the culture, the depression and the voices started, and we never got around to making the trip. It's where my father came from.'

'Do you know much about him?'

'Only what Mamma told me, that they had a short affair of which I was the unexpected result, but he was married and went back to his wife. Mamma also said he was good-looking and that I resemble him, particularly in my dark colouring and hazel eyes. She always encouraged me to be aware of my Italian ancestry; introduced me to their art and music, and we studied the language together for a while, anticipating the trip.'

'Such a shame you never got there; Venice is one of my favourite cities,' said Lucas with wistful fondness. 'I went with your aunt, many times. It can smell a bit ripe in the full heat of summer, and she preferred to go in the early months of the year, but my availability was tied to the school holidays. I was Head of History at a local private school.'

'And will you travel more now that you're retired?'

Sadness crossed his face, and he put down his cutlery. 'We'd planned to do so much, Mayan ruins in South America, temples in Vietnam, but it wouldn't be the same without Emilie.'

For dessert, Lucas served home-made meringues with raspberries and cream. The bought ones are never quite right, but these were crisp yet melt-in-the-mouth chewy. As we ate, he apologised again for bombarding me with too much information earlier.

'When I got back home it dawned on me what a surreal experience it must be for you, not having known Emilie at all, or that she even existed. Then I come blundering along; it must have been a bit much.'

I flushed. 'That might have been an overreaction on my part; I panic sometimes. The hospital described me as having a volatile temperament; must be my Italian ancestry.'

Lucas raised a doubtful eyebrow and sat back. 'Or it might run in the family? Emilie didn't often get angry but when she did, I could only describe it as volcanic.'

'I'd love to know more about her, but is it OK if I ask you questions as and when I'm ready?' I asked, setting aside my dessert plate with a contented sigh.

'Any time,' he said, topping up my glass.

'OK then, what was her favourite colour?'

'Pink. No, don't pull a face, not pale pink, fabulous deep fuchsia. It was her signature shade, and she wore it often, especially as her hair went grey, which it did quite early.'

'Favourite food?'

'Fish every time, any kind, but she enjoyed a good steak too, ate them nearly raw.'

'Star sign?'

'Virgo like Sofie, of course. And very true to type – a perfectionist. It's why her writing was so good; she honed and polished every sentence.'

I paused. Something had struck an odd note. 'So they were both September birthdays – why "of course"?'

Lucas gave me a puzzled look. 'Well, because they were twins. Wait, are you telling me you didn't know that either?'

'Hell, I didn't even know Mamma had a sister, let alone a twin. It's beginning to feel as if my mother's life was a work of total fiction. What else wasn't she telling me?'

'Mattie, Sofie's choices might appear odd to you, but...'

'Damn right they do. Twins usually have such a close bond, yet they seem to have spent very little time together, at least as adults.'

'They weren't that kind of twins, not identical, I mean,

but physically alike in the way siblings often are. Very different people though.'

'I'm beginning to understand that. Did they fall out the way Mamma and I did? More of the family volatile temper?'

'That's not quite how Emilie described it.'

'Then why? I'd have loved to know my aunt; she sounds like a fabulous person, if a bit strong for some people's taste. She didn't have children of her own, so why wouldn't she want to be in my life?'

'She did, of course she did, but…' Lucas's voice tailed off as if he'd said too much.

Anger was growing in me. 'You know, don't you? You know the whole story.' The flush rising up his neck answered my question. 'Then why the fuck won't you tell me?'

'Not won't, can't,' he said with sadness. 'Emilie was very specific; it has to be Sofie's decision to explain, or not.' He ran his hands through the thick silver hair, which stood on end, making him look unexpectedly boyish, not to mention guilty. From under the table, Mutt, who'd been sitting on my feet, gave a low whine, picking up on the charged atmosphere.

I stood up, trying to damp down the molten lava of rage rising within me. It had been such a pleasant evening, spoiled now because I was furious with Lucas, Mamma and Emilie, all of them, for the stupid family secrets and lies I'd never known about.

'Thank you for dinner, it was delicious, but it makes me deeply uncomfortable when you know more about my family than I do myself. I didn't sign up for any of this nonsense so I'm going home now.'

'Mattie, talk to Sofie, please. She can explain – if she chooses to.'

It was childish but I let the front door slam and Mutt barked insistently as I walked away.

SIX

Over the next few days, my anger cooled as I got over myself and began to be ashamed of the way I'd behaved. Lucas had gone to so much trouble to make a special dinner. It certainly wasn't his fault that Mamma had chosen to keep her sister's existence secret, though Emilie had known all about *me*. The poor man had been put in an invidious position, trying to follow through on Emilie's wishes, with an incomplete picture of what I knew or should be told.

Intending to go out for a morning run, it was clear that what I ought to do instead was go next door and apologise. Great minds really must think alike because Lucas and Mutt chose that moment to appear on my doorstep. He was accompanied by a strong whiff of cigarettes, and, at a guess, had fortified himself with a crafty smoke in the garden before setting off.

'We come in peace, and I'm so sorry,' he said, holding one hand up in mock surrender. The other had a firm grip on Mutt who strained at his lead, keen to explore my house. 'I seem to have managed to do everything wrong, but could we start again? Please?'

Heat ran through my body as I flushed with shame. 'No, it's me who should be apologising to you for being so cranky, and rude. None of my family skeletons are your fault. Won't you come in? I've got chocolate biscuits.'

The anxiety lines disappeared from between Lucas's brows, and he smiled his relief.

'Not while I've got this fella with me; he's been promised a walk and will behave very badly if I make him wait. But could I come this afternoon? That is if the chocolate biscuits will still be on offer?'

'It'll be touch and go, but I might not have eaten them all by then.'

'I could always bring more. There are some things I want to give you including a box of photographs Emilie left for you, and it might help to have a chat about the trust before you meet with the lawyer next week.'

'Later then. I'll try not to scoff all the biscuits before you get here.'

He set off at a brisk pace, with Mutt pulling ahead, taking no notice at all of Lucas's admonitions to behave. Puppy training classes were an urgent necessity.

I went for a run anyway; my stamina was improving every day and, to my surprise, the exercise had even become something to enjoy. Given my previous scathing remarks about joggers on the pavements of York, I was ever so slightly shamefaced about it. Other regular walkers and runners had become recognisable, many accompanied by their dogs. Some nodded and others called out greetings and acknowledgements as we passed one another; it was all a tentative start that might one day grow into a sense of belonging.

The big sea and sky worked their magic on my soul as I headed towards Granny's Bay, a favourite place to pause. I sat on the wide stone steps lining the curve of the sand and breathed in the distinctive smells of the shore. The forward creep of the waves as the tide inexorably came in put me in reflective mode.

Everything I'd been taught about managing my depression had to do with routine, structure and safety, with the avoidance of stress a primary concern. Yet inside a couple of weeks, I'd navigated more challenges than was strictly wise but hadn't relapsed or crumpled in a heap. Gazing across the estuary and breathing in the fresh air, I made a conscious effort to be thankful for all the good things Auntie's bequest had brought with it. I now had a secure home, and even a few pupils for maths coaching would bring in some extra money and keep me occupied, at least until I decided what to do next.

After lunch, Lucas duly arrived on my doorstep with Mutt in tow. He kissed me on each cheek in a continental-style greeting.

'I apologise for having to bring Mutt, but he's taken to howling when I leave the house. My neighbour mentioned it; must be a total pain for her, I hope he grows out of it.'

'He's as welcome as you are,' I said, making a big fuss of the puppy. Let off his lead, Mutt dashed inside the house and into the kitchen, where the good smells were, but then seemed ill at ease, whimpering and staying close to Lucas or myself. This behaviour puzzled us both, but by the time I'd made coffee, we'd had to give in and let him out into the garden.

'Given that the vet diagnosed separation anxiety, he seems keen to leave me today,' said Lucas. 'The two of you got on so well the other evening, I was sure he'd be fine here. Contrary creature.'

I looked out to see Mutt's tail waving like a flag from among the ferns. 'It is odd – he went from being eager to come in and explore, to unhappy about something once he was inside. Shall we have our coffee and biscuits in the conservatory?'

'Emilie would have objected to you using that word.' Lucas grinned. 'She always insisted it was an orangery. I got my knuckles rapped for it many a time, but never quite understood the difference.'

The May weather was so warm I left the French doors standing open and put our mugs of coffee on the table as we watched Mutt snuffle in the borders, much happier outside.

'It doesn't seem to be you,' said Lucas, 'it's as if the house is the problem. Oh well, what goes on inside a puppy's brain is deeply mysterious.'

My neighbour had brought a bright-pink archive box which he put on the table in front of me; I'd seen others like it upstairs in the study, but all of those were empty.

'Emilie's instructions were to let you have these photographs, whenever or if the moment was right. What you do with them is your choice; I hope they might make you feel better about the twins rather than worse.'

'Family pictures? Should I go through them now, or can it wait until I'm ready?'

'There's no need to look at them at all unless you want to. You can burn the lot if you prefer; Emilie never wanted you to feel burdened by the past, and I don't want to upset you again.'

I rubbed at a non-existent mark on Emilie's table. 'It isn't being upset exactly – confused and angry would be nearer the mark, but absolutely not with you.'

'Don't shoot the messenger?' Lucas smiled.

'Exactly. And I took out my frustration on the person nearest to me, which happened to be you. That was unfair and I'm so sorry.'

'You don't need to be. I've been trying to imagine how it must feel, and you described it very well – like an avalanche falling on you.' He reached out a hand toward mine, his almost as brown from gardening every day, with fingernails a little grimy from the vestiges of soil and compost.

'Someone once accused me of being a control freak, and maybe that's true,' I said, 'but only because feeling out of control isn't a good place to be for someone with depression. Structure and routine maintain my life within safe boundaries.'

The worst times had always seemed to happen when I was out and about somewhere, never at home or work, which is why my featureless flat had become a place of safety. I avoided crowds, though this was difficult to achieve in a busy city like York. If I retreated for too long, Polly would eventually persuade me out of my cave and take me for a drink with friends and colleagues, to restore my social skills and remind me that the world wasn't all bad. Memories of being assaulted by the voices were all too vivid, a cacophony of sound, making it impossible to function. The anguish caused just by thinking about those bad times must have been visible because a shiver went through my body. Lucas came to my side of the table and put his arm around my shoulders. I don't always want physical contact but right then I genuinely needed that hug.

'It was a huge decision to leave York and move here, not to mention amazingly brave,' he said. 'Weren't you taking a massive risk it might destabilise you all over again?'

'All the medical people worried about that, but, surprisingly, it hasn't happened, at least so far,' I said, making a mental note to get more of Emilie's delicious brand of coffee. 'While I was in hospital, Polly collected the post from my flat, and she brought the letters about losing my job and inheriting the house on the same day. The two together seemed like a message that it was time for change. The truth is that, far from throwing me off course, it provided the fresh start I hadn't realised was what I needed. Living in this house has been fun from the very beginning, and no it's not at all lonely; I text and chat with Polly most days.'

'Emilie would be thrilled to hear you say that; it's what she hoped her legacy would provide, a sanctuary which can be temporary or permanent, whatever you choose.'

Mutt was running happily around outside, so I got out the

promised chocolate biscuits, and we chatted about the garden, which Lucas had helped Emilie design. I got up to make us another drink, and as the coffee machine spluttered and hissed, I was thinking that my York flat had never been a real *home*, only a place to hide and sleep. Why had I ever settled for its dull, beige anonymity?

'You know, Lytham could be a place to put down roots,' I said, and Lucas's smile was so delighted I felt the need to qualify my statement. 'It's too soon to be sure and depends on my finding work that will provide a reasonable living. But since there won't be rent or a mortgage to cover, I wouldn't need a high-flying salary.'

'There's always the university in Preston? You could get the bus; in winter the station would be a stiff walk from here.'

'It's a thought. But I don't know if I want to be a junior lecturer anymore or engage in the endless departmental politics that always go with uni life. Not now I know my so-called career will never go anywhere.'

Lucas's expression became serious. 'Ah, well that brings me to the other reason for my visit; I wanted to explain a bit about the trust Emilie left, before your appointment with the lawyer. She was insistent you should feel free to keep the house or sell it. Understanding that your illness must constrain your life choices, she set up the trust in two parts. Broadly speaking, if you decide to sell up, there will be either an income or a lump sum to help you go forward, with the balance left to various charities. If you choose to stay, there are other provisions, but there will be a regular income for you either way. You will receive the ongoing royalties from her books, and a substantial sum from various investments.'

I was stunned by this information. 'But why would she do that? Emilie didn't even know me!'

'She did in a way; with Sofie's help, she followed your life and was proud of you. The two of you were all the family

Emilie had, and she wanted to secure your long-term future. All the more so when you developed… vulnerabilities.'

'*Don't you get it?*' said Lee's voice unexpectedly. '*She loved you; she* always *loved you.*'

I almost told him to piss off in response to this intrusion, but Lucas might have thought I meant him. Anyway, his words rang true; Emilie had cared about me, enough to leave me not only her special house but money to go with it, she'd even been at my graduation. Had there been other times when she was a presence I'd never known about?

The implications of what he'd told me slowly sank in. I was free of the necessity to build an academic career and could choose my own path. This simple fact was just huge and changed everything. Stunned would describe my reaction.

'Thank you, Lucas. I'm so glad I heard about this from you and not in some dusty lawyer's office.'

'Mr Haltwhistle will explain the nuts and bolts, as he's the other trustee, but I wanted to give you the broad picture myself. I do hope it isn't unsettling you all over again, I seem to have a talent for that.' Lucas's face was full of regret.

'No, I'm still trying to take it in, but my first reaction is to feel incredibly grateful that she did this. It's liberating because I needn't beat my brains out at some random job just to keep a roof over my head – that is what it means?'

'Emilie was successful and rich; she sold a lot of books and many of her backlist titles are still in demand as a new generation discovers her work in the digital sphere. She bought the rights to those back from her publisher and put all the older titles online. There's an income from the audiobooks as well.'

'You two were such long-time friends. Why didn't she leave something to you?'

'Mattie, she left me so much more than money – a rich inheritance of wonderful memories.'

*

Lucas's cleaner, Ruth, came the following day, a tall and stringy person. My mamma's instinct would have been to feed her up because she gave the impression of someone who needed a square meal and a long sit down. Nothing could have been further from the truth, because the woman had the energy levels of an athlete. I watched in wonder as she zoomed around with a duster and vacuum cleaner, and hoped I'd still be able to afford her by the end of the year.

Ruth rang the doorbell on arrival but had her own set of keys, provided by Lucas, and I was happy to let her keep them. She was also a person of few words, not much given to chatting except to tell me she preferred to "get in, done and out" if I was happy with that. Since I couldn't have coped with anyone garrulous invading my personal space, I figured we'd get on fine.

At my appointment with the lawyer a few days later, Mr Haltwhistle put much more detail on the bones of what Lucas had told me. Whatever I chose to do with my life, there would always be the cushion of Emilie's money behind me. The figures mentioned were beyond my wildest imaginings and gave me an unexpected freedom in that there was even a choice about whether I needed to work at all. But I enjoyed teaching, and there might be scope to make a satisfying career out of tutoring – with three pupils booked in already – so could afford to see how it went. The lawyer encouraged me to think about what he'd explained until I'd come to a final decision either way about making Lytham my permanent home, at which point there would be some documents to sign.

In the evening, I went next door to Nigel and Davina's house, once again dressed in the black-and-white outfit with George's jewellery. I hadn't yet returned it and was sure she wouldn't mind my wearing them both again.

Nigel opened the elegant front door wearing a quilted smoking jacket. '*Buonasera*, Mattea.'

I pinned on my best smile to hide a distinct lack of enthusiasm for their invitation. Did that make me a snob? I just couldn't seem to warm to these people or feel relaxed in their company.

Davina came forward in the sort of little black dress Mamma would instantly have identified as designer. Her blonde hair was expertly highlighted and cut in a beautiful classic style, but so much Botox had been injected into her face that it was frozen into near-total immobility, with eyes like flint set in the smooth, featureless landscape.

'Darling, lovely to meet you at last,' she exclaimed, coming close in a cloud of perfume and kissing the air by my ears. 'We've been so looking forward to this evening.'

Proffering the bottle of wine Lucas had helped me to choose, I said, 'I've brought elderflower cordial too; I'm not supposed to drink much with my medication.'

Davina gave an artificial tinkly laugh. 'God, how positively tragic, that must be awful for you. Nigel and I do like to think of ourselves as wine connoisseurs. Are you taking antibiotics?'

'Painkillers,' I said shortly. This was a big, black lie, but the truth was none of their business. Then I had to tell myself to stop being so prickly with friendly neighbours who'd been kind enough to invite me over.

'Well, a little champagne won't hurt, will it?' said Nigel, holding out a flute glass with a silver edge as I gazed around the huge open-plan space where most of the walls had been removed. Much like Davina herself, everything in it screamed high-end and expensive. Black leather sofas and lots of chrome teamed with striking modern chandeliers composed of silver balls and glass, all somehow at odds with the Victorian house. I'd once admired the look, thinking it stylish and chic, but now actively preferred Emilie's eclectic, lived-in style. I was ushered through to the rear of the house, where a glass table was set for dinner. Looking around, I realised that what was bothering me was the absence of books or anything personal at all, not even family photographs. The setting was just that, staged the way a hotel interior would be, but lacking in soul.

'Like it?' asked Nigel, his eager expression suggesting he expected praise.

'It's so cutting-edge contemporary,' I managed, trying to look suitably impressed.

Davina shot a triumphant glance at Nigel. 'We do our best to keep up with trends, don't we, darling?'

His fingers stroked her bare neck. 'Nothing but the very best for my girl.'

He looked at her with such naked adoration; whatever my private opinion of either of them, this was undoubtedly a man besotted with his wife.

She received his adulation as no more than her due. 'Nigel always says "what Davina wants, Davina gets", isn't that right, darling?'

I was shown around the garden, also ultra-modern, with a steel-ball water feature, lots of straight concrete paths and spiky sculptural specimen plants. Natural foliage didn't stand a chance in that environment, where even the grass was artificial.

Dinner was served from a gleaming hostess trolley; a starter of cheese and tarragon-stuffed field mushrooms, followed by baked monkfish with lemon and parsley butter. I was wondering which of them had prepared the food before it occurred to me that the answer was neither; they'd probably had it all delivered. The ultra-modern kitchen, with its glossy black units and marble worktops, didn't look as if it was ever used.

'I believe you're a teacher, Mattea?' asked Davina. 'Nigel doesn't want me to work; isn't he sweet? I'm a lady of leisure but manage to keep busy, and there are my charity committees, obviously.'

Anyone could see that the maintenance of her face and figure must take hours; it would keep anyone fully occupied. Then I was ashamed of being so judgemental; if that was how she chose to spend money, it was none of my business, especially when I put minimum effort into my own appearance.

While we ate, Davina and Nigel asked a lot of impertinent questions about how I'd come to inherit the house from Emilie. I responded with as little information as possible without actually being rude.

'Have you been on holiday?' I tried to head them off by changing the subject.

'You've noticed my lovely tan?' asked Davina. 'We have a sunbed in the gym upstairs. Are you naturally olive-skinned, Mattea? Nigel thought an Asian person had moved in next door at first!' She laughed, as if the very idea was hilarious.

'I go much darker than this in the summer,' I said, carefully casual. 'People often make that mistake.'

'But with your curly hair...' protested Davina. 'Giancarlo at our favourite Italian restaurant could be your brother.'

'Really,' I said through gritted teeth, wondering how soon it would be reasonable to make excuses and go home. *Be nice*, I kept telling myself.

The conversation was stilted, what with us having zero interests in common. After almost two hours, we'd staggered our way to the coffee-and-mints stage before Nigel got around to their agenda. I'd had a shrewd idea these two would have one.

He fiddled with a gold coffee spoon, leaning forward in his seat. 'The thing is, Mattea, you've been here a few weeks now, and we were wondering whether you've made any long-term decisions yet? If you should plan on selling the house, we'd be extremely interested in buying it. Davina wondered if you might feel more at home in a multicultural big-city setting, where there are more opportunities for someone like yourself. We'd make you a generous cash offer, and no agent's fees.'

'Very generous,' said Davina, watching me closely to gauge my reaction.

I let that sit in the silence for a few breaths. 'Actually, I'm considering making this my permanent home,' I said, looking from one avaricious face to the other, and crunching into the chocolate mint served alongside the coffee.

Davina gave another tinkly laugh, but her grey eyes were now solid steel. 'You must understand that it's always been my dream to buy the other half of the house. It's no exaggeration to say my heart is set on it. You can imagine what a magnificent home the two together would make.'

'Oh yes, I'm sure you'd have lots of amazing ideas for it,' I said, with exaggerated sweetness, 'but I do rather like it as it is. No final decisions made, but settling here would make me feel so close to my dear departed aunt.'

Davina opened her mouth to say something, but Nigel reached out a hand and quietly silenced her with a warning look.

'Of course. You'll want to take your time thinking about it; only natural when you're grieving her loss,' he said, at his most urbane and smooth. 'But I've written down the figure we had in mind.' He produced a white envelope and slid it towards me. 'You might want to reconsider when you see it.'

'I'll open it later,' I told him. 'Now, you must forgive me, it's been so lovely, but I'm afraid the combination of champagne and medication has made me sleepy. I wouldn't want to snore.'

'God no,' was Davina's response. Then she remembered her company manners. 'Must you go?' It was evident she couldn't wait to be rid of me.

'I'm afraid so, before I turn into a pumpkin. Perhaps we'll do this again some time.'

'I hope so,' said Nigel, escorting me to the front door. 'It's been lovely getting to know you better; please do give serious thought to our offer.'

'*A presto*,' said Davina, switching on the charm at the last minute.

'Oh, you speak Italian,' I responded with a wide smile. '*Arrivaderci, vaffanculo!*'

It was clear from their faces they had no idea I'd just told them to fuck off.

SEVEN

In the days that followed, my mind kept going back to the things I'd learnt about my family, over and over. There was so much to puzzle me, and Lucas had made it clear that Mamma was the only person who could answer my questions. But would she, when so much had been kept hidden for so long? There was only one way to find out.

How do you reopen a dialogue with your mother after a two-year silence? It took a long time to put together what I wanted and needed to say.

Dear Mamma,

This is to let you know that I've moved; Aunt Emilie left me her house in Lytham and I'm living in it, for now at least. You never told me about having a twin sister, and all this raises a lot of questions only you can answer – if you're willing to talk to me about things.

Sorry it's been such a long time, but it would mean a lot if we could build a bridge, I miss you.

Love,

Mattie x

PS my mobile number is still the same.

An understanding of just how much I did miss my mamma only came when the words were written. Memories of my happy childhood crowded in, of a time before depression had cast its shadow over both of us. I'd said some very harsh words about her failure to come to terms with it, but Polly had forced me to recognise that it must have been an agonising experience to see an adored daughter struggle. She wouldn't be the last parent to cope by pretending it wasn't happening or hoping that she could make me better just by loving me enough. As with so many failures of communication, our mutual pain had driven us apart rather than brought us together, but I hoped she might want to reconcile and there was only one way to find out.

I read my message aloud, to see if I was happy with it, then pressed send quickly, before I could change my mind.

'*Good girl, you've done the right thing,*' said Lee.

'Get lost,' I said. 'Your opinion is not required.' That shut him up.

While in the study, I checked through the preparatory work I'd done for my first two pupils, who were due the following day: an assessment test based on the A-level syllabus to find out where each of them was, and what areas they might be struggling with.

Done, I looked around for another task and the pink box of photos Lucas had brought sat there accusing me of cowardice. I still hadn't nerved myself to open it. I had no idea what was stopping me, only a vague sense of unease. My finger traced the neat label, "family photos", and I realised this must be Emilie's handwriting, which I'd never seen before.

'*It's not going to bite,*' said Lee. '*Don't just sit there, open it.*'

His voice was no longer a source of fear and threat as it had initially been, and my reaction had reduced to mild irritation at the intrusion. I might be growing accustomed to it, but even so didn't appreciate comments from my subconscious prompting me to do things. It was *my* brain, and I was determined to be in charge of it.

'Just go away, I'm trying to think.'

Along with the box, I'd brought upstairs the white envelope Nigel had given me. I hadn't opened that either, some kind of denial or avoidance going on in my head. Did I even need to know what they were offering when selling the house didn't form any part of my hopes for the future? On impulse, I tore the envelope open, and the figure on the piece of paper left me gaping like a stranded fish. *How* much? I hadn't realised property in Lytham was worth that kind of money, except for the ones on the seafront. Davina would be planning to spend a fortune ripping the guts out of the place to make it match next door, and that would cost a fortune as well.

Emilie's eccentric interiors had appealed to me from the beginning, and in just a few weeks I'd grown to love them even more and appreciate every quirky little detail. I couldn't bear the thought of all her precious collections being boxed up and sold at auction. Living with her things around me every day provided a sense of who she was, and a growing certainty we'd have got on well, though from Lucas's comments we'd undoubtedly have clashed too.

'Mattie, don't be such a coward. Look at the photos, it's what she wanted.'

I took the lid off the box. Inside were several tissue paper packages, each tied with ribbon and neatly labelled in my aunt's writing. Emilie must have done all this when she'd known she was dying, preparing to hand the story of her life over to me. I set them out on the desk and plumped for one labelled "early days". The pictures inside were of the twins' childhood, from black-and-white images of two adorable chubby blonde babies, through coloured school pictures and family groups. The sisters were always together, their closeness evident from the way their hands were often entwined, or their arms around each other. Non-identical or not, most people would have guessed they were twins, although there were small differences if you studied them closely. Emilie had written dates and locations on the back of each picture, but I had no way of sorting out which of the girls was which. She'd also spelt mamma's name as Sophie and their last name as Lombard, the way it was on the lawyer's documents, another curiosity.

They were around the same height, but the sister I decided must be my mamma had fairer hair, and as they reached their teens was more petite in build. Emilie's hair darkened over the years, and from her body language she was confident and striking in a way Mamma had never been. These were small things, and all I had to go on to make the distinction between them was the photograph we'd had in my childhood home, a picture that might have been Emilie, not Sofie as I'd always supposed. What could have driven such close sisters apart, even though they must have remained in regular contact?

There were a few pictures of them as young adults, including the standard graduation shots. They'd attended different universities, which must have been the first time their lives diverged. Studying the happy faces made me wish I'd had a sister to make me feel less isolated. I'd been additionally stigmatised for being a maths prodigy; proof, if it were needed, of the adage that nobody likes a smart-arse. Mamma always said I must have inherited the gift from my father's side because she'd had to retake maths to scrape the pass necessary for a career in teaching.

Another package was labelled "travels with Lucas" and showed him and Emilie over many years in various locations, each of them gradually greying over time. Judging by the dates, they'd been friends for almost three decades. I set the other pictures aside when my phone pinged, thinking it would be a text from Polly. We messaged each other most days.

But it was an email from Mamma, less than an hour after I'd sent mine.

Darling Mattie,

I can't tell you how wonderful it was to hear from you – I cried. For the longest time, I've hoped we might find a means to reconnect. Not back to the way things were when I didn't understand what you were going through, but a way to move forward. A year ago, I met a friend at the Geographical Society who'd been a mental health nurse. He helped me to see how difficult your adolescent experiences were, and how brilliant your academic achievements have been, considering everything you were up against. I'm ashamed now of how I behaved; hoping I could make you better by pretending your problems didn't exist, instead of walking alongside you through them. Can you forgive me?

I was able to attend Emilie's funeral but assumed she'd have left everything to Lucas, they were always so close. Now I think things through, it makes perfect sense that she chose to give you a secure future, and I will always be grateful she made you that final gift.

Of course you have questions, and maybe the time is right to provide the answers. It was always my intention to do so but when you became ill, I was afraid to put you under stress over things you didn't necessarily need to know.

We can continue our conversation by email if you prefer, but I've put my mobile number below in case you want to talk directly.

With love always,
Mamma x

The warmth and generosity of this response took my breath away, especially when I'd been so horrible to her during the final row which had led to our estrangement. It was typical of me; whenever I felt threatened or insecure I became angry and defensive, so it should have been me making the apology, not Mamma.

I sat at the desk, staring into space. Through her legacy, Emilie had not only given me financial security but also reasons to renew contact with my mother. There was so much to thank her for.

'*Now it's time you talked to Lucas; he'll listen,*' said Lee.

My subconscious was right again. At that moment, Lucas was the person I most wanted to share all this with, so I called him.

'It's Mattie, are you busy?'

'Trying to teach Mutt to sit and stay. With a singular lack of success. Is something the matter?'

'I'd like to talk, if you have time to listen. Can I invite you to a soup and pâté lunch?'

'Beats my boiled egg plans – I'll be there in half an hour.'

I gathered up the packages of opened photos and took the box downstairs. When Lucas came to the door, I hugged him. Learning to be physical with new people and feel comfortable about it was a big thing for me, amazing progress from my spiky hedgehog past. Like a lot of vulnerable individuals, I'd kept people at a distance, fearful that if they found out about my mental health problems, they'd reject me. My general tactics were to get in first. Those who could get past my booby-trapped defences tended to be the ones who would stay the course.

'I sent Mamma an email this morning, and she's already replied,' I told my guest, serving up a fragrant sweetcorn chowder Polly had brought. 'She was so sweet about everything; I think it's going to be all right.'

'My dear girl, of course it is,' he said warmly. 'It's what Emilie hoped would happen, that her death might somehow provide a catalyst to bring you two back together.'

After demolishing the soup and bread, we studied the pictures I'd already opened. Lucas had seen very few childhood snaps of the twins but appeared to have a strong instinct for which was which. It matched my own, but then each of us had known one of the pair very well. He also listened patiently while I recounted the tale of my dinner with Nigel and Davina. When I got to the bit about my parting shot, he exploded with laughter.

'Oh well done, Mattie. I applaud your command of the language, but I'm sure your Italian classes didn't teach you such a rude expression?'

'No, it was a girl at university, she came from Naples. I learnt a few other useful phrases from her, including *fottuto bastardo*. I do feel a bit mean about next door now though; you must think I'm a dreadful snob.'

Lucas smiled. 'I was always doubtful you'd get on; Davina is horribly pretentious, and one of those women who can never be content, always seeking the next big thing in terms of super-cool gadgetry, clothes or cosmetic surgery. Nigel's sole mission in life is to make her happy by getting them for her. You don't have a thing in common with them apart from being neighbours.'

'They made me an offer for the house.'

He put the photos down and his head came up. 'Did they indeed, and what do you think?'

'I'd leave it to the dogs' home rather than sell to them,' I said between gritted teeth. 'Never mind "Davina always gets what she wants", not this time, she doesn't. They'd change everything I love about this house, and I hate the thought of that. Anyhow, I've pretty much made up my mind to stay. I love it here, especially having you next door.'

His face lit up when I said those words. Maybe having Emilie's niece around eased his grief a little too; I hoped so.

Lucas leaned towards me, his face serious. 'Nigel also made Emilie an offer for the house last year when it became obvious that she was very ill,' he told me. 'The aneurism was leaking, and she looked dreadful. Emilie was all too aware there wasn't much time. I'm afraid she told Nigel in no uncertain terms to stick it where the sun doesn't shine. He wasn't best pleased to be turned down and bothered her about it until she threatened him with legal action for harassment.'

'They're still after the house, but no way are they going to get it. This could be what the estate agents describe as a "forever home" for me and, with the rest of my inheritance from Emilie, I can make it work.'

'Even though it means leaving your friends in York?'

'There weren't that many; my circle was always small and work-related. There's nobody special, apart from Polly, and now she's fallen madly in love, so won't be missing me too much. It's an incredible coincidence, but her new girlfriend is from Lytham, though she dreams of living in New York. I'll miss her if they go but... well, life changes, doesn't it?'

'Emilie hoped you and I might be friends: we are, aren't we?' asked Lucas.

I picked up the soup bowls and took them to the sink.

'Absolutely, don't even think about trying to get rid of me.'

'*I'm so pleased about that*,' said Lee, but I ignored him.

'Mattie, it's fabulous news that you might want to settle here,' said Lucas when I brought back mugs of coffee, 'but you should speak to the lawyers again. As you know, the trust has two sets of provisions, depending on whether you plan to sell or stay. I'm so glad you love Lytham; Emilie and I came on a visit years ago, she was doing a book signing, and we were both so taken with the place we moved here. I sold my cottage in the

83

Yorkshire countryside, and Emilie had a large house in Malton. We never lived together, except briefly while there were builders in this house. She always insisted on separate residences.'

Taking a deep breath, I asked, 'But you were lovers, yes?' I was afraid of offending him by asking but wanted to know.

'For a while,' Lucas said calmly. 'Emilie wasn't suited to monogamy, but we were always best friends, which is even more important.'

'You loved her.'

'Once I'd met her, no one else could ever measure up,' he said, with devastating simplicity. 'There were a few other relationships, but nothing ever lasted because I couldn't give another woman my whole heart. It was always Emilie's, and they soon cottoned on to that basic fact, however hard I tried.'

'And neither of you ever had children?'

He smiled, but his eyes were sad. 'Emilie was forthright about choosing not to have a family, and I only wanted one if it could be with her. Anyway, I spent my working life with children, so don't feel as if I missed out. I've also been fortunate to have a very close relationship with my nephew, and if I'd ever had a daughter, I'd have hoped for someone just like you.'

He couldn't know what that meant to me. 'When I dreamed of meeting my dad as a child, I imagined someone strong the way you are, that I could always turn to, a rock I could lean on.'

'You *can* depend on me, Mattie. I made Emilie a solemn promise I'd look after you. Now we're getting to know each other properly, I'd care about you even if you weren't... well family.'

He got another hug for that.

*

84

The following morning, I had my first two pupils, for an hour each. Although both boys were seventeen and had recently done AS levels, they couldn't have been more different. Pranit was physically still a boy, with a fluffy, dark moustache on his top lip, earnest and serious. He was fine with pure mathematics but struggled with probability and statistics. Jordan was a total contrast: tall, blond and athletic, but had produced disappointing AS results. He'd need a good A-level grade if he wanted to study aeronautical engineering. His test answers indicated a sloppy approach rather than ignorance, so I figured that a giant kick in the pants to work harder was the primary requirement in his case.

They were both great kids, and our sessions were enjoyable. Jordan was inclined to be a bit cocky and arrogant, but he'd soon learn the painful lesson that the world didn't revolve around him, even if his parents had so far given him the impression that it did. A third pupil, Sienna, was coming the following week, and, all being well, they'd be with me until exams. It was a start, and my postcards might yet produce more customers if positive feedback from these three got around.

When Jordan had gone, Lee commented, '*That one thinks he's God's gift to women.*'

'So what? Better to be a confident kid than bullied and scared, the way I was.' Another conversation with the inside of my brain, but there was time for a run before lunch, which always helped to blow the voices out of my head. I was already dressed in a tracksuit, as the intended wardrobe renovation remained on the to-do list. Trotting along Cavendish Street, a gleaming soft-top Bentley purred to a halt next to me and Nigel climbed out of it.

'Thought it was you, Mattea. Lovely weather for a run.'

'Yes, summer's almost here,' I said, jogging on the spot to suggest I was keen to be on my way.

He was stroking the bonnet of the car as he leaned against it, and with the top down I could smell the immaculate cream leather upholstery.

'Davina and I were wondering if you've had time to look at our offer.'

'I have considered it, yes.'

His confidence in the outcome was visible. 'I hope you found it generous?'

'Definitely. I had no idea the property was worth so much.'

'It is to us,' he said, his face eager. 'Davina's dreamed of doing the whole house for years.'

'Then I'm sorry to cause disappointment, but I've decided to make Lytham my long-term home.'

Nigel frowned, and then his face cleared. 'You could sell to us anyway? This town is full of incredible properties, and that kind of money would get you a flat overlooking the sea.'

'True, but I happen to be very attached to the house, and all the mementoes of my aunt; she feels almost present in every room.'

Something shifted in his eyes, causing a chill to run through my body, and he took a step towards me, standing a bit too close. I involuntarily retreated a pace and stopped jogging.

'What can I say to make you reconsider? Davina's set her heart on this. We can increase our offer if that's the game you're playing. Name your price.'

'I'm not playing any games, just telling you the truth. I love the house and want to stay. It's not for sale, however much you offer.'

His eyebrows raised in evident disbelief. 'In my line of business, I've found everyone has their price. Like I say, name it.'

'Perhaps I'm not the kind of person you usually deal with.' His face showed total incomprehension at this statement. 'I'm not all that interested in money or material things.'

'Of course you are; who isn't?'

'As I've told you, me for one. You're wasting your time, Nigel, and now I want to be on my way.' He was blocking the pavement, and I was beginning to feel threatened when he grudgingly stepped back towards his car. With one hand on the door, he gave me a strange, almost panic-stricken look.

'Davina isn't going to like this at all. I don't want her to be unhappy.'

'She'll get over it,' I said, beginning to jog on the spot again.

'Look, I can't tell her you said no, she'll go apeshit. Promise me you'll at least think about it.' His voice was pleading, almost desperate.

'I'm sorry, Nigel. For the last time, the answer is no.'

His face twisted with anguish. 'She'll leave me if I can't get this for her.'

'Have you considered marriage counselling?'

'This isn't the end of it; I don't give up easily,' he told me.

'Don't you? How interesting. Well, you'll eventually get the message that I mean what I say. End of discussion.'

I set off down the street again, feeling his gaze boring into my back as I reached the corner. His car roared past and, once he was out of sight, I came to a halt, angry with myself when I realised my legs were shaking. Life in my new home was off to a great start if I'd already managed to piss off the neighbours.

EIGHT

Being in Emilie's study, no, *mine* now, always brought a feeling of calm and peace; one reason why I preferred to keep the room private. With the view over rooftops and gardens, it had become a safe space, a refuge, and after Nigel's veiled threats I needed one.

Trying to think about something else, I worked on a reply to Mamma's email. After discarding several drafts, I stopped trying too hard and just wrote what was in my heart.

Dear Mamma,

It meant so much to hear that you now understand my illness better, rather than trying to deny it was happening or saying I'd grow out of it. When you couldn't accept what was going on, I felt so isolated and alone, all the more so when the doctors were telling me what I was experiencing wasn't real.

After a recent hospital admission, I'm in a better place – physically and mentally. I have a new CPN who is supportive and encouraging, and, with her help, I hope to build a life here.

Yes, I do have questions – so many I hardly know where to begin. Auntie left me a box of photographs which includes shots of the two of you growing up. What happened to cause

*the rift between you, and why did she spell your name
"Sophie" and our surname differently?*

Love,

Mattie x

I hit "send" and tried not to speculate about how this message
would make her feel. I was in the study to work, so made a
determined effort to put Mamma and her twin right out of
my mind. I'd almost finished putting together some sample
exercises on statistics for Pranit when my phone pinged with a
text from Polly.

*Will ring later when we can talk but had to share – Harriet
asked me to marry her and I said yes! So happy!*

P xxx

*PS Don't go thinking it's a bit quick; when you meet the
one, you know. Corny but true.*

I was thrilled for her; Polly had been ready to settle down for so
long. If I'm honest, there was also more than a twinge of envy
on my part. OK, a whacking great big green jealous hill of it.
Few of my relationships had ever lasted more than six months –
almost a year in one memorable case – but Sven had gone back
home to Sweden at the end of the academic year and hadn't
asked me to follow or stay in touch. It would be exciting to hear
all about Polly's fiancée later; her text hadn't given much away.

I was deep in histograms and cumulative frequency for
Pranit's next session when my phone pinged again with another
message.

*Picking up nephew Tom from the station this afternoon.
Fancy joining us for a roast beef Sunday lunch? I'd love you
to meet him. L.*

I sent an enthusiastic acceptance – pure self-interest because how long was it since I'd had a roast dinner? It's not something you cook for one, even if I'd known how to set about it. My mamma always made gorgeous gravy; I might ask her to teach me the secret. If our email correspondence continued to be positive, maybe the next step should be an invitation to visit. I missed her, achingly so since the anger I'd been stupid enough to hold onto for so long had begun to dissipate. I'd nursed the pain to justify our separation and convince myself I was right. With a painful clarity that cut like a blade, I saw that I'd been wrong. Again.

With Pranit and Jordan's next sessions planned, I sketched outline lessons for some weeks ahead in case their parents were keen to continue, as I hoped they might be.

*

George arrived by appointment at 4.00pm. 'Hey, Mattie,' she said with a friendly smile.

'Before you start, I've got a good excuse for wearing a tracksuit this time; I went out for a run this morning.' No need to mention that I hadn't got very far.

'Hey, there are no rules about what you choose to wear, as long as it makes you feel good,' said George, dumping her enormous tote by the kitchen sofa and pulling out a file I assumed was mine.

'But it doesn't anymore. Comfort used to be my primary concern,' I admitted, 'but now, thanks to Polly, I've developed a horror of looking like a games teacher. I need a makeover. How about a tutu? Fairy wings? Full ballgown? Seriously, I should buy some summer dresses now the weather is so warm. I can't live in T-shirts and trackie bottoms any longer.'

Perched at the kitchen island, George studied me as I made the coffee. 'You look well though, happy even?'

The word made me stop in the act of returning coffee beans to the cupboard. Happiness wasn't a term I'd used to describe my life in a very long time, but now it fitted me comfortably. Distracted by this thought, it became necessary to refocus on the coffee machine before the mug overflowed.

'It surprises me to say it, but yes, I am. Happy, I mean, or maybe contented would be nearer the mark.' Even the words sounded unfamiliar coming from my mouth.

'Getting any problematic side effects from the medication?' she asked.

'Very few beyond sleeping like a brick; it's one of the least zombie-inducing drugs I've had so far. So many of them stopped the world sparkling.'

'That must have been hard.'

'It was, but it's genuinely better right now. I'm functioning well enough to prep maths lessons and enjoy doing it.'

George beamed her delight. 'You got some pupils then?'

'Three so far, two came this morning and they're both good kids I'll enjoy working with.'

'Mattie, this is excellent; you're doing great. No troublesome voices?'

'Nothing to bother me, no.'

'*I always make a point of being helpful,*' said Lee.

'*Not always,*' said the other, more distant, voice.

My coffee went down the wrong way as I choked. When the coughing fit subsided, I hastily covered up by saying, 'I've been making friends with my neighbour on the other side. He's an old flame of my aunt's and I'm invited for lunch on Sunday.'

'And how did dinner with the people next door go? Was the outfit a success?'

'It was, and your necklace and earrings are here in this envelope. I was afraid of forgetting to give them back.'

'Keep them,' said George with a wave of her hand. 'I never wore the set anyway and had an idea it would work on you. Look, can I use your loo before I burst? I wanted to go at the last appointment, but the health hazards of his grimy bathroom were too much to contemplate.' Her pained expression made me laugh.

'Help yourself; it's out in the hall under the stairs. I hope you find it hygienic.'

She would, of course; Ruth was a demon with the bleach. When George left the kitchen, my eye was inexorably drawn to the open file. It was too much of a temptation – and I don't feel comfortable with people writing things about me at the best of times. The most recent entry was from a week earlier.

Mattea is compliant with the medication regime but hostile today and seems resentful of the mental health system. Experiencing auditory hallucinations which she claims are not threatening. This requires monitoring and frequent visits in the short-term since it was hoped the medication would control these.

I pushed the file back to its original position on the coffee table. It was an accurate assessment of where I was at, but such notes always reminded me of a zoo specimen being observed. Peeking at the file hadn't made me feel any better, but I was faithfully taking the tablets, so it couldn't be my fault if they weren't working. It required my best efforts to look innocent when George came back, saying, 'That is the most awesome loo ever!'

For the remainder of the visit, we chatted about innocuous subjects, such as my cookery experiments. She also recommended a shop in Lytham where I could look for a new outfit, since I didn't want to wear black and white again for Sunday lunch.

*

I was able to present myself at Lucas's front door in a simple, calf-length dress in a soft shade of pale blue, worn with the white sandals the helpful shop assistant had persuaded me I'd need. The whole exercise had taken no more than fifteen minutes; some of the easiest shopping I'd ever done. I should have bought more, they'd had some nice things, but by then had been in a hurry to escape. The local stores were such a different experience to trawling desperately up and down the busy streets of York. I didn't much enjoy shopping online either, never able to imagine myself in the clothes on display. The few I'd ordered didn't fit and the sizing was always inconsistent: clothes for men aren't like that; at least, according to my former male colleagues. Yet another item to add to the long list of things that are more difficult for women.

Waiting on the doorstep, my anxiety levels were rising, especially knowing that Lucas was heavily invested in my meeting his much-loved nephew. I could hear Mutt barking, and Lucas's voice rebuking him sternly, but it was a stranger who filled the doorway with his tall frame, 6'5" or more, and broad, reminding me of a big bear. His beard was red, in contrast to the brown hair; late thirties perhaps, kind of ordinary-looking except for the impressive set of muscles under his T-shirt. Not that I looked or anything.

'You must be Mattie. I'm Tom, do come in,' he said with a wide smile. 'I've been hearing so much about you.'

'Ah, so you'll be expecting the worst.'

'Definitely.' He laughed. 'Come on through, Lucas is in the kitchen basting roast potatoes. I only call him Uncle on formal occasions, or when he's in trouble.'

Mutt was jumping around my knees, desperate to make me feel extra welcome. I can be awkward in social settings, especially with strangers, though I try not to let it show, usually by talking sharp and smart. But Tom had the same quality of quiet strength as his uncle, which put me at ease and dampened down my anxiety. The dog liked him too, always a good sign.

Lunch was delicious; Lucas's Yorkshire puddings were the best, perfectly light and fluffy, and the beef a delicate pink, served with creamy home-made horseradish sauce. Just because I'm a rubbish cook doesn't mean I can't appreciate good food.

It seemed Tom agreed because he leant back in his chair saying, 'Lucas, that was epic. You make the greatest roast dinner ever.'

'Tom is between jobs at the moment, so I persuaded him to come and spend some time with his old uncle,' said Lucas, his fondness evident. 'He's not long out of the army and could do with a breathing space before embarking on the rest of his life.'

Tom picked at a thread on the tablecloth. 'I'll have to decide what I want to do with it first. Being a military police officer doesn't qualify you for very much in civilian terms, except more police work, but I fancy a change and I'm too big to be an inconspicuous private detective.'

'Did you always want to be in the army?' I asked over the stilton and fruit which followed the main course.

'Not at all, I was desperate to join the Metropolitan Police, so I did criminology and forensic science at university, but then the Met weren't taking people on, so I joined the Home Office for a while.'

'Bored out of your tree, weren't you, Tom?' said Lucas.

'Absolutely. It was dry and dusty stuff, and I hated being stuck in an office. One day, on impulse, I walked into an Army recruiting office and the rest is history.'

'Have you considered doing a master's degree – then you could lecture?' I suggested, cutting a corner off the cheese, but Tom pulled a face.

'I want to do something different, but I don't know what yet. And it has to be something I can manage with this busted-up knee.' I'd noticed he walked with a slight limp.

'No rush,' Lucas told him, gathering up the plates. 'Better to take your time and find the right thing. Mattie, I hope it wasn't wrong of me, but I told Tom you had a history of depression.'

Understatement of the century, I thought as he headed into the kitchen. It made me feel uncomfortable, wondering what Lucas had been saying. Tom gave me a straight look, well aware of my discomfort, and when he spoke his voice was deliberate and unemotional.

'Please don't think Lucas has betrayed any confidences; he only mentioned your experience because I've been suffering from post-traumatic stress. Got into a nasty situation in the Middle East and came out alive, if not quite undamaged.'

Then I understood; Tom was another member of the walking wounded. 'Not quite my experience, but I can certainly empathise. Flashbacks?'

'Yes, and sound triggers such as loud noises. Nightmares too, but they're less frequent these days.'

The doctors had given him very similar advice to the kind I'd received: medication, rest, fresh air, gradual exercise for the knee, and minimum stress. His uncle had suggested a few weeks by the sea might help.

'Are you seeing someone?' I asked.

'No, happily single.' He grinned cheekily, knowing that wasn't what I'd meant. At my raised eyebrows, he coughed. 'Yeah, I did have some cognitive behavioural therapy while I was still in the army, and I've been working with a counsellor since. It does help, but so often it's two steps forward and one back.'

'It's brave of you to work through it; remembering can be a challenge.'

Lucas came back and the conversation moved on, but Tom had my sympathy. Some of the medication I'd taken had given me terrible dreams, and I wouldn't wish those on anybody.

*

On Monday morning Ruth was back, so I left her dusting upstairs while I worked with my next pupil. Sienna was all black eyeliner and attitude; she didn't want to be there, but her strict parents had threatened to withdraw her allowance if she failed to comply. I'd been told her ambition was to study pharmacy, enabling her to walk into a job at her father's chain of chemist shops, so I pointed out that most courses would want A-level maths.

'Daddy says the same,' she said, folding her arms and clearly unimpressed. 'But I'm already doing chemistry and biology, and they're more relevant.'

'No, Daddy is right. Maths is what they call a facilitating subject, so it's a requirement for a lot of biomedical courses.' Sienna showed me her best "don't care" face.

As we went through the assessment process, it was clear she was a bright girl who just wasn't all that interested in maths. I might be able to persuade her to cooperate. Maybe the games teacher outfit wasn't helping my credibility with such a fashion princess; I'd try to look more professional if she came again.

Afterwards, it was a relief to get out and run along the seafront, where the gulls were crying overhead, hovering on the wind currents. The big sky and ozone smell from the water always soothed me, not to mention provided perspective; a reminder that the world was bigger than my small, everyday concerns.

Arriving home, I opened the door and stepped into the porch to be confronted by a disgusting stench, and while I was reeling back from it, managed to plant my feet straight into a puddle of vomit on the floor. For God's sake, someone had puked through my letterbox while I was out. It was gross; requiring heroic efforts not to heave, I took off my trainers, then gathered together rubber gloves, a bucket and disinfectant to clean up. It seemed odd that there was nothing on the outside of the door at all, although the puke had trickled down the inside and onto the tiles. It must have happened while I was out, but who would do such a thing – kids on their way home from school? It was a bit early in the day for drunks, but then you can't judge what goes on with people, even behind the smart exteriors of Lytham houses.

My trainers and socks went straight in the bin; I had several more pairs upstairs, all identical because of my brand loyalty or – more accurately – lack of imagination. The door was open to the fresh air as I mopped the floor with strong disinfectant when along came Davina, tottering past on vertiginous heels.

'*Ciao*, Mattea,' she called out, and I waved back.

She came up the path towards me, smiling as much as her frozen face would allow.

'Such a lovely dinner; I do hope you'll come again?' she said.

Leaning on the mop, I saw no reason not to be direct. 'Nigel will have told you that I turned down your offer – I hope it wasn't too disappointing for you?'

'Well naturally, a little, and if you ever change your mind, I'm sure you'll let us know. We must have a girls' lunch in town some time; get to know each other better.' Davina was making a determined effort to be friendly, so I found myself agreeing to the plan. Much better to be on good terms with the neighbours.

'*That one is up to no good*,' observed Lee. '*Nasty little madam.*'

This had to be my subconscious speaking; the shaming truth was I'd taken against Davina and her husband in an irrational way, which was totally unfair. I had to stop doing that.

After generous doses of air freshener around the ground floor, I retreated up to the study, where the smell hadn't reached. The running must have paid off because I wasn't even out of breath from climbing the stairs.

'*Somebody doesn't like you: that vomit stunt was bloody vile,*' said Lee.

'Get out of my head, I'm busy,' I told him. His running commentary was an unwelcome intrusion; a constant reminder I wasn't in full control of my brain.

Opening my inbox, there was an email from Mamma, which took my mind off everything, including Lee. Before reading it, I glanced at the photos of the twins' early years I'd left spread across the desk and wondered again why such close sisters had broken apart.

Darling Mattie,

I am so glad to hear you're in a better place mentally now. It sounds as if the move to Lytham has been good for you. It's only natural you should want to know about my sister, and why she wasn't part of our lives.

It must have been university that started it; we found it liberating to be in different places and study our own choice of subjects. It allowed each of us to be an individual, rather than always half of a pair.

It's hard to explain, but around the time you were born, Emilie and I disagreed over something so fundamental there was no mending it. Maybe it was partly hormonal new motherhood, but it was months before we were back in touch and although over time we reconnected and negotiated a truce, things were never the same. I thought it was easier if you never knew about her, rather than try and explain to a small child the complexities of an adult argument. It took some time before we began to speak regularly on the phone and meet a couple of times a year, but our lives had become very different.

As for the name changes, they had to do with your father. Even though we weren't married, I hoped it might be easier for you if your surname sounded more Italian – you were always so distinctively dark and foreign-looking. It was all done officially by deed poll, and while I was at it also changed the spelling of my name to the one that sounded more Latin.

I wanted to share the bare facts rather than get into too much detail here, I hope this goes some way to answering your questions. If you want to know more, perhaps we can speak on the phone?

Ti amo, piccolo.

Mamma x

She'd always called me *piccolo*, Italian for "little one", and it had become a joke between us in my teens when I became much taller than she was. From some deep well of connection came a huge longing to hold her close. I wrote back on impulse, without over thinking it.

Dearest Mamma,

Thank you for answering my immediate questions, but I'd love to know more about my father and there is so much I want to hear – and say. How would you feel about coming to visit me in Lytham? I still don't drive, and trains between here and Yorkshire are complicated.

You can say no, I won't be offended.

Love,

Mattie x

It was a start, but she hadn't given me much new information, or any clue about the nature of the disagreement which had driven the twins apart. Was it something to do with me, or perhaps my father? Maybe Emilie hadn't got on with him or been supportive of her sister's decision to raise me alone? I hoped Mamma would explain more, but I couldn't force it if she chose not to, especially when our fragile reconciliation remained a work in progress.

*

Lucas warned me that the continuing warm weather wasn't typical of Lancashire summers, which he said were more often cool and showery. Having grown up in Yorkshire, I considered myself a hardy Northern girl, so this didn't bother me one bit. Now I had a garden of my own to maintain, I'd begun to look around and take notice of what grew well locally. One day before breakfast, I'd been tidying up the front bedroom in the hopes of a forthcoming visit from Mamma, and saw Tom set off on his regular early walk, with Mutt pulling eagerly ahead.

Less than half an hour later, they were standing on my doorstep, the puppy jumping up in his eagerness to shower me with love. I bent down to make a fuss of the little dog but stood up to see Tom's pleasant face creased with worry.

'Mattie, I'm sorry, this is awful, but there's something you should see.'

He led me to the street side of the low wall which bordered my small front garden, where I saw that some charming person had spray-painted the word "Paki" in Day-Glo orange.

'Oh, for fuck's sake,' was all I could say.

NINE

Lucas must have heard Tom's voice and Mutt's anxious barks, so came to see what was happening. A waft of cigarettes suggested he'd been having a crafty smoke in the garden again. Tom had told me he discouraged this habit out of concern for Lucas's health but didn't want to turn into a nag.

Then Nigel arrived from next door, presumably alerted by us gathering in the street. Seeing the paint on the wall, he spluttered with indignation. 'Mattea, how bloody awful,' he said. 'Some people just let the whole neighbourhood down. And all the more so when Davina and I have been at great pains to explain to everyone that you're Italian.'

Lucas swivelled his head to look at Nigel, his expression hard to read, but I had a shrewd idea what he was thinking.

'How can I get it off?' I said through gritted teeth.

'There's a product you can put on it,' said Tom, picking up Mutt to keep him away from the wall. 'Can't remember what it's called but the hardware store might have it, or something similar. You put on a few coats to degrade the paint, and then it will power wash off; we had to do it on the outer wall of the military base, at regular intervals.'

'If you don't have your own, I've got a power washer you can borrow,' offered Nigel. 'This is supposed to be a nice area. Bloody vandals.'

Lucas put his arm around my shoulder. 'You're shaking,' he said. 'Don't let this upset you, Mattie.'

My whole body was reacting, with hot and cold waves of anger and revulsion. 'I'm not upset, I'm bloody livid,' I told him.

'Here, take Mutt,' said Tom, putting the wriggling dog into my arms. 'I'll nip to the shop now and see if they stock anything.'

Other people were beginning to appear at their gates and windows, so I dragged Lucas inside my house, where he promptly set to work making strong coffee. Mutt whined a couple of times and insisted on sitting on my knee, but was otherwise less unhappy than on his previous visit. The soft little body on my lap was comforting, and in that way animals do he picked up on my conflicted emotions and kept licking my hand and whining.

'This is such a rotten thing to happen when you've been settling in so well,' said Lucas, handing me a mug decorated with a blue flamingo wearing a crown. 'Don't worry, we'll get it off somehow. Tom will find a way.'

'It's the stupidity of racism that gets to me – why would it matter even if it was true? We're all just people, aren't we? I'm used to being called a "Paki" by ignorant people,' I told him. 'It's been happening all my life because I'm so dark. Before, I might have assumed it was kids messing about, but this is the second time…'

'What?' asked Lucas, a sharp note in his voice as he turned from the coffee machine to look at me.

I hadn't intended to tell him, or indeed anyone, but Lucas was too astute for me to lie with any conviction. The vomit incident was described in the minimum necessary detail, which grossed me out all over again.

'You and Tom were out for the day, and I soon had it cleaned up. The porch still smells of industrial-strength disinfectant.'

'Mattie, this is disturbing. Once is nasty, but twice is something else.'

'*It's that bloody Nigel*,' said Lee.

'It can't be Nigel,' I said. 'I don't think he'd go that far.'

'*Davina might*,' observed Lee.

'This is ridiculous,' I told both Lee and Lucas. 'There is no way I'm going to let these petty incidents upset me, but should they be reported to the police?'

Lucas frowned, looking into his coffee mug as if it might provide answers.

'Not sure it's worth bothering, to be honest, they simply don't have time to investigate small stuff of this kind.'

Tom eventually returned with an aerosol can. 'The bloke in the hardware shop says three applications of this should get it off, so I've given it one spray already and I'll do another later. It needs six hours between coats.' He gazed around the kitchen in delight, taking in the eccentric details. 'This house is just wild, on an epic scale. I've only ever been in the garden before, never seen anything like it.'

That cheered me up. 'My friend Polly described Auntie's taste as absolutely bonkers, but I do love it.'

*

It took Tom a couple of days to get the paint off, after which I was determined not to give the vandalism any further thought. It couldn't be allowed to disturb the balance of mind I'd tried so hard to achieve. My subconscious brain did not seem to agree.

'*You've got to watch out for that Nigel,*' said Lee. '*He's trying to drive you away, scare you into moving on.*'

'If they're trying to force me to sell the house to them, it makes no sense because I won't; not if hell froze over.'

'*But he doesn't know that.*' Lee's tone was triumphant.

'He does because I told him to his face. I won't sell – not to them, not to anybody. They both seem to have accepted my decision, so that's the end of it. Davina even invited me to lunch.' By then I'd had enough of arguing with a voice in my head. 'Now go away and leave me alone,' I told Lee. 'You're making it worse.'

He did, which I fervently hoped meant I was gaining some control over my condition. It's such hard work focusing on remaining generally optimistic, but it's always an improvement on the dreaded "everything is pointless" feeling. Not easy when I seemed to be under attack from somewhere – or perhaps it was only paranoia on my part conflating the two incidents, but it made me jittery.

By the time George came for her regular visit, I was doing my best to put both events behind me but underestimated the power of local gossip.

'I heard about the paint job,' she said without preamble. 'From the looks of the wall, you got it off all right. But how did it make you feel?'

'One of those things,' I said, attempting to dismiss it. 'Probably kids larking about.'

'*No it wasn't,*' said the distant voice that wasn't Lee. He was always faint enough for me to ignore him.

'This is such a lousy thing to happen when you're only a couple of months out of hospital,' said George, settling herself on a stool at the kitchen island.

Go on, remind me that I'm potentially unstable, I thought, trying to look and sound relaxed about what had happened. Inside, I was like a messed-up hedgehog: prickly and threatened.

'Just leave it, George. I'm trying very hard to forget it ever happened.'

Accepting the coffee I held out, she raised an eyebrow. 'Buster – that is, Barbara – at the St Annes Law Centre will give you free legal advice if you need it. She's really nice and knows her stuff. Denial might not be the right coping strategy.'

'Is there an alternative which doesn't involve allowing it to make me anxious?' I snapped.

George held up her hands in mock surrender. 'I only wondered if you might need to talk about it, but you don't have to. Now, before you shoot me down in flames, I do have to ask: any more trouble with voices?'

'Nope,' I said briefly, and she didn't press me on the subject. This meant there was no need to admit that Lee was a strong and frequent presence, but one who could be persuaded to go away if I insisted. It wasn't clever of me to keep the truth from her when she was only trying to help, but I hadn't told any lies. Lee's voice wasn't troublesome, more at the level of irritation when he interrupted a train of thought.

It was still a surreal experience having "conversations" with him and I didn't want to talk about it. George might see it as the medication not doing a good job, but the evidence was there because I *was* coping with everyday life, even teaching again. It was also true that the unpleasantness had disturbed my inner equilibrium, even if I didn't want to admit it. Walking or running down the street always left me wondering which of my neighbours might be hiding their racist hate behind shiny front doors and neat exteriors. George had suggested I make a greater effort to get to know the people around me, but far from wanting to knock on doors and introduce myself, recent events only made me want to hide behind my own.

Whenever I'm feeling anxious or threatened, it always ends up with me pushing people away, so George and I parted with some awkwardness. She would probably write down that I was being hostile again. At least her next visit the following week was better; there'd been no more toxic events, so I was marginally less tense. It wasn't quite back to our easy relationship, but progress of a kind.

To make up for my bad attitude, I'd bought doughnuts from the deli to go with the coffee.

'Peace offering,' I said, 'and I'm sorry for being such a grumpy cow last week.'

She smiled at me, before happily munching into a squidgy chocolate doughnut. 'If you think that was grumpy or hostile… all I can say is my visits to other patients aren't always well received. Some won't even open the door, but you have to be persistent in this job.'

'It's a genuine apology. I didn't mean to be cranky.'

'Mattie, give yourself credit for being in a difficult place,' she said around bites of doughnut. 'Quite apart from the graffiti on your wall, it's hard starting all over again, and you've done so well. Have you given any thought to getting out more? Not only running but getting to know people. Social isolation can be a real issue when you have depression; I don't want it to be a problem for you.'

My lack of enthusiasm must have shown because George put the doughnut down.

'Maybe I could go and look at the library noticeboard,' I said hastily, hoping this might head her off.

'Great idea, you might find some groups to join. Didn't you say you were interested in knowing more about local history?'

'Yes, but what I had in mind had more to do with reading up on it than joining groups.' George's frown was back, so I added, 'OK, it's true, I do tend to hide, and maybe I should get out more. I promise to give it a go but don't expect me to do a complete 180-degree turn and suddenly become sociable and extrovert.'

She had to be content with that, and I suggested she eat the other untouched doughnut too, which got her off the subject in a satisfactory fashion.

*

It was a full ten days before Mamma replied to my email, leading to a suspicion that she didn't want to answer questions about my dad, and it seemed I was right.

Darling Mattie,

I've thought long and hard about your request to know more about your father, and I hope you can understand how conflicted I feel about the whole episode. I managed well enough on my own, but being a single parent is tough, and without Emilie's financial help it would have been even more difficult. He was a good-looking man, and you have his beautiful hazel eyes, but more than that I can't give you.

I know it's not much and must be frustrating. If you want to withdraw your invitation to visit, I will understand, but it would mean a lot to hold you in my arms again and see how you've made Emilie's house into your home.

Love always,

Mamma xx

What the hell was I supposed to do with that? I wanted to be angry with her, but my understanding had always been that it had been my father's choice to leave, with Mamma the one left holding the baby. Things might be easier when Mamma and I could hang out together and have a face-to-face conversation to help me understand the hurt she'd experienced.

I emailed back within the day.

Dear Mamma,

Yes it's disappointing, and I had hoped you'd tell me more, but I do get how you feel and have to respect your decision. Of course the invitation is still open – why not come next month in June? July will be a busy time for tourists here, so, now you're retired, make it before the schools chuck out for the summer.

Looking forward to us being together again.

Love,

M xxx

The summer weather in Lytham proved to be every bit as mixed as Lucas had predicted, and I soon learnt to make the most of good days and save up any indoor projects for the frequent wet ones. My life was quiet, all the more so when one of my pupils went away on holiday, though there were two more booked in from August. I was settling into a contented routine and allowing myself to relax, even thinking about inviting some neighbours for coffee.

Then the letters began to arrive.

The first was easy enough to shrug off, typed in capitals on a strip of paper which said, "WE DON'T WANT YOUR KIND HERE". I threw it in the bin, not sure what "kind" I was supposed to be, but with a pretty good idea of the direction of travel. The second, a few days later, was also typed, and much worse.

"YOU DON'T BELONG HERE, BLACK BITCH. WHY DON'T YOU GO BACK WHERE YOU CAME FROM? I SEE YOU OUT RUNNING ON YOUR OWN. BETTER WATCH OUT FOR DARK ALLEYS WHERE YOU MIGHT GET WHAT'S COMING TO YOU."

The sheer venom behind this sent a shock of cold down my spine, throwing me seriously off balance all over again. Who was doing this, and, more importantly, why? All my instincts rejected Lee's belief that it had to originate from Nigel, he just didn't seem the type. It had to be the work of some unhinged individual who'd taken against me for reasons which wouldn't make sense to anyone, let alone me. However, it was the first time I'd been physically threatened, and feeling afraid sent me next door to talk to Lucas.

'Hello, Mattie, come in, this is nice. Tom's gone to the physio; the knee has improved enough for him to drive himself in my automatic…' His voice trailed off at the look on my face. 'My dear girl, whatever's the matter?'

Mutt had jumped into my arms, and I was holding onto him for comfort, silently handing Lucas the strip of paper.

'It's not the first. The other one went in the bin, but this…'

'Is vile stuff. No wonder you're upset.'

I had to resist a strong temptation to fling myself into the safety of his arms and cry my eyes out. In the peace of the light-filled kitchen, and even though it was only mid-afternoon, Lucas fed me brandy and chocolate cake (made by Tom). As remedies for general angst go, these were pretty damn good and, as a short-term solution, a great improvement on antidepressant drugs.

'Maybe it's time to involve the police?' said Lucas.

'What's the point when there's no evidence to give them – I cleaned up the puke and Tom sorted out the wall. The first letter went in the bin, so this is all there is.'

'You're forgetting Tom's military police background. He took a picture of the paint on the wall before he cleaned it off.'

'He did? I should have had the common sense to do that myself, but a photo of the wall and one nasty letter isn't a lot to go on, is it?'

'True, but I do think you should report it. Mattie, you've been threatened, which makes it much more serious.'

'Let me think about it,' I said, unsure what to do. What Lucas didn't appreciate was that claims of harassment from someone like me weren't necessarily going to be treated with real seriousness by the police. Once you have a history of mental health problems, everything is viewed through the prism of that lens, and anything you say or do can and will be attributed to an unreliable state of mind. If I reported harassment and hate mail, it might not get me very far, or worse, be written off as some kind of persecution complex.

I accepted more cake as a distraction from my troubles and told Lucas about Sofie agreeing to come and visit in a couple of weeks.

'I asked her about my father, but she hasn't told me much more than I already knew. She's still nursing a lot of anger towards him, even after all this time.'

Lucas gave me a sideways look. His breath smelt of mints. 'It's hardly surprising she feels that way. I'm sure you can empathise?'

'In some ways, but from a purely selfish perspective, I need to understand who I am. Did Emilie ever mention my dad, or meet him?' I asked.

'Yes, I believe so. She always said you had his eyes.'

'Mamma told me that he came from Venice, but that's the only information I have. I don't even know his name. The few times he was mentioned she always called him "your father", or once "Addi". Maybe a diminutive of an Italian name like Adamo or Adriano, but I'm guessing.'

'Having so little information must feel strange.' Lucas was carefully non-committal.

'It never used to bother me,' I said. 'Plenty of kids at school came from broken families and had no contact with the other parent. Maybe Mamma will be willing to say more when she comes to stay? At least we'll be together in the same space, and that seems such an important step towards healing our relationship.'

'I so hope the visit turns out well for you both,' he said. 'Look, I've been thinking about Venice and wondered if you might like to go with me. It would be an enormous pleasure to introduce you to Italy.'

'But you don't know me very well,' I protested, with a cheeky grin. 'I might be a terrible travel companion who'd demand English food and complain about everything being foreign.'

'Oh dear, I hadn't thought of that – good job you warned me before our plans were too advanced. Seriously, I'm confident we'd enjoy each other's company and it's a genuine offer, Mattie, please think about it.'

'I will. Thank you.'

'Some online research suggests that late October when it's cooler sounds promising. We could get an apartment overlooking one of the canals. My treat, of course.'

'I'd love to go but can't let you bear the expense. Anyway, thanks to Emilie, I can afford to pay my way.'

'Which reminds me,' he said, 'have you been back to the lawyer to discuss your intention to stay? Remember, it makes a difference to how the trust operates. And before I do any more research on this trip, do you have a passport?'

'No, because I've never needed one before; Mamma and I always had our holidays in the UK. I'll need to apply for my original birth certificate to get one, won't I? Wait a minute, it might tell me my father's name. Why didn't I think of that before?'

Lucas's expression was doubtful. 'If Sofie was angry about him abandoning her, she might not have registered him?'

'Well, there's only one way to find out.'

Sending off for my birth certificate turned out to be more complicated than anticipated, and the online form required very specific information I didn't have. I had to give up on technology – a wonderful thing, but only when it works – and go the snail-mail route. A letter explaining what I did know went to the General Register Office, giving my date of birth and other necessary information, and enclosing a cheque for the fee.

A week later, woken by Ruth vacuuming the hall, I came downstairs in search of breakfast. There was a small box on the island unit, wrapped in fancy paper with an extravagant gold bow. Maybe something from Lucas; it wasn't as if I knew many people who'd be hand-delivering presents.

Ruth brought the vacuum cleaner back to its home in the kitchen cupboard, and when I picked up the package told me, 'That was sitting there when I arrived.'

That meant she hadn't brought it in, and the realisation that the box had been inside my house was disturbing. I put it down with exaggerated care as if it might contain a snake.

'A gift?' asked Ruth, who didn't know about the hate mail or the rest, unless she too had picked up on the local gossip.

'But who could have got into the house, and why doesn't it have a label?'

Something wasn't right, but sheer curiosity had me reaching for the box again.

'*It must be a bomb; don't touch it, Mattie,*' screeched Lee's voice, loud enough to make my ears ring. I had to be losing the plot to come up with that.

'Go on, open it,' said Ruth.

It was a mistake, but I did. Inside was a small black plastic bag, knotted at the top and tied with a parcel tag which said, "YOU DESERVE THIS". Ruth leaned in to read the label and both of us were puzzled by this oblique message.

I should have known; a part of me did know something wasn't right, and the stench which floated out of the bag made us both take a step back.

'Dog shit,' said Ruth unnecessarily, and reached out to tie the bag again. 'I'll get rid of it for you.'

'No.' I put a hand on her arm. 'It might be evidence; I've had some horrible letters too and other stuff. Please, just get it out of my sight. Put it in the shed or something.'

She carried it at arm's length into the garden and came back with a troubled look in her eyes.

'Somebody's being proper nasty.' She got the air freshener spray out and gave the kitchen a liberal dose of it. 'Who'd do a thing like that?'

The image of someone sneaking into my home to leave such a "gift" brought up goose bumps on my arms and the cosy kitchen seemed suddenly cold, despite the warm day.

'That's what I'd like to know,' I said.

TEN

After Ruth had gone, I went upstairs to my attic sanctuary. Sitting at the desk, gazing unseeing into space, I tried to imagine what kind of extreme hatred and prejudice might lie behind the campaign of harassment. Nigel had said it himself, it *was* a nice neighbourhood, but the area was overwhelmingly white and a long way from multicultural. There would undoubtedly be people to whom I might appear as some kind of immigrant invader. It made me want to stand in the street and shout, "I was born here, and my dad was Italian", but why would I even want or need to defend myself against a charge of being Indian or Pakistani? Many of my old friends were, and why the hell should it matter anyway, as long as I was a good neighbour.

But even if I went door to door to say these things, it wouldn't do any good or change anything. Racism isn't based on any recognisable logic or solid intellectual foundation, it's visceral, tribal and instinctive. Which left me with a problem.

Up in my sanctuary, I'd begun to create a wall of special pictures, none of which seemed to be hanging straight – a few of York, a line drawing of Malton where I'd grown up, Polly and I laughing outside some random pub, and a photo of Mamma.

'Who would even do this?' I asked them, still thinking about the harassment.

'I keep telling you, it's Nigel. Why won't you believe me? He's got a motive for trying to drive you out of the house,' Lee insisted.

'Look, I know he's disappointed because I won't sell, but would he seriously hate me enough to do all this? What's spooky is the nasty parcel being inside my house. How the hell did it get there?'

'Working that out isn't rocket science. No signs of a break-in. So, who has a key?' asked Lee.

'Lucas, for one, and so does Ruth, but...'

'You can rule Lucas out, which leaves Ruth.'

'But she's been his cleaner for years, and he trusts her. Anyway, she offered to return the key once she first came, but I told her there was no need. It's not always convenient to be here to let her in.'

'Everyone has their price.'

Nigel had said the same thing, but even if he'd been upset about my refusal to sell, he'd been neighbourly enough to lend me his power washer. Then Davina had invited me for lunch, but perhaps what she wanted was a liquid lunch after which I'd be amenable to another attempt at persuasion.

'I don't know what to think,' I said.

'Please, Mattie, be careful. You're too trusting.'

Polly had told me the same thing, more than once. I'm a straightforward person who sees things in terms of black and white, so tend to take people at face value. It goes with the maths and the logic I'm used to applying. I tell the truth, try to be nice and assume others are doing the same. By my early thirties, experience should possibly have taught me otherwise, but despite my visceral dislike of Nigel and Davina, I still leaned towards believing the best of people.

'When you have eliminated the impossible, whatever remains, however improbable, must be the truth. Sherlock Holmes, or was it Poirot?

'Go away, Lee, I can't think about this now.'

'*Talk to Lucas*,' was his parting shot.

By way of distraction, I got out my aunt's box of photographs, which I'd been avoiding for reasons I couldn't articulate. There was a package marked "friends", showing Emilie in various locations. In these, she was invariably accompanied by a good-looking man and had written names or initials on the back: "with N in Sri Lanka", one taken on a white beach with a beautiful Indian man in a very close embrace, marked "in the Maldives". I leafed through them, finding another which had a temple in the background labelled "with James in Vietnam", and many more. Lucas was in some of them, but his assessment had been right; she wasn't suited to monogamy.

There were photos taken at awards ceremonies for her books, and some professional publicity shots, including the one on the back cover of her most recent books. I decided to keep that one out and get a frame for it; she could join Mamma on my wall. Studying the picture, there was a clear family resemblance: Emilie, Sofie and I all had the same-shaped eyes and nose, though Mamma had chosen to have her chin-length hair highlighted blonde as she aged, and my aunt had opted for a stylish short grey crop.

I studied the graduation picture again; Emilie had cared enough to come, so why hadn't I even known who she was or why she was there?

'*There are more photographs, on the computer*,' said Lee.

'But the hard drive was wiped,' I protested. 'There aren't any files on it, except for her manuscripts.'

'*Look again.*'

In the word-processing programme, there was a long list of folders with the titles of her many novels, in alphabetical rather than date order. It began with *A Life in Ruins* and I could see the one I'd read, *Eye of the Storm*. I'd inherited the copyright for all of these, most of which were still in print.

'*The one you want is* Precious Child, *scroll down a bit*,' instructed Lee.

I didn't remember that being one of the titles on the shelf, and when I clicked on it a dialogue box asked for a password.

'*Princess, capital P*,' said Lee.

It was ridiculous, my friendly auditory hallucination couldn't possibly know any of this, except he'd done it before…

I tapped in the letters, the file opened up like a flower, and there I was… in full glorious technicolour. My entire life was recorded in loving detail, from babyhood to my late twenties. It took ages to go through them all, and there were many I didn't remember ever seeing before. Me as a curly headed child, perhaps six years old, laughing outside the primary school gates with a friend. Another showed Mamma and me admiring the Babbage Difference Engine when it went on display at the Science Museum in London. We'd made a special trip to see what was, in effect, the first-ever computer. I would have been around eight, and already a maths geek. Mamma must have got a passing tourist to take the picture.

Lucas had been speaking the truth when he said that Emilie cared about me, following my life in great detail and, I could only assume, with some kind of pride. Many of the pictures might have been taken by her sister, and yet she'd been excluded from our everyday lives. I'd be able to ask why very soon, but would Mamma be willing to open up when she'd kept silent all this time?

*

As much for therapeutic value as anything, my culinary explorations continued – I was onto the pasta section of the cookbook – and my confidence grew enough to invite Lucas and Tom for lunch. I fed them home-made pasta (Emilie's kitchen had a machine) with a cream, dill and smoked-salmon sauce. For Mutt there was a rawhide chew for distraction as he remained a little ill at ease inside the house and much preferred the garden.

'This is delicious,' said Lucas, smiling his appreciation of my efforts.

Tom nodded in agreement, adding black pepper to his dish. 'I buy fresh pasta from the supermarket, but this is so much better.'

'It's so nice that you're impressed, but it's super easy,' I told them. 'Fiddling about with the machine is fun, and winding out the lengths. There's something satisfying about it. The sauce is incredibly simple too, only takes a couple of minutes, and the salmon is straight from the deli. The people in the shop raved about it; from Lochgilphead, I think, somewhere in Scotland.'

They cleared their plates with gratifying enthusiasm, and after a cheesecake also supplied by the deli – the chapter on desserts came nearer the end of the book – Lucas offered to make coffee.

'Sit down, Mattie, we want to talk to you,' said Tom, as he handed me my favourite mug.

'Sounds ominous, have I done something wrong?'

'No, of course not, but we're both worried about the harassment and hate mail.' I'd told them about the reeking poo parcel, of course. 'We're concerned that you aren't taking it seriously enough.'

'Mattie, please listen,' for once Tom's broad face was unsmiling, 'I've come across this kind of thing in my military police work. It's not just a mild annoyance but, in my experience, something much more sinister. We have to consider the possibility that you might be in danger, and since you live alone…'

Lucas nodded. 'Someone has been in this house without your knowledge to leave that revolting package, and I've been worried about you ever since.'

'But I took the box and letter to the police, with a printed photo of the wall. They gave me a crime number and said I should consider getting a security system installed or changing the locks. I told you about it.'

Lucas pushed his glasses to the end of his nose and gazed at me over the top, visibly unimpressed. 'Yes, well that didn't seem like an adequate response from them, so I asked Tom's advice, and he suggested getting you one of these.'

The object he held out was matte black and at first sight appeared to be a wristwatch, except that it had no face, just a blank disc.

'It's a personal alarm made to look like a fitness tracker,' explained Tom. 'The top has a kind of panic button which can be linked to any mobile phone you choose – maybe Lucas's and perhaps mine, as long as I'm around, anyhow.'

When I didn't respond, Lucas fidgeted with the coffee mug while Mutt whined at his feet.

'You aren't offended, Mattie? We just don't want anything bad to happen to you.'

'No, of course I'm not, it's sweet of you to care, though I'm surprised you think this is necessary.' I draped the black strap across my wrist. 'But if it will make you feel better, I'll wear it.'

'Mattie, this is not about humouring us,' Tom's face was serious, and his voice urgent. 'It's to keep you safe and I'd rather be over-cautious, even if it's not needed. The casing is waterproof so you can keep it on even in the shower.'

'It did make me uncomfortable that someone got into the house without forcing entry,' I reluctantly admitted. 'But only Lucas and Ruth have keys, so I must have accidentally left a door or window open.'

'Ruth has a key?' Tom's head came up in alarm.

'Yes,' said Lucas, 'I gave her a copy of mine after Emilie died when she agreed to keep the house in order before Mattie moved in. I've known Ruth for years; she must be beyond suspicion.'

'And she was so upset about that nasty parcel,' I added.

The look on Tom's face told us we were innocent in the ways of the world.

'Look,' he said. 'The unpleasant truth is that most crimes aren't committed by a stranger, but by someone close to the victim. You can never rule out the obvious people, so we should ask her about it.'

I remembered Lee's comment, that what remained must be the truth.

'Look, ask Ruth if you like but please don't involve me. Call me a big chicken if you must, but I hate confrontation and prefer to avoid it.'

'Fair enough, but please wear the alarm, Mattie, it would make us both feel so much better,' said Tom.

*

On her Friday visit, George surprised me by recognising the device on my wrist.

'A personal alarm – so what's making you feel unsafe?' I could almost hear her thinking "signs of paranoia" and had to come clean with the whole sorry tale of the letters (there'd been another), the vomit donation and the gift box.

George was shocked. 'Why didn't you tell me any of this before? What a horrible experience. How did it make you feel?' she asked. Bloody standard counsellor question.

'Uncomfortable; disturbed,' I said shortly. 'A normal reaction, I'd say.'

'What about your anxiety levels?'

'Again, elevated of course, but yours would be too. I took what little evidence I had to the police but don't hold your breath for any answers from that direction; they weren't much help. I get it, you're wondering if I'm sinking into depression again or even a fantasist making it all up for attention?'

George sighed. 'Can you please believe that I don't think anything of the kind. There's no reason to doubt what you're saying when the police have evidence, and you even have witnesses to some of it.'

I sighed in irritation; yes, of course it made me feel threatened and anxious, but I wasn't about to admit it, most of all not to my CPN.

'There's nothing else to be done. Unless the police get back in touch, it's just an unpleasant experience to put behind me.' I was being prickly and defensive again.

'And you're taking your medication?'

'Of course. Look, you have to trust me here, I'm an intelligent woman and am dealing with the situation, being sensible and practical, working through my feelings about it. When I told my neighbour, he suggested I wear the alarm as a precaution. End of story.'

George sighed again but said no more on the subject.

After she'd gone, Lee said quietly, '*George was only trying to help.*'

'I know, but I can't stand it when they start with the formulaic questions, "how did that make you feel" stuff. If I tell her I feel unnerved, threatened and suspicious of every stranger in the street, she'll only see me as paranoid.'

'*I don't think that's what you are. Be careful, Mattie.*'

*

Three days later, I was working upstairs in the study on a lesson plan. Pranit continued to be blocked on the calculation of probabilities, and I was trying to come at it from a different angle to help him understand. When the doorbell rang, I was frustrated by the interruption, but found Tom on my doorstep, his big frame blocking out the light. He'd trimmed his bushy red beard down into a neater spade shape. At that moment, I glimpsed the serious military police officer in the uncharacteristically grim and set lines of his face.

'Mattie, could you come next door for a moment? There's something you need to know.'

Intrigued, I followed him into their kitchen to find Lucas sitting at the table with Ruth, her face tear-streaked. At the sight of me, she gave a strangled wail and would obviously have preferred to be anywhere else.

Lucas patted her hand, and with a lot of prompting from Tom, the story came out in fits and starts – how Nigel had asked her to lend him the key while the house was unoccupied, saying he was interested in buying it. Ruth had rightly told him to go to the lawyers or ask Lucas, but then he'd offered her an envelope containing £500 in cash.

'It was a bad year.' She sniffed. 'I'd lost a few of my elderly clients and was struggling for money. Then, as promised, he gave me the key back a couple of days later.' Her eyes darted anxiously between the three of us.

'Nigel must have made a copy,' said Tom.

Ruth nodded, her head bowed, shoulders slumped, and misery written in every line of her body language.

'When all those bad things were happening to Mattie, it proper upset me. After that box of dog shit arrived, it took me a while, but I figured it had to be him doing it because nobody else could have got in. Oh, Mr Fallon, I've let you down and messed up big time. Are you going to sack me?'

Not only was this the longest speech ever to come out of Ruth's mouth, but it was clear to me that I'd been a total gold-plated idiot. Lee had told me repeatedly that the culprit was Nigel, and I should have trusted what were after all deep instincts coming from inside my head.

'I've always believed in second chances, Ruth.' Lucas's voice was artificially calm. 'We've known each other long enough for me to be convinced this was a one-off. So, no, as long as Mattie agrees, you're not going to be sacked.'

'But there are conditions,' said Tom, turning to Ruth. 'This is how it's going to work: I'm going to type up a statement which you will sign. All three of us can witness it, providing solid evidence against Nigel. With any luck, that will be enough to warn him off, without having to involve the authorities. In return, you can keep both jobs, but there will have to be a period of probation, so we want the keys back, and the property owners have to be present at all times when you are cleaning.'

A tearful Ruth eventually left, having agreed to everything and signed on the dotted line, pathetically grateful not to lose the work. Maybe I should have been angry with her but part of me genuinely understood. I'd lived through some lean financial times myself when teaching hours were scarce, and only frugal living and a diet of tinned soup had got me through. A lot of us would have done the same if we were desperate and someone offered an envelope of cash.

As the door closed behind Ruth, Lucas gave way to the feelings he'd been bottling up. His face was dark with anger as he launched into a tirade against the evil doings of my neighbour. 'I'm going to tell Nigel exactly what I think of him; the bastard set out to intimidate and frighten Mattie in the worst possible way...'

Tom held up a hand to silence him.

'Not helpful, Uncle. Let's keep this calm and professional. *I* will meet with Nigel, challenge him with the evidence, and insist he returns the key. It will be made plain that any further harassment would trigger immediate legal action. At least then the situation can be resolved on reasonable terms; you've both got to live near him, so no point in making things worse, for now at least.'

Tom took the opportunity to confront Nigel within days. Over coffee in Lucas's glorious garden the same afternoon, he related the bare bones of what had to have been a difficult confrontation.

Mutt ran around joyfully while Tom sipped a drink and gathered his thoughts.

'You won't be surprised, but he denied everything, except for the part involving Ruth. Claimed he wasn't behind any of the harassment, but I made it clear we didn't believe him. He left the room for some time and just as I was wondering where the hell he'd got to, came back with the key. Nigel's had a warning and with any luck, that's the end of it since he knows what will happen if there are any more incidents. I also took the opportunity to make sure he understands once and for all that you have no intention of selling.'

All I'd wanted was to draw a line under an unpleasant episode but, even though I disliked him, still couldn't quite picture my neighbour pushing vomit through my letterbox or any of the other stuff he'd done. This forced me to the inevitable conclusion that I must be a bad judge of character. It took a massive effort on my part not to dwell on what had happened and instead make a conscious decision to move on.

*

Two weeks later, Mamma came to visit. She announced her imminent arrival with a text sent from the station. Waiting for her on the front step, it was a surprise to feel so nervous that my feet couldn't seem to keep still, and I twiddled with the buttons on my cardigan so much that one fell off. It had been two years since we'd been together, and although our recent emails had prepared the ground for a new relationship, at some deep level I was anxious about how the visit would go.

The taxi had barely come to a halt before Mamma had the door open and was running up the path with outstretched arms. She hadn't changed at all, her blonde bob and dark, rose lipstick as familiar as my own face in the mirror. Resting my cheek on her head, and smelling her trademark perfume, was a kind of homecoming.

When our initial excited exchanges came to an end, she paid off the grinning taxi driver, who unloaded her case and the potted plant brought as a housewarming gift. I ushered her inside, knowing she'd never been to Emilie's home, and wondering how she'd react to the fantastical interior.

As we got into the hall, her eyes widened, and a smile of pure wonderment spread across her face. 'Oh, this is all so Emilie. I remember the moose head, and she's had that sign since her university days. This is such a hoot.' Mamma's taste ran to mid-century modern, classic brands like Ercol, which she'd always said were a good investment. Turned out she was right too.

'Do you like it?' she asked, turning to me.

'Yes, which surprises me because I always preferred my rented flats bare and impersonal. It's strange, but the wonderful chaos of this is liberating,' I confessed. 'Though my cleaner says it's a bugger to dust.'

'*Oh, Sofie,*' said Lee's voice, '*you're here at last.*'

There was no time to think about this as we embarked on a tour of the house, putting her case in the front bedroom as we passed, and ending with drinks in the garden. Sitting there, Mamma held my hand and looked into my face with such love, her eyes brimming with unshed tears.

'Mattie, my darling girl,' was all she could manage before her voice choked up. A glass of her favourite Franciacorta wine restored the smile I'd missed so much, and then she studied me, assessing. I was wearing the blue dress again, just for her.

'*Piccolo*, you are too thin. Are you eating right?' Mamma remained a sharp dresser, but her plump figure had expanded a little. That might have been my fault because she was an inveterate comfort eater, and I'd made her miserable.

'I'm learning to cook, Mamma, instead of living out of tins and packets, so it must be all the running if I've lost weight; I've been going along the shoreline every day.'

There was so much to say, words tumbled out of both of us, all through a simple dinner of antipasto and salad, followed by cheese; everything easy and all courtesy of the deli in their trademark brown paper carriers.

Later, we sat companionably on the big sofa in Emilie's parlour. By mutual unspoken consent, we didn't immediately talk about the past or the row which had caused our separation. The little she did say made it clear how much her understanding of my illness had grown, making it possible to begin again from where we were, together again.

Mamma wanted to hear all about my new life in Lytham, the maths students, and Lucas next door. I minimised the story of what had happened with the other neighbours, only saying they'd hoped to buy the house and there'd been some unpleasantness when I turned them down.

It turned out Mamma had moving plans of her own. 'I know it was your childhood home, *piccolo*, so I hope it doesn't make you sad, but I'm thinking of selling the Malton house. I don't need to be near the school now I've retired, and it's been my dream to buy a cottage somewhere more rural. Still in Yorkshire, of course.'

'Of course I don't mind, you've got to do what makes you happy,' I said.

Mamma was also gradually persuaded that I wasn't just coping but finally in a good place, not least because of the financial cushion provided by Emilie. At last, the stupid wall between us came tumbling down, making me wonder why I'd ever constructed it in the first place.

Everything led to the moment we both knew would come, when I tried to ask questions about my father, but it was no surprise to encounter resistance.

'Please, Mamma, I need to know more. Our personalities have always been so different – you're laid back and easy-going and I'm not. My facility with maths and languages must have come from him, along with my colouring, and it would help me so much to understand who I am; otherwise, I feel like half a person.'

Her face was set, and she hid behind her wine glass. 'He left us, Mattie, went away and didn't come back or get in touch. What kind of a person does that?'

'*Someone who didn't know he had a child,*' said Lee, who'd been silent for hours.

'But he knew about me?' I asked.

'*One day she'll have to tell you everything,*' Lee observed.

Mamma hesitated, and a range of emotions crossed her face, before she said, 'Forgive me, Mattie, but it's painful to talk about him. He was gone before you were born. Anyway, we did OK, the two of us, didn't we? I worked hard to give you the best life I could.'

'You did,' I said with complete truth. 'It was a magical childhood, full of love and encouragement.'

And that was as much as she would open up, but I wasn't leaving the subject, or reminding her that as, an adolescent, I'd turned out to be broken beyond her ability to repair. *Let it go for now*, I told myself.

Over the weekend, we played at being tourists, shopping in Lytham and lunching at some of the excellent restaurants. One of the smarter shops was having a summer sale, and Mamma insisted on buying me some new clothes. She'd seen inside the armoire in my bedroom and been aghast at its limited contents, then further horrified to discover I was a size smaller than when my diet had been junk.

'Too skinny for your height,' was her verdict, but it was said with a fond smile. I did try to look interested in the clothes she exclaimed over or held up against me. I even let her buy me a couple of dresses, plus some trousers and lightweight tops. In the face of my evident lack of enthusiasm, she admitted defeat and we went for coffee and cake instead. Poor Mamma would never turn me into a stylish, fashionable woman, no matter how hard she tried.

On Monday morning a reply came from the General Register Office, and everything changed. You might say "the shit hit the fan" because nothing else quite covers what happened next.

ELEVEN

Mamma slept late on Monday, after generous quantities of Franciacorta the previous evening. I'd had very little to drink because of the medication, and, in any case, liked to stick to one (big) glass, leaving the rest to her.

In those light summer mornings, I always woke early, so had got into the habit of getting up and going for a run while it was quiet. The post came early on our street, and the letter was waiting on the doormat when I got home, an official communication from the General Register Office. It made a change from hate mail, but it might as well have been for the tsunami it caused.

Before anything else, I needed a shower and a change of clothes; the day was warming up and running had made me sticky and sweaty. I opted for cotton trousers and one of the tops Mamma had bought me, thinking to please her by wearing them, then came downstairs and made toast. Half an hour later, I was still sitting in the kitchen with the unopened letter in my hands; it might provide answers but part of me was scared to find out.

'For God's sake, just read it,' said Lee, so, at last, I ripped open the envelope, thinking it might tell me my father's name, or at least I hoped so.

It did, but also way more than I wanted or expected.

The Certified Copy of an Entry of Birth showed I'd been born on the 9th of February 1991 – not in Harrogate, as I'd been told, but Scarborough on the Yorkshire coast. My birth name was given as Adeline Sophia Lombard... Who? It was reading the rest that made me feel sick, and my body went first hot all over and then cold.

Mother: Emilie Alicia Lombard.

Father: Aadi Gurdeep Rajani.

I stared at the certificate in my trembling hands, as if hoping the words might rearrange themselves, but the hard facts wouldn't, couldn't, change. My brain refused to process the information that everything about the identity I'd grown up with, right down to the woman who'd given birth to me, was a lie. Then there was my father's name. All my life, people had said I looked Indian, and now it was clear why.

'*Oh, Mattie...*' said Lee softly. '*She should have told you.*'

He'd got that right, as with so much else.

There was a second document, a copy of a Deed of Name Change, by which, at around four months old, I became Mattea Francesca Lombardi.

Impelled by rage, I stormed up the stairs, but there was no sign of my mother getting up. Hesitating on the landing outside her door, I was torn between wanting and needing to challenge her with what I'd discovered, but there was also a sick fear in the pit of my stomach. Consumed by a furious urgency to understand what lay behind all the deceit, at the same time there was a deep reluctance to hear the answers. Talk about conflicted.

I bottled it and instead went next door to see Lucas. He opened the door with tousled morning hair and wearing a dressing gown.

Without preamble, I demanded, 'Did you know? Have you been hiding the fact that I'm Emilie's child all this time?'

His jaw dropped in such genuine shock I had to believe it when he said, 'No, Mattie, no! Emilie never had any children.'

'Oh yes she did.' I waved the papers in his face. 'I've just received a copy of my birth certificate.'

When he read the words on the page, Lucas blanched and sat down hard. He looked ten years older, and almost as shattered as me.

'Emilie never told me. I promise you, Mattie, I had no idea. I was aware of her relationship with Aadi, she mentioned him as someone who'd been part of her life long ago, but she never said…'

'Emilie lied, to you, to everyone. So, if she was my birth mother, how did I end up with Sofie? My mamma's got some explaining to do and I'm going to haul her out of bed right this minute and demand an explanation, no more excuses. How could she do this to me?'

Lucas put a restraining hand on my arm. His expression was still dazed, while I was shaking with rage, a pressure cooker about to hit full steam.

'No, Mattie, please, stop and think. Don't do anything hasty, not while you're so angry. You might say something you'll regret later, just as the two of you are restoring your relationship.'

'Which was built on a fabrication! She's not my mother and I'm supposed to be half Italian, with a father from Venice. Instead, he turns out to be from a different continent, so what the hell is going on here and what else hasn't she told me?'

'Please, darling girl, take it slow. You need time to assimilate this information before you can be ready to hear Sofie's explanations. Sit there while I get dressed, then I'll make some coffee.'

After a quick change of clothes, he came and sat next to me in the kitchen; the handsome, vital man I'd grown to love, suddenly older and somehow deflated. His eyes had a broken look that hurt my heart.

'I'm so sorry, Lucas, I've been looking at this from a purely selfish perspective. She was the love of your life, but Emilie deceived you along with the rest of us.'

Lucas nodded miserably. He needed support too, but I couldn't be the one to give it, not while wrestling with my own inner turmoil.

'Tom's not here?' I asked. The car was gone.

'No, he got up very early to drive to Leeds; an appointment with the surgeon who did his knee operation. He'll be back later.'

It was still a real temptation to go storming home and confront Mamma, but Lucas was right. What was needed was time, to take it all in slowly and adjust to a new reality.

'I'm going out,' I said. 'I have to somehow process this and rearrange my brain before I can think straight. Tell Mamma… Sofie, I'll be back later; we can talk then. In the meantime, maybe you'll be able to help each other since Emilie was important to both of you.'

'Are you sure you want to be on your own, you must be in shock?' asked Lucas doubtfully.

'Yes, but I need space inside my head, it all feels too unreal. I know it must be true because this is an official document, but it doesn't seem possible.' My body was trembling, as anger and disbelief waged war with my emotions.

'Mattie…' began Lucas.

'For fuck's sake,' I all but shouted. 'Every single time I think there's some solid ground to stand on, it turns out to be quicksand. I don't think I can bear any more.'

I went home to grab my shoulder bag then fled the house, leaving the paperwork on the kitchen island. Sofie would see it when she came down. Running to the end of the street, I jumped on the first bus that came along, heading towards

Blackpool; it didn't matter to me where I went as long as it was somewhere else. I sat upstairs at the front, a habit from childhood, as we jolted through urban areas, protected sand dunes, and then into the suburbs of the resort. Pacing the unfamiliar streets, I must have scowled in such an intimidating way that tourists and passers-by all avoided me. I didn't want the jollity of the promenade and tower area, so turned east and just kept walking. Registering the local population out and about, there were a few people of Indian heritage, and all I could think was, *I'm one of you, you're my people, my tribe.* All those years of racist bullying, and it turned out I belonged after all, but with no cultural inheritance to bridge the gap, I remained an outsider even among my "own" people.

Time passed without my knowing where I went, but somewhere in the process I managed to move from fury and disbelief to grief, then some kind of acceptance. With a sandwich and takeaway coffee, I sat in a beautiful park away from the tourist areas. In the centre was a small space dotted with benches; a green oasis of mature trees where I could stop, breathe and calm my mind. The coffee helped but later, on the return trip to the bus station, I gave the unopened packet of sandwiches to a homeless person.

It was late afternoon when I got back to find Sofie and Lucas sitting in my front parlour. Mamma's eyes were red from crying, and though her bottom lip trembled at the sight of me, she sat up straight and put her shoulders back, resolved to face up to the coming storm.

'*Piccolo*, I meant to tell you, it was always part of the plan, but...'

Lucas had Mutt on his knee, man and dog a picture of anxiety as they looked between the two of us.

'Perhaps we should leave you to it?' he began.

'That might be for the best,' said Sofie.

'No, I want Lucas to stay. He has a stake in all this too.' I sat far away from Mamma, on the opposite side of the room, lodging myself in an armchair between an aspidistra on a plant stand and a Moroccan side table, putting physical distance between us.

Mamma visibly braced herself. 'You must have so many questions; ask anything you want, I'm ready to give you the answers.'

'*About bloody time,*' said Lee. '*She owes you that.*'

Sofie's face was pale, her eyes fearful as she stared at me. I'd imagined venting my fury during the bus ride home, had even rehearsed the scalding words I would use, but the anger which had burnt me up all day simply drained away. At that moment, I didn't see an aunt who'd told so many lies and betrayed my trust, but the woman who'd brought me up and been my mother, kissed me better and been a source of all the love any child could ever hope for.

'Oh, Mamma, I only need to understand why?' I choked, tears scalding my eyes, and she crossed the room in an instant to kneel beside me.

'I didn't even know Emilie was pregnant,' she said, her warm hands squeezing my unaccountably cold ones. 'Always insisted she was no more cut out for motherhood than monogamy. It wasn't planned, of course, and once the doctor confirmed you were on the way, she left her house in York and went to Scarborough, where she wasn't known, somewhere to hide until you were born. The first I knew about a baby was when she made a panicky phone call from the hospital pleading with me to come immediately.'

'If I wasn't wanted, why didn't she have a termination?' My voice was hoarse.

'That was her original intention, but at the last minute she simply couldn't go through with it. That's when she decided to rent a temporary place in Scarborough. An adoption plan was in place, but once you were born Emilie flat-out refused to sign the papers or hand you over and called me instead. She put you into my arms and begged me to take you.'

'She just gave me away!'

'It wasn't quite the way that sounds,' said Mamma.

'*Damn right it wasn't,*' growled Lee.

'Then how was it? She refused to give me up for adoption, but wanted you to take me? It doesn't make sense.'

'*It did, actually,*' Lee said.

I shut my eyes and silently told him to get lost, unable to cope with intrusive voices along with everything else.

Sofie took a deep breath. 'Even in the few days since giving birth, Emilie had grown to love you, but she was brave and honest enough to acknowledge that it wasn't in her to be a good mother. She'd just made the USA Today top-sellers list, and the publishers wanted her to do a book tour over there; all her energies were focused on the writing career she was building.'

'But you had a life too, and your teaching; why did your sister expect you to give up that life to raise me?'

'Because she didn't have a moment's doubt I'd want to,' said Mamma, with a compelling simplicity. 'Emilie knew just how much I'd once longed to have a child but couldn't. Investigations showed I wasn't ovulating, so there was pretty much zero chance of my ever conceiving; back then, the fertility treatments which exist now were in their infancy. And anyway, I'm a lesbian.'

'*You never told her that, either,*' said Lee.

'I kind of guessed that part,' I said, stroking her blonde hair. Grey roots were beginning to show, which only made me feel a deep tenderness towards her. 'There were never any boyfriends that I was aware of, but you did have some very close women friends.'

She nodded, looking up into my face. 'I did have a few special relationships but wasn't willing to upset your life by bringing a long-term partner into our household.'

'Is there anyone now?' I asked.

'Yes, someone very special.' Mamma's voice was charged with emotion. 'One day I'd like you to meet; we're talking about moving in together, which is why I'm going to sell up.'

Lucas had left the room without my noticing and returned with food and a pot of coffee.

'Eat something,' he told us. 'The sandwiches are that Lochgilphead salmon you're so fond of, Mattie.'

During the long hours of my absence, the ever-thoughtful Lucas had figured out nobody would want to cook, so he'd gone to the deli and stocked up. With the plate in front of me, I discovered how hungry I was. The blessed man had even brought doughnuts and followed up with a bottle of chilled Chablis.

Once restored by all this, Mamma and I sat side by side on the sofa while Lucas took my seat by the aspidistra, Mutt staying close to his feet.

'So, let me get this straight,' I said. 'One of a pair of twin sisters had a baby she didn't feel able to raise, so she gave it – me – to her infertile sibling?'

'Well, yes, but it wasn't quite that simple,' said Mamma. 'I adored you from the moment we met and wanted you very much, but I couldn't allow Emilie to make such a decision while she was all hormonal and emotional right after giving birth. What if she'd regretted it later? You both came home with me while we tried to work it out. My GP signed me off work with stress and depression when I went to him in floods of tears.'

'And what did you come up with? Was there a formal adoption?' I asked.

'It never seemed necessary, though Emilie signed documents making me your legal guardian, in case anyone ever asked. Apart from when we changed our names, nobody did. She sold her home in York and used some of the money to buy us the house you grew up in outright, and she made me a monthly allowance until I was able to go back to teaching. After that, I insisted on financial independence, but she funded some extras such as summer school for advanced maths coaching, and the specialist psychiatrist you saw in your teens. Later, she paid for the private sixth form college when you were so unhappy at that high school.'

'The kids there found out I was having mental health issues, so they called me "Looney Tunes" or "Nut Job". It was hard when I was still struggling with the diagnosis myself. They called me "Paki" too, of course, but...' I began to laugh, a hysterical edge in the sound. 'I am one.'

'No,' said Mamma. 'Not Pakistan. Aadi was from the South Indian province of Kerala. It's a gorgeous place, very green, but he and Emilie met in Venice during the winter months; she'd rented an apartment to write her latest book and escape from a very cold England. Aadi was attending a course of some kind.'

'And I was the unintended result? But he left her?'

'That's not quite how it was.'

There was a low growling sound which might have come from Lee or Mutt, I couldn't tell.

'Aadi was married, and Emilie never told him about the pregnancy. She did love him but knew it wouldn't last, not on her side anyway. Plus, she didn't want to force him to choose between her and the family, including two sons, he already had.'

'So, all the stuff about my father abandoning us and you being angry with him was complete bullshit?'

'*Creative fiction*,' said Lee.

'I was trying to explain my actions in a way that would make sense to a child. Emilie always said we should tell you the truth when the time was right. But then you developed depression, and, ever since, I've been afraid of precipitating some kind of crisis.'

'I was very angry this morning when the paperwork arrived. Then, as soon as I got home, all that rage melted away. Looking at you made me remember how much you've always loved me, and I knew there must have been good reasons for what you did. But why the Italian part?'

Mamma blushed. 'That was my idea, part of the Venice connection; Emilie never approved, but I insisted. When she and I were at grammar school there wasn't the same multicultural mix there is now. The two Asian kids in our class had a horrible time, with overt racism of the worst kind, and, mostly, the teachers did nothing. I didn't want that for you, and with your curly hair… So, the Italian part was invented because I hoped it might make your life easier.'

'It didn't stop them saying "Paki" when I passed in the corridors; they meant it as an insult but were well off target. Some of my few close friends were of Indian heritage, and, later on, so were many of my university colleagues. I liked them a lot more than the white bullies who tormented me. As a group, we were the serious kids who wanted to do well. And you know what? Even if I'd been a blue-eyed blonde, I'd still have been a misfit, because of the maths prodigy part.'

'Mattie, I'm so sorry about the bullying; I didn't know how bad it was for a long time, but I should have done.' Mamma stroked my hand. 'Kids can be so bloody cruel, as I know all too well from working in a school, though I hope it's much better these days.'

My laugh had brittle edges in it. 'It had better be.' A wave of weariness washed over me, and all I wanted was my bed, but there was one more thing I needed to understand.

'How come Emilie wasn't part of our lives? Why didn't I even know about her?'

Sofie grimaced. 'We had a huge row, worse than we'd ever had, and Em could be volatile.'

Lucas coughed. 'An understatement if ever I heard one.'

'*She lived life at high intensity,*' said Lee. '*It was part of what made her a good writer.*'

'What did you argue about? Me, I suppose?'

Mamma's face twisted with regret. 'Emilie did love you, very much, but while we were living together in those early weeks and months, she was claiming the right to dictate how you were brought up and every little thing I did. She even told me the formula feed I was using wasn't the best brand, so I said if we were going to do this "exchange", she had to step back and give me a free hand to be your mother in my own way.'

'She would have been reluctant to cede control to you,' observed Lucas.

'Yes.' Sofie nodded. 'I told her she couldn't parachute in and out of your life, like a fairy godmother bringing gifts, not to mention demanding I did everything her way. She hated my idea about claiming Italian heritage, but I was trying to protect you – without success, as it turned out.'

'So she just left?' I hadn't expected that.

'When Em stormed out of the house, I believed she was only going on the American book tour for a few months, but she stayed away for three years. The lawyers had control of everything, the money and so on. By the time she came back to the UK, you were *my* little girl, so I couldn't allow her to interfere. And she would have done.'

'*Yes,*' agreed Lee.

'No doubt about it,' said Lucas. 'I adored Emilie, you both know that, but she was incredibly strong and dominant, controlling even, and selfish enough to want her own way all the time. It couldn't have worked, Sofie, so don't blame yourself.'

'But I always have. She was my twin sister, and I should have tried harder…'

'*You did the right thing*,' said Lee, but Mamma couldn't hear that.

We were all exhausted, and Mutt was snoring on Lucas's knee, so he went home while we simply abandoned the detritus of our evening meal and headed for bed. As I crawled under the covers, I heard Mamma talking on her mobile, but nothing could keep me from sleep, even if my dreams were tangled visions of Emilie and Sofie shouting, each of them pulling one of my arms.

*

The next morning, Mamma and I walked along the shore, picking our way along the tideline and laying a number of things to rest.

'You genuinely aren't angry with me?' she asked.

'How can I be? You gave me the incredible gift of a happy childhood. Everything you said or did, even the parts that weren't true, were only ever to protect me. When I look back, I always felt loved and precious.'

'Because you were – are.'

'And whatever that birth certificate says, you'll always be my mamma.'

'My darling, you were a dream come true for me, and the nearest I would ever get to having a biological daughter. Emilie gave me the most precious thing she had, and I can never thank her enough for that.'

Picking up a driftwood branch, I swung it idly, giving a passing dog the exciting idea I might throw it for him. 'Emilie gave me something too: not only my life, but the stable, loving home she couldn't provide. I can see now that it was a brave and generous thing to do.'

'That's how I came to look at it,' said Mamma. 'Never ever doubt how much she loved you, but she was also sufficiently self-aware to see she'd make a lousy mother. I hated being estranged from her, but I couldn't let you be caught in the middle between us. When it came down to it, I had to choose you over my sister and, although it was painful, I don't regret one day of it.'

*

It seemed all wrong when she left later that day, but the visit had always been planned as a brief one, to test our restored relationship. Neither of us had imagined the past exploding in our faces, and there was so much more to say, but Mamma had an appointment to view a property with her partner.

'Rachael called me last night. She's found a house which could be perfect for us. It might even be better for you and me to take a break from all this emotional upheaval. I wouldn't leave you this way while you're still getting your head around everything, but I know you can rely on Lucas. He's an amazing man, pure gold.'

'I think he cares about me because I'm a kind of connection to his lost love.'

'Perhaps, darling, but that's not the whole story. He loves you for yourself too, he told me, not only because you're Emilie's child, but the daughter he never had. He admires your courage in the face of adversity and sees a lot of Emilie in you.'

So now I had not one, but three parent figures in my life. On the whole, it felt pretty damn good.

TWELVE

When I rang George to postpone our next appointment, she was *not* happy about it.

'Mattie, you committed to full cooperation with the mental health team.'

'But I am being cooperative. I'm faithfully taking my medication and exercising regularly too, exactly as I promised. And that's before we get onto learning to feed myself properly and the ongoing wardrobe makeover. But some family information has come to light, and I need to see the lawyers today and discuss the trust my aunt left. I promise to tell you all about it next week.'

'I'd prefer to see you sooner, but my diary is crazy with appointments shifting about. People will insist on going away on holiday at this time of year,' said George ruefully.

'Honestly, I'm well, doing great, but this family stuff can't wait. Please trust me, George, I'll even bake you something special to make up for messing you about. I've got my eye on a chocolate brownie recipe which sounds easy.'

'Ah, now you're talking. OK then, but you will ring the Mental Health Team if there's anything?'

'Absolutely, yes. And there will be loads of juicy information to share next week. My family history is turning out to be a bit like one of Emilie's novels.'

*

In his wood-panelled office, Mr Haltwhistle studied me over the top of gold-rimmed glasses, his face half-hidden behind the carefully trimmed grey beard and moustache.

'It's good to see you again, Mattea – may I call you that? Ms Lombard put this trust together with considerable care, being at great pains to provide for your future, whatever your life choices. As you're already aware, it is in two parts, depending on whether you decide to sell the house or settle here in Lytham.'

'That's what I'm here to tell you; I'm going to stay.'

'May I ask if you're sure about this? You would be required to sign a legal document to the effect that the house will become your permanent home. That was made clear at our previous appointment.'

'Seriously?' More evidence of my birth mother's controlling personality. I didn't remember that part but had probably been too preoccupied by the fact that I was inheriting an income as well as a house.

'I'm afraid so, yes. The trust is very clear – one set of provisions if you stay, and another if you choose to move on, but you have to commit to one or the other.'

'Lucas – Mr Fallon – told me that much, but I didn't understand that I'd have to sign something legal. What if I meet someone or my life changes? I might even get another lecturing job and need to settle elsewhere.'

'Which is why you should give the matter very careful consideration before you sign this document.' Mr Haltwhistle squared up the papers to one side and put his glasses neatly on top. 'If you were to sign and then later wish to change your mind, it becomes complicated. The financial provisions change.'

'I don't understand.'

'Whatever you decide, the house is your property without conditions. But if you sell up or leave, the income provisions for your future are altered, and any residue of the estate will go to charity. However, if you stay, your income from the trust will be greater and, fundamentally speaking, you inherit everything. It is a considerable amount of money, including the royalties from the... er literary estate.'

His evident ambivalence about the kind of books Emilie wrote might have been funny under other circumstances, but I was feeling manipulated and forced into making a choice for the rest of my life.

I studied the blotter on his desk, and the fountain pens precisely laid out. A man with the same organised, orderly mind as myself, but perhaps without my regrettable tendency to panic.

'I'm not sure what to do now except take more time to think about it. Can I do that?'

'You may indeed.' There was a pause in which Mr Haltwhistle steepled his fingers and rearranged his expression, before saying carefully, 'I was very fond of Emilie; she'd been my client for many years, and we did not often disagree. However, I was obliged to point out to her that the conditions she was placing on the trust were unduly restrictive. She meant them for the best, allowing for your mental health history, intending only to protect you. However, I persuaded her that you would need time to consider the options. As a result, there is provision for the interim income you receive at the moment to continue for up to five years. After which, a final decision will have to be made.'

I sat up straight. 'That makes it much easier. I'm pretty sure this is what I want, but not quite enough to commit to it on a legal document.'

'Which is why I insisted on the time frame.' Mr Haltwhistle's smile transformed his face into that of a friendly garden gnome. All he needed was a pointy hat and a fishing rod. 'I hope you will feel able to place your trust in Lucas Fallon and myself. As trustees, we are here to guard your interests at every stage of whatever lies ahead.'

'Thank you,' I told him, getting to my feet. 'Right now, the future is something of an unknown quantity.'

Walking back home, I wondered if that were true; in many ways, my life was more secure now than it had ever been under a series of short-term teaching contracts. The trust provided me with a basic income which would more than cover all the routine expenses of daily living, if not an extravagant lifestyle, and I didn't hanker after one of those. My client base of pupils was building up and I was becoming known among local parents. From these small beginnings, it was reasonable to hope my reputation as a tutor would grow. I found the one-to-one sessions satisfying in the same way small group or individual tutorials at the university had been – an opportunity to genuinely get to know my students and respond to them on an individual basis.

Best of all, my mental health remained stable, despite recent events, and I was as surprised as Mamma that the truth about my father hadn't left me feeling depressed again or caused my mood to plummet. By any logic it should have, because, at one level, everything had changed. In real terms, the revelation of my true biological parentage made no difference to either my past, present or future life.

*

When George came to see me a week later, I was able to greet her wearing a different outfit (one of Mamma's contributions) rather than my tracksuit uniform.

'Gorgeous dress, Mattie! The fuchsia pink suits you.'

'Turns out it was my aunt's favourite colour… Well no, not my aunt,' I said. 'You'd better sit down because I've got a lot to tell you.'

Two cups of coffee and a whole box of coconut-and-choc-chip biscuits later (I'd never got around to making brownies), George expressed herself gobsmacked by the machinations of my family.

'I suppose it does make a kind of sense,' she said. 'I mean, you hear of sisters having babies for each other, but generally via a surrogacy arrangement rather than by accident. Don't look at me like that – yes, I *was* about to ask how it had made you feel, but I'll keep it zipped.'

'I'm not angry about being rejected by my real mother if that's what you're thinking.'

George nodded. 'You'd be entitled to feel that way; she gave you away to her sister.'

'Yes, that's true, but as I've learnt more about Emilie, I realise she was trying to do her best for me. You might even say she was heroic, making that decision.'

'I don't get it.' George's expression was puzzled.

It took some time to gather my thoughts together. 'I've come to understand that Emilie was a strong, powerful woman, very talented but monumentally selfish. She could never have made the huge sacrifices necessary to bring up a happy child. Knowing those things about herself, she chose to let me go to the one person who could be trusted to give me all the love I'd ever need. Emilie did love me and put my happiness before her own.'

In the silence while George digested this, Lee's voice said softly, '*You* do *get it. Darling Mattie, I'm so glad. It makes everything worthwhile.*'

'Mattie, that's a very generous response.' George was frowning. 'But might you be suppressing your real feelings because they're too painful and difficult to face up to? I worry this is a form of denial and it might all hit you later...'

I interrupted her, saying, 'Don't imagine I haven't wondered about that myself, but, honestly, a part of me feels liberated to simply be myself. I'm not the same as Mamma – Sofie – she's calm and thoughtful; I'm much more volatile, if not to the degree Emilie was. Maybe I'm like my father, or rather the sum total of the random genes I inherited, and simply myself.'

George studied the photo taken at my graduation, which was now in a frame along with Emilie's portrait; I'd brought it down to show her. 'Physically, I'd say you resemble the twins except for your colouring. Does it trouble you to find out you're mixed race?'

'Not a bit; I've never cared about skin colour or understood why some people do. Other people have seen Indian heritage in me all my life, but the Italian story was the only one I had. Knowing who I really am feels so much more comfortable. I've done some research on Kerala, and it's somewhere I might want to visit one day. More coffee?'

'No thanks, or I'll be hyper with caffeine by the time I get home.' George was frowning. 'Are you thinking of going to look for him? Your father, I mean.'

'*Not the best idea,*' said Lee.

'No, I don't think so. Emilie chose not to tell him she was pregnant because he already had a family. It wouldn't be helpful for me to turn up and cause damage to their lives.'

'*Good decision,*' Lee affirmed.

'*No shit, Sherlock,*' said the other voice.

George shuffled her files, a frown between her eyes. 'You've worked so hard to achieve this current stability, but I have to be concerned about anything which might threaten that. You're taking your medication?'

'*You won't need it for much longer,*' said Lee.

What on earth did that mean? I had to focus on the conversation with George; my brain could never sustain two at once, let alone the other distant commentator. The voices I heard when out in town were different – a sort of half-heard background jumble of conversation.

'You can look at my medication box if you like,' I told her.

'We should make an appointment with Dr Parks anyway; she hasn't seen you yet.'

I pulled a face. 'Another bloody shrink.'

'You'll get on fine with her,' said George. 'She's great; the whole team thinks so.'

'Go on then, make the arrangements. As you say, we have to meet sooner or later.' I grinned naughtily. 'See how cooperative I'm being?'

'Yes, duly noted, and thank you, Mattie.' George smiled back. 'Please try to understand that the Mental Health Team only want to keep you safe.'

'I do know, honestly. I just hate feeling controlled or confined.'

There was a snort from Lee. '*I wonder who you take after?*'

When George had gone, I pictured her trying to write the complex family history into my file. She'd have a hard time keeping track of the twists and turns of the story.

I threw together an omelette from what I had in the fridge, going into the garden to eat it in the sunshine. There was a lot to think about. An hour later, I went back inside to make coffee, deciding not to sit in the kitchen as usual, but Emilie's front parlour. I continued to think of it as her room, not mine.

'Lee? Are you there?' I said into the silence.

'*Always,*' he said.

'I've been thinking. You're not an auditory hallucination, are you?'

'*Told you so.*'

I took a deep breath. 'Then what?'

'*I'm not sure of the right word to describe it.*'

'Are you a ghost?' It fried my brain that I was even asking such a question, having never previously believed in hauntings or anything supernatural, but, in this situation, elementary maths said two and two made four.

There was a long silence before Lee replied. '*Probably, a sort of spirit in place, if you will.*'

'You're part of the house? I never hear you anywhere else,' I said, thinking it was a good thing George wasn't present for this conversation. She'd have me back in a psychiatric unit, pronto.

'*You could say that. I can't leave or go anywhere else.*'

'Have you been here a long time?' I was half imagining some Victorian presence, a kind of sitting tenant long connected to the house.

'*Many years, twenty-five altogether if you count my life here.*'

I spluttered into my coffee, and then my brain made further connections which moved smoothly into place, as if I'd dialled the combination on a safe, allowing the door to swing open.

'You said your name was Lee!'

There was a pause. '*It's what Lucas called me. Lee, short for Emilie.*'

'But your voice...'

'*Sounds masculine? It was always this way; when I was in the school choir, I could sing the baritone parts. A fondness for cigars didn't help.*'

Stunned isn't a strong enough word to describe my reactions, physical, emotional, the lot.

'You're my mother. But why are you here?'

'*I've wondered about that myself. Maybe because I had to know you would be all right – some deep need to watch over you?*'

'Sofie said you loved me, and I wanted to believe it...'

'*My darling girl, always, it's why I let you go.*'

I sat very still, faced with a shattering but simple truth.

'Thank you,' I said eventually. 'I had a very happy life, but then you were aware of that.'

'*I watched you from afar, whatever Sofie would permit. When I knew that the aneurism was going to get me, I wanted to make sure you were provided for. After I "passed over", I was just here, in the empty house, waiting for you. Lucas came sometimes, that was nice.*'

'So does that mean... are all the other voices I've heard ghosts too?'

'*I can't tell you that, but I always wondered because your granny was the same.*'

Yet another startling revelation. The ground under my feet was beginning to wobble again.

'Who's the other one – I hear him distantly?'

'*You mean Hal? He comes with George.*'

It was an effort to breathe, and my chest was growing tight.

'Look, I'm struggling to take this in. Would you mind going away for a while, so I can think properly? Please.'

'*Whatever you want.*'

I climbed the stairs to the study and sat there in the gathering dark. Like the Babbage Engine we'd been to see, with its thousands of cogs, my brain had processed the myriad elements of my experiences into a logical conclusion. The moving parts which constituted all the disparate parts of my knowledge finally reached their destination and then went click to stop at the right place.

All those years in which I'd been medicated, tranquillised, told my voices couldn't be real, but they *had* been, still were. When nobody believes what you say, it makes you doubt yourself. The worst times had almost always been in older buildings, I realised, beginning at secondary school where the main building was at least one hundred years old. No voices had ever troubled me at the newly built sixth form I'd gone to, and everyone (including me) had supposed it was because I was "better".

My undergraduate course at the University of York had been chosen because it was near our home in Malton in case I had another depressive episode. Over the years, I'd grown to love the ancient city but, given how much history oozed from every stone, it was no wonder that the clamour of voices I'd heard had sometimes felt like an assault, overwhelming and crushing me. Later, I'd delivered my tutorials and lectures in the modern buildings of the university maths department and rented a flat in a newly built block. So many things were beginning to make sense, but I found myself wishing I'd known my granny, who might have explained it all to me, and, more importantly, how to cope with it.

*

In the following days, I retreated into myself, not seeing anyone except my three pupils – and received bookings for four new ones, which was seriously encouraging. I was even contacted by the head of maths at a local school, a potential source of more pupils who might need additional support.

I hardly left the house, except to run or shop for food. Far from being overwhelmed and panicky, my head was full of the huge realisation that I wasn't – and never had been – mentally ill. OK, maybe sometimes I genuinely had suffered from depression, but only as a result of the continual violation of my mind by the voices. A memory returned of asking the child psychiatrist I'd seen as a "disturbed adolescent" if my depression was caused by hearing the voices, or whether I was hearing voices because I was depressed. She'd favoured the latter explanation, but she was wrong. I was psychic the way my grandmother had been, and though I've never been much interested in supernatural things, my mathematical brain now recognised a genuinely inescapable logic.

This simple fact changed everything I'd ever believed or been told about myself – that I was vulnerable, needed medication, should live a careful life and avoid stress. A mental and emotional transition of such magnitude couldn't just happen overnight, and I needed time to get my head around it. I'd often used the analogy of standing on quicksand and now, for the first time since adolescence, there might just be solid ground on which to build a future.

There was a moment when I thought about flushing my tablets down the toilet but didn't. The information leaflet which came with the medication was full of warnings about the dire consequences of sudden withdrawal. Instead, I began to reduce the dose to wean myself off them gradually. What I didn't know, and was a little afraid to find out, was whether, without medication, the voices would increase in volume, leaving me overwhelmed again. Such episodes had happened more than once, but at least now I was beginning to understand why.

Lucas was away on a history society trip, visiting medieval buildings as part of a group tour, so I couldn't pour my heart out to him. Polly and I exchanged texts most days, and at the end of a challenging week, I rang her because I simply had to confide in someone.

When she answered, my friend dominated the conversation, full of the wonderful Harriet and how happy they were.

'I'm ashamed of neglecting you,' she confessed. 'I'm so sorry but honestly, it's like all the romantic books and films say – when you meet the one, you know. I never believed it before.' She even mentioned wedding plans, and it shamed me to realise that I wasn't exactly listening, only waiting for the chance to talk about myself.

'We're going to wear long dresses, but they'll be coloured, not white, no virgins here. And tiaras, obviously, but since we plan to be the stars of our own show there won't be any veils or bloody bridesmaids either. I'm telling you so you're not disappointed when I don't ask you to be one.'

As soon as she paused long enough to ask how my life was going, I leapt in and poured out the tangled story. It was a huge relief to let it all go and Polly always was a good listener, but even she gasped when I got to the part about the sitting tenant in my house.

'Bloody hell. How does that make you feel?'

'Don't you start,' I told her with mock seriousness.

'So you're not a mad cow after all? Dammit, Mattie, after so many years of pills and hospitals. You didn't need them at all.'

'I know, right. Mega, isn't it?'

'I've never forgotten you saying the drugs took all the sparkle out of life. If only someone had told you about your granny earlier, it might have been so different.'

'When senior doctors diagnose a serious illness, everyone goes along with it. I was only thirteen when it began, and very frightened. Nobody in my whole life ever suggested there could be another reason for the voices.'

'I suppose hearing dead people might be equally hard to cope with. The good news is, you're not mentally ill, and the bad news is that if you tell people you're psychic, some of them will still think you're crazy. Bloody hell, what an impossible place to be! Hang on, Harriet's been listening and she's trying to tell me something. What...?'

Polly must have put her hand over the phone because I could hear them speaking, their voices sharp and raised, but not make out the words. Then she came back on. 'Mattie, something's come up, and it might be important. Sorry, but can I get back to you?'

'Of course,' I told her, and she disconnected without further explanation.

Early the following morning, she called again. 'Mattie, I hope you're not busy this weekend because we're coming over. Cancel everything; Harriet's packing the car right now and then we'll be on our way.'

'I've got no plans, and it will be fabulous to see you and meet Harriet, but why the rush?'

'No time, just trust me. Harriet says we have to do this, but absolutely not over the phone. Should be with you in a couple of hours or so – possibly nearer three in this July holiday traffic. York is crazy busy right now; you can't move for tourists.'

Not at all sure what was going on, I went to make up the spare bed with fresh linen before going out for some essential food shopping. Lucky for them, I was onto the next chapter of the cookery book – meat and fish – but what lay behind this sudden cross-country dash? I'd find out soon enough.

THIRTEEN

Polly and Harriet finally arrived with tales of endless queues of traffic made even more hideous by the July heat. Their elderly car didn't have air conditioning and opening the windows had only made things worse.

'It's so awesome to meet you, Mattie,' said Harriet, bouncing gratefully out of the stuffy car. She couldn't have been a greater contrast to the tall, elegant Polly, being short and round with curly blonde hair. She also talked very fast and rarely stood still, a bundle of pent-up energy.

'As soon as Polly explained what was happening, I told her you needed help and we had to come immediately.'

Standing there, confused, I hadn't a clue what she was on about, which must have shown, because Polly said, 'I can see you don't get it, but you will, and we've brought some books that might be useful.'

As soon as we went into the house, Harriet ran about like a headless chicken, exclaiming over everything.

'I knew she'd love it here,' said Polly, watching her beloved with a fond eye. 'It's so her sort of thing – she's a collector of eclectic objects too, especially steampunk. We're going to need a bigger house.'

After they'd both showered away the stickiness of the journey, we had a simple lunch and talked a little about my new understanding of the voices.

'I always knew you were crazy, but you're absolutely fucking nuts!' said Polly cheerfully.

'Call yourself a scientist?' I said, munching sourdough bread with my home-made liver pâté. 'The empirical evidence is logical and irrefutable.'

Polly rolled her eyes at this, but Harriet delivered a stern look and commanded her to go for a walk; a long one.

'Look at antique shops or walk on the beach, anything,' she instructed, and her fiancée obediently headed out of the door. 'I've already explained everything to her, last night and in the car today, so she doesn't need to hear it all again,' said Harriet. 'Now come and sit down with me, because I'm worried about you.'

We sat in the parlour, where Harriet's small figure was lost in the enormous sofa. With her little feet tucked underneath her body, she resembled a pixie perched in the corner.

'It's kind of you to be concerned, but there's no need,' I said. 'As I told Polly on the phone, the liberation of knowing I'm not mentally ill is indescribable.'

'*I like this one, her aura is a beautiful colour,*' said Emilie. '*She can help, you need to hear what she has to say.*'

'Ha, listen to your mother,' said Harriet, with a mischievous gleam in her eye.

My jaw dropped as I stared at her, unable to believe what she'd said. 'You can hear Lee? I mean Emilie?'

'Yes, it's why I came – because I'm like you. But our gift can be something of a mixed blessing, and the idea of you trying to control it without help or any understanding of what was happening, it's not surprising you ended up half out of your mind.'

'*Sofie listened to the doctors and never made a connection with your granny… Though I wondered sometimes,*' said Emilie. '*I'll go away now and let you two talk.*'

'Thanks, Emilie. She's safe with me,' said Harriet.

'*I know.*'

The weight I'd been carrying drained away, as relief flooded through me, leaving my arms and legs unaccountably boneless. It was completely unexpected to be understood without question, and I sank into the other end of the sofa, overwhelmed and grateful.

Harriet dived straight in. 'First, you should understand that I don't practise as any kind of psychic, never wanted to, and I rarely tell people anymore, not even Polly, though it was always something I intended to "confess" when the time was right. Your story precipitated that, so we were up late last night, talking. Then on the way here she got the full explanation of why I was worried for you. When my gifts emerged, also in adolescence, there was someone to guide and teach me control and mastery of it. I can't imagine how hard it must have been for you on your own, without anyone to help you.'

'Everyone told me I was ill, and that none of it was real,' I said, remembering my experiences with something close to horror. 'Some of the drugs did help block the voices out, but they left me in a fog, which was horrible.'

'Mattie, I'm so sorry.' Harriet scrambled across the sofa and reached for my hand. 'That must have been a terrifying experience. Were you able to develop any coping mechanisms at all?'

I winced. 'Now you're using psychology phrases like George, my psychiatric nurse, but I guess you're both talking about the same thing, just coming at it from a different perspective.'

'Exactly. Whatever name you give to the things you hear and experience, you have to find ways to be in control, or else it can take over your life. The advice you were given as a supposedly mentally ill person does make sense, given it's all about finding ways to dampen down the voices and emotions, allowing you to live a normal life and function day to day.'

'And you can teach me how?'

'There's no guidebook if that's what you're asking. All I can do is make suggestions, and the books I've brought may help. Everyone's gift is different, but, from what Polly told me, you and I share a similar experience; I'm a "psychic medium" which means I hear people but don't see them. In some societies, we'd be revered for our wisdom as shamans, and our connection with the dead. But you were told over and over that what you experienced wasn't real, and all in your head. That didn't happen to me, but I did get fed up with people asking me to tell them the future. As if. That's why I stopped being open about it, and it's also the reason I only pass on messages when there's no choice because it's something urgent and important.'

We talked the whole afternoon, not stopping even when Polly came back with gooey cakes from the bakery. With a raised eyebrow at the two of us, she even made coffee to keep us refuelled, before going out to the garden to read her book.

Of necessity, it was only a flying visit, and they left after breakfast the following day, by which time I was beginning to understand what was needed. Learn what strategies worked for me, and how to set boundaries for myself on when and how I chose to "listen", or when it was necessary to tune out.

Emilie had remained quiet but now said, *'She's right, you know. If you summon all your will and tell me to leave, I kind of have to, there's no other choice.'*

Harriet put her number into my phone and made me promise to call her if I needed to talk again before they set off to do battle with Harriet's mother over the size of wedding she had in mind, versus their own hopes for a small and intimate celebration.

I waved goodbye, with heartfelt thanks for coming to my rescue, and envied their obvious closeness and deep bond. It's something most of us want, but that doesn't make it easy to find.

*

Lucas had been back from his history trip for some days before I summoned up the courage to share everything that had happened with Lee/Emilie. With considerable trepidation, I invited him for lunch (more of my home-made pâté) and sat him down in the parlour afterwards, leaving Mutt to play in the garden.

'Look, there's something you need to know, but I think it might be difficult, even painful for you to hear.'

'Sounds ominous,' he said, eyes searching mine.

Even choosing my words with the greatest care, he was shocked and visibly upset by what I told him, his face very pale.

I went back over the whole history of the voice that had come with the house, Lee knowing the passwords, and how, over time, she'd helped me put together what was going on. When I was done, tears rolled silently down Lucas's face, as if he didn't know they were there. All I could do was hold him close. And to think I never used to hug people. Mutt had joined us after his adventures outside and now whined his anxiety, pushing at Lucas's hand with his nose.

'I have to believe what you're saying is true,' he said slowly, absently scratching the little dog's scruffy ears. 'How else could you have known that I always called her Lee? It was only ever between the two of us, and she called me Lou. So does that mean Emilie was there those times when I came and sat in the house? But why didn't I know? We were so close, you'd have thought…'

I waited, giving him time to let it all sink in. I loved this man and knew my story had upset him. After a long silence, he said, 'I don't know whether to be glad that Emilie's spirit lives on or horrified if she's somehow trapped here.'

'*Not trapped, I needed to stay,*' said Emilie.

'Harriet told me it's sometimes the result of a very strong attachment to a person or place, positive or negative, and, the way Emilie puts it, is that she needed to know I would be OK. After all the care she put into planning how to provide for me, there was a compulsion to see it through.'

Lucas took off his glasses to brush tears away. Looking around Emilie's parlour, an expression of pure love spread across his face, almost painful to see in its raw, naked intensity.

'She's here now, isn't she?' he said, hope lighting his eyes.

It was tempting to lie and spare him further agony, but his face was so full of longing I just couldn't.

'Yes.'

'*Oh, darling, dearest Lou. Always my truest friend, I love you so,*' said Emilie, her voice choked.

Lucas must have seen my face change. 'I can't hear anything, but she's here?' he asked.

I nodded. 'She loves you; I just heard her say so. Look, I'm going to go outside for a while and take Mutt with me. If I leave you on your own maybe you'll feel something, I don't know.'

Closing the parlour door, I heard his voice breaking as he said aloud, 'Emilie, the love of my life, it was always, only, you.'

An hour or so later, a very pale Lucas came upstairs to the study and persuaded the dog to allow him to sit in my one spare armchair. He was calm, and although his eyes had a painful lost look, seemed to be at peace.

'I don't know whether I was truly aware of her presence, or if it was only how much I wanted to be, but you saying she was there was enough. I sort of... breathed her in. It was so thoughtful of you to share this.'

Relief flooded through me. 'It's taken me a while to feel brave enough, but there was no choice. You had a right to know.'

'I should go home now; there's a lot to think about.'

'Is Tom there? Maybe you shouldn't be alone.' He looked exhausted, with dark shadows beneath his eyes.

'No, he's taken off for a while. The surgeon in Leeds didn't have good news for him; there's nothing else they can do, but I know he'd hoped for one last try. Anyway, the bottom line is that his knee isn't ever going to be any better than it is now, and he has to find a way to live with that. He plans to see the counsellor he worked with before.'

'Poor Tom,' I said. 'It must have been awful for him to hear such news.'

'He's made of strong stuff,' said Lucas, standing up. 'I might just be a very fond uncle, but Tom amazes me with his depth and wisdom. I have every confidence he'll find a way out of this; he's been through much worse. Now, I should go.'

'Are you sure you want to be by yourself?' I was worried about him, protective even.

'*You love him,*' said Emilie. '*We both do.*'

'I'm used to my own company, and Mutt will want feeding,' said Lucas. 'Anyway, I need to be quiet for a while. No, don't come downstairs, we'll see ourselves out.'

When he'd gone, I sat at the desk, gazing unseeing into space, my mind whirling with all the new understanding I'd been given.

*

Jogging along the shore some days later, I watched the gulls feeding as the tide receded. My route meant trying to navigate the assorted detritus left by the water. The smooth surface of the walkway which stretched all the way to St Annes was generally preferable, but in the summer season there were too many bicycles, family groups, prams and tourists. Sitting down to pause for breath on the wide steps at Granny's Bay, a small dog, not much more than a puppy, dashed over and made friendly overtures.

'Hello! Well, aren't you cute?' The collar tag said her name was Mary, and she leapt trustingly into my lap, trying to lick every inch of my face. I was fondling the soft, wiry coat when her owner appeared.

'Mary, what have I told you about invading people's privacy?' He was tall, blond and gorgeous. Probably in his thirties. I vaguely remembered seeing him out and about before.

'It's fine.' I smiled. 'I love dogs and Mary is a darling.' She was a wire-haired Jack Russell, all white except for dark ears, and an endearing patch of tan over one eye.

'I've seen you out running before, haven't I?' he said, plonking himself down on the steps and putting a reluctant Mary back on her lead.

'Yes, I'm here most mornings, usually by 7.00am to dodge the crowds.'

'You're a local then? I'm a temporary resident, friendless and alone.' He grinned. 'Here on a short-term work contract and staying in a soulless hotel room.'

'I haven't lived here long myself, only a few months. I'm Mattie.'

'Maybe I'll see you tomorrow? My name's Simon.' He stood and stretched before running off towards St Annes with Mary's in his arms, and disappeared around the curve of the bay. Not that I was watching, obviously, but he did have a very nice bum.

On the way home, I went to the butcher's shop for a pork pie, still warm from the oven and leaking meat juices onto the paper bag. Coming out, I walked straight into Nigel from next door.

He had the grace to look embarrassed. 'Mattea, I've been hoping for a chance to apologise,' he said.

'You certainly owe me that, but why not write a letter?' I so didn't want to be having this conversation, skin prickling with discomfort in his presence.

'I am truly sorry,' he said. 'It was wrong of me to make a copy of the key. I wanted access because I was certain Emilie's family would choose to sell the house. She never let me inside, so it was a chance to snoop about before it went on the market. Like I say, it was well out of order.'

'But when I turned down your offer, it was only the beginning – the things you did were loathsome, an attempt to intimidate me,' I said, desperate to be on my way.

'But that's what I told Tom – Major Weller. All those things, the letters, the graffiti, and some parcel he accused me of sending; I didn't do any of it. Yeah, I can see you don't believe a word and why should you. I'm no innocent, I've made the odd shady deal, or a given a backhander to grease the wheels, but I wouldn't write nasty letters or anything like that.'

'You're right, I don't believe you,' I said, my voice cold.

'Mattea, please, listen to what I'm trying to tell you, it *wasn't* me. Which means you have an enemy out there who's trying to frighten you. So, if not me, then you have to ask who, and why?'

Only a complete tosser would lie to my face about the harassment. 'Sorry, your apology is accepted but I don't want to discuss this further. Let's just leave it there. Goodbye, Nigel.'

Jogging off down the street, I was still clutching my pie, which, for some reason, I didn't fancy anymore. The encounter had taken some of the shine off my new-found sense of liberation and self-understanding. I still had a poisonous neighbour to deal with, but the evidence was safely stored away, and if there was any further trouble from him, I'd make a formal written complaint to the police.

*

Setting off for my run the following morning, it wasn't a total surprise when Simon caught up with me by the windmill on the seafront, Mary in his arms. The wind off the waves was fresh, and there weren't many people about. Simon didn't say much, just smiled, but then I prefer a man who doesn't gabble on. When we got close to St Annes, by mutual agreement, we turned back, and as we approached the windmill again, he asked, 'Coffee?'

As chat-up lines go, this was refreshingly straightforward. When he led the way to my favourite haunt, it scored another point on my approval index. He was tanned and almost movie-star handsome, not the kind who'd normally have time for a low-maintenance woman like me. Mary sat under the table at our feet and went to sleep. She'd run a long way for a small dog.

'The coffee is so good here,' he said, 'exactly the way I like it.' More points. I was very taken with this guy. And his dog.

'So, what do you do for a living?' I asked. An unoriginal conversational gambit, but a fair question.

'You'll think its dull,' he said, pulling a face. 'I'm an accountant, sort of.'

'What does "sort of" mean, exactly?'

'It's a particular branch of the field – forensic accounting, looking into fraud and money laundering. I don't want to bore you with technical stuff.'

I laughed. 'You won't if it's maths; my field is data science and analytics, so there'd be some crossover with what you do.'

His face lit up. 'Seriously? Are you a numbers person? Most women glaze over the minute I start talking about my occupation.' He had such a nice smile and a dimple in one cheek.

'Not me,' I said. He seemed genuinely interested and asked more questions, so I ended up telling him about my academic work, and how inheriting the house had brought about a change of direction.

'And you enjoy the tutoring, even though it's below the level you're used to working at?'

'I do – turns out those cliches about shaping young minds are all true. It's a great feeling when one of my pupils "gets" something. I like being able to give them individual, tailored attention.'

Simon nodded approval. 'On the bad days, when I'm tempted to give it all up, I wonder about taking up one of those incentive deals and retraining as a teacher. Temporary contracts are all very well, and they're lucrative, but I'm never in one place for long. Lately, I've been feeling an urge to settle down.'

He was relaxed and comfortable company and after another coffee, we agreed on a time to meet the next morning. Just like that, the morning run became a regular arrangement, and even though I wasn't sure if the attraction was mutual, I certainly fancied *him*. His easy friendliness and our common interests, including Mary, made me comfortable with him. He'd told me his temporary contract was three months, but not how much of that time had already elapsed. It became necessary to stop myself speculating about him, though he did have a very nice bum.

*

When my next Friday appointment with George came around, I was able to offer the cake I'd promised, in the form of brownies. There'd been a couple of failed experiments until I realised that Emilie's high-end oven was super-efficient, and I needed to turn down the temperature and reduce the cooking time to keep the fudgy texture.

When George arrived, Emilie commented, '*Pity that girl can't hear her brother. His name is Hal and he died in a car accident when he was fifteen. He's always with her, but she doesn't seem to be aware of his presence.*'

'*Wish she was,*' said the distant voice. All this time I'd been hearing George's brother without understanding who he was, and that it only happened when she visited. That must be what Emilie had meant by saying "he comes with George".

I couldn't think about it then, not with my CPN being such an acute observer, but it was sad. I understood then why Harriet might choose not to pass on messages or information; it would be so hard, and a huge responsibility.

All unknowing, George munched appreciatively on a brownie. It was early enough in my culinary journey to be a delight when people enjoyed my kitchen experiments.

'Maybe I ought to visit more often,' she said, brushing dark crumbs from the corner of her mouth. 'You're in danger of going downhill fast; I should monitor your condition with great care.'

'Hmm, is it me you're concerned about, or the supply of brownies?'

'Both,' she said with a smile. 'Actually, I was thinking that, far from going downhill, you're brighter than I've ever seen you. Living here seems to suit you.'

'I've decided to make it my long-term home,' I said. 'York is a wonderful city, but now I realise it might not have been the best place for me.'

I wasn't about to explain why or talk about being psychic and hearing the dead, so instead described my encounter with Nigel and his denials.

'Did you believe him?' she asked.

'Not for a second; he's a total shit, and I can prove it if necessary.' That made me laugh because a sample of the actual turd was wrapped in layers of plastic in Lucas's freezer.

'*Her aura's gone a funny colour, be careful,*' said Emilie, which was no help at all. I might not always tell her the whole truth, but my CPN was one of the select group of people I did trust.

George hesitated, before saying, 'Look, I'm sorry to ask, but you're still taking your meds?'

'Faithfully,' I told her with perfect truth, failing to mention I'd gradually halved the dose as I weaned myself off them.

'It's just that you seem brighter, more alert, it might be the start of a "high"; we have to watch out for the signs.'

George was way too perceptive, so I distracted her with another brownie.

'I'm happy, that's all,' I said, with my best approximation of a guileless and innocent look. 'It's a great feeling and an unfamiliar one. I've got some more pupils too, which keeps me busy.'

'There's something new about you, but I can't quite identify what it is. Unless you've got a secret lover I don't know about?'

'As if,' I told her. 'A boyfriend would only make my life even more complicated.'

'It's a pity I couldn't get you a consultant appointment sooner.'

'October isn't far away, and you can see for yourself that I'm fine.'

When had I become such an accomplished liar?

FOURTEEN

Despite poring endlessly over the books on psychic abilities Harriet had brought me, they weren't as much help as I'd hoped. Her core advice had been to put my greatest efforts into developing control, as in not letting the voices beat me down, or allowing them to intrude when I preferred to keep them out. Bitter experience had taught me just how overwhelming the clamour could be, but thinking back the worst assaults on my senses had taken place in or around old buildings. York certainly had its fair share of those, from Roman to medieval; no wonder I'd preferred the edge-of-town modern shopping malls to the old city centre. My excuse had been avoidance of the tidal waves of tourists who thronged the ancient streets in all seasons.

Harriet had been taught in her teens to clear out the mental clutter, only allow the strongest voices through and send them away when she didn't choose to listen. She'd described it as tuning in or out but couldn't give me a precise explanation of how this was done, only that I'd get better with practice. The books tended to focus more on expanding your abilities, rather than dampening them down.

I turned to Emilie for guidance, but she was no help at all. *'How the hell would I know?'* was her answer. *'I never believed in ghosts and I'm not even sure how I came to be here, I just am. It seems like one moment I was in the hospice, and then I was here at home. It took me a while to realise I'd croaked, died, passed over, or however you want to describe it.'*

'But you meet people on the "other side", don't you?'

'You mean Hal? Only because he comes with George.'

An internet search only produced offers to enhance my gifts, help me speak to lost loved ones, or courses on subjects such as aura viewing or crystal healing. In the end, I rang to consult Harriet but found her bubbling with excitement and packing for a last-minute trip to New York.

'It was a bargain, too good to miss, probably because it'll be stinking hot in August. Polly and I don't care, even if the Manhattan types all escape to Martha's Vineyard at this time of year. And, just so you know, the wedding's off again, even though we've bought our dresses. My mother is being intransigent, but we're holding firm; no way are we going to do the big production she has in mind. We might yet elope to Vegas and get hitched by an Elvis impersonator.'

It didn't seem the right moment for a long conversation about controlling the spirit voices, though we did manage to have a brief discussion about establishing dominance.

'You are the conduit,' Harriet told me. 'It's your choice whether to open yourself to them or not. Establish who's in charge, and make sure they go away if their presence is unwelcome.'

It was true Emilie always disappeared when I told her to go, but my authority hadn't been tested on any other voices. I briefly wondered about visiting some old buildings to see what happened but chickened out. What I needed was someone to talk to who would take my questions seriously and might be able to offer advice. None of the people I was close to had the first idea how to help, and the most practical suggestion came from Lucas, who suggested consulting another psychic.

'You see them advertising in the local free newspaper, so it might be worth contacting somebody from their pages. I can tell it's worrying you and wish I could help, but it needs to be someone who understands what you're experiencing.'

Armed with some back issues from Lucas's recycling box, I rang a couple of numbers, but the minute I began to explain the kind of help needed, the phone was immediately put down on me.

'*Bloody rude,*' said Emilie, '*and doesn't suggest they have any real gift at all. I imagine most of them are making it up.*'

'But there must be some genuine people out there?' I protested. 'After all, me and Harriet are the real thing, even if we aren't necessarily good at it.'

I kept trying. Another woman, improbably named Romani Lee (they all seemed to be female), was sympathetic but unable to help.

'I use a crystal ball, sweetheart, or tarot cards sometimes, and there's either something to see there or not. I wouldn't be of much use from what you've told me. Evelina in St Annes might be worth a try; she's got a good reputation and has been at it for years.'

Trying the number, I opted for a more cautious approach after my previous experiences of metaphorical phone slamming. Instead, I asked if she was available for a reading, and a pleasant voice offered to fit me in at the end of her normal working hours, two days later.

Evelina's home was a modest Victorian terraced house, in a street near the park and supermarket, and she turned out to be a tiny elderly lady wearing an excess of black drapery. Both hostess and house smelt vaguely musty as she led the way into a room at the rear of the house, facing onto a small patio surrounded by brick walls and dotted with concrete donkeys. The window had pink frilly blinds, and the carpet was deep purple. Not quite what I'd been imagining, but then my vague expectations came from watching movies and involved beaded curtains.

'Your aura tells me you are feeling anxious, Miss Lombardi. No need to be, I'm very experienced.' She gestured for me to take one of two floral armchairs. 'Is there someone you'd like me to contact?'

'Not exactly,' I said, unsure how to begin.

'Ah, perhaps a matter of the heart? Give me your hand.'

I couldn't help wondering what Simon would say if he could see me now. A year ago, I'd have laughed at the very idea of consulting a psychic. Now I knew better than to judge.

'Ah, there is someone... a dark man. No, your aura says he is not the one.'

Since Simon was a blue-eyed blond, this was well off the mark.

Evelina looked up from my hand, studying my face intently. 'Why are you here? Your colours are strange, but I see you have questions.'

'*Tell her to give it a rest,*' said a strong voice. '*She's no more got the family gift than one of those bloody pot donkeys outside.*'

I did my best to ignore this input. 'Someone recommended I should contact you; I am looking for help, yes, but perhaps not in the usual way...'

'Your aura says you are fearful,' Evelina told me.

'*Ha, so does hers! No wonder when she's scared of what you might have come for. Tell her Tabitha says to stop messing about.*'

I wasn't about to relay this and silently willed Tabitha to make herself scarce, hoping my skills in this direction might have improved.

'Look,' I said, 'perhaps I should come right out with it. The truth is I've recently discovered that I'm psychic, but I don't seem to be able to control it, and the voices I hear can sometimes be... difficult. I hoped you could help.'

Evelina stood up; the pleasant expression wiped off her face. She opened her mouth to speak, but then she stopped. Eyes widening, she stared at me in astonishment.

'Hell's bells, you're telling the truth. Your aura…'

'I can't see those; I just hear voices. The doctors told me I was mentally ill.'

'But you're not, are you?'

'No,' I said, 'and that's why I've come. I need someone to help me.'

'*You're on a loser there,*' put in Tabitha, who hadn't gone away at all. Her voice was very strong. '*All she can do is see colours, but she's made a modest living out of it.*'

'There's a dark cloud behind you, it suggests danger,' said Evelina. 'You want to be careful.'

I was wasting my time with this woman. 'Is that what you tell everybody?' I said, deeply disappointed with the way things were going.

Evelina was stony-faced, but she sat down again. 'Don't be so bloody quick to judge, lady. When you live on a basic state pension, you need the extra money to get by. My mother and sister had stronger gifts than me, but I do what I can. There is a dark cloud, and I'm not a fraud, though it's obvious you think so.'

'*Evelina my arse – she's plain Phyllis Archbold from Fleetwood. I should know, I'm her sister,*' said the voice.

'No, I don't think you're a fraud; you see auras, I can't.'

Evelina appeared to be mollified, up to a point. 'I've always seen them; I can tell when people are lying, or troubled about something. I've been called an empath, and sometimes a genuine instinct for what someone wants or needs just comes, but I can't do it to order, which is a bit of a pain. And I'm not kidding about the dark cloud – but I guess you won't believe me. I don't suppose you'll be paying either and I could do with the cash; my roof leaks.'

I realised with shame how shabby and worn down both the elderly lady and her house were. She was only trying to get by on not enough money. I'd been there.

'Of course I'll pay; you've given me your time, even if you can't help.'

'It's not that I don't want to. My mam or sister could have, but they've both passed over now. They'd have helped you in a heartbeat, and probably not charged neither.' Evelina sat up straight and put her shoulders back; she was proud but vulnerable and needed help herself.

'Could you tell me how it works for you,' I said. 'I'm genuinely interested because I only know one other person who's psychic, and she's more like me. It seems to come out in different ways from person to person?'

Evelina relaxed a little, probably because I'd promised to pay. 'It was very strong in my mother and sister; they could hear voices too, and channel spirits. My mother's gift went even further – she had a natural intuition, second sight. It made her a lot of money, but it's not been the same for me. She left us this house, which helps, but I've never earned enough to do more than get by. While my husband and sister were alive, we managed better, but she had breast cancer…'

'*My poor Phyllis,*' said the voice, softer in tone now. '*It's been bloody tough since her Eric died, I know, but I can help. Go on, tell her.*'

'Her name was Tabitha, and you're Phyllis,' I said reluctantly.

The colour drained from Evelina's face, and I was afraid she was going to faint. Eyes wide, she stared at me. 'Saints preserve us, you do have the gift, don't you?'

'Yes, but I'm not sure I want it. Tabitha is here, she says she can help.'

Evelina/Phyllis sagged and suddenly looked old, grey and exhausted.

'We fell out; I wanted her to get treatment, and have the cancer operation, but Tabitha wouldn't. Said it was her time. Maybe I understand that better now, but I never got to tell her so.'

'She knows,' I said softly.

'There's so much I regret…'

'She knows that too.' I moved from the chair and knelt by Evelina's feet, holding one small, claw-like hand.

She smiled feebly. 'Tell me about yourself, Mattie; I'd like to know. Well, if you're not going to be late for your tea?'

'Shall I go out and get us some chips?' I suggested, and her face lit up.

I went to the place she suggested, coming back with what turned out to be some of the best fish and chips I've ever eaten. Evelina had laid the small kitchen table with a cloth and cutlery, and made a pot of tea, with her best bone china cups and saucers. I loathe tea, and most of all the strong builders' kind she'd made, but drank it bravely, hoping my aura didn't reveal how little I enjoyed it.

For a skinny, frail old lady, Evelina fell on the generous portion of fish and chips like a hungry bear, putting away more than you'd ever imagine possible.

'*She doesn't eat enough; worrying about money and that dratted roof,*' said Tabitha.

After we'd polished off the chips, she listened to the whole sorry story, the hospitals and psychiatrists, the medication, and how I'd come to learn the truth about myself.

'Turns out my granny was the same, but nobody ever mentioned it until now,' I concluded with a sigh.

'It often goes that way in families – sometimes misses a generation,' said Evelina. 'You poor kid, it must have been hard. It's a wonder you're not off your head, but you seem to have it screwed on all right. I'd like to help, but maybe your boyfriend can be a comfort.'

'Oh, you can see there's somebody?' I was surprised.

'It's the colours, you have strong feelings for him.' It wasn't a question.

'We haven't known each other long but… it might be special.'

Evelina sighed. 'I lost my lovely Eric a couple of years back; daft sod fell off a roof. I could do with him now, to fix this one.'

'*Tell her I can help,*' said Tabitha, her voice urgent. '*I know where Mam's share certificates are. Mattie, it's why you're here. Tell her, please.*'

Uncertain of her reaction, I did, and Evelina's lined and seamed face blossomed with hope. 'I've been trying to find them buggers for years; they have to be here, somewhere safe. Can't seem to dig them out though.'

With Tabitha's help, I explained.

'In the coal shed rafters all this time? My God, the very the last place I'd have looked, especially since we had the gas fire in.'

'*Should be worth a few bob by now,*' said Tabitha. '*Fix the roof at the very least, and maybe more.*'

'Mattie, you're like an angel sent from heaven,' said Evelina. 'I can't thank you enough.'

Being able to help gave me an unexpected glow of satisfaction; maybe Tabitha was right, and I'd been "sent". That was a nice feeling.

'Thank your sister, not me,' I said.

'Pity I haven't been able to do more, you're a nice lass.'

'Tell me about your mum, she sounds awesome.'

'She'd have liked you; your colours are so clear, not muddy the way some folks' are.' Evelina smiled, showing ivory-yellow teeth. 'She always told me the world was crowded with spirits, and some of them weren't very nice.'

'I've heard voices saying nasty things,' I said, remembering one particular assault with a shiver of revulsion.

'Mum said a lot of them were angry, either because something bad had happened to them in life, or they were kind of stuck and unable to move on.'

'I've heard those too, and my mother's spirit can't leave the house we live in. But there's only her and one other there, and he comes with one of my regular visitors.'

Evelina gave me a sympathetic look. 'Our Mum would cry out at night sometimes, when they crowded in too close.'

'What did she do about it?'

'Mum was strong, the same as you. Commanded them to leave. When she told them to, they had to go.' Evelina gave me a straight look. 'I can see you're doubtful about being a strong person, but you are, the colours don't lie.'

'It's not how I feel, most of the time, maybe because I've been told so often that I'm vulnerable.'

'Now this is something I *can* help with,' said Evelina with new confidence. 'Mattie, your aura is beautiful, the colours clean and clear. You might be confused right now, but you have a huge reserve of inner strength to draw on; I don't often see that in people, not to the degree you have it.'

I hoped she wasn't just saying what I needed to hear, but, if true, then it was good news; a different way of thinking about myself.

'Perhaps I get it from my birth mother, Emilie? I'm told she was fierce and powerful – too much so at times. I can feel it from her presence, and sometimes the things she says.'

'But you're not fierce; some of your experiences have made you angry and impatient, with good reason, but there's gentleness in your colours too, empathy,' said Evelina. 'I can also see that you prefer order, sequence and pattern.'

'I'm a mathematician, it's how my mind works; one reason why this has been so hard to get my head around.'

'You're there now though, aren't you? The edges are

indistinct, but I don't see turmoil in you, only strength, growing resolution and confidence.'

It wasn't what I'd come for, but this in itself was a powerful revelation. Mattea Lombardi was not a vulnerable, mentally ill person, she was – or could grow to become – powerful and strong, but in the right way.

'There's not much more I can tell you, dear. I hope it helps.'

'It really does. Talking like this has made me feel better about myself and it's been an honour to meet you.'

I gave her all the cash in my purse, and when she protested, told her, 'No, any money from selling the shares may take a while to come through. This will help, for now at least. I can get a taxi home and use my credit card.'

We parted friends, and on the journey back to Lytham it was blindingly obvious I had learnt something. Evelina had given me a peace I hadn't had before, and a new sense of my inner strength, but I did hope she was wrong about the dark cloud.

*

In the following days, Lucas commented on how much my visit to Evelina appeared to have helped – I'd shared the whole story with him.

'You've got a spring in your step which wasn't there before,' he observed. 'You look lighter, I suppose.' Simon might also have had something to do with it, but I was keeping that to myself.

'Evelina couldn't teach me how to manage my voices, but I did learn something, more to do with my inner strength if I can learn to trust it.'

'So it was worth going?'

'Yes, absolutely.'

'That's good, and I've got something to show you.' Lucas produced a brochure about Venice. The photographs were beautiful, and I studied them with a pang of sadness that Mamma and I had never made the long-promised trip. But it had been planned when I'd thought there was a strong reason to connect me with the place.

'The water looks the most amazing colour; is it really that opalescent green?'

'Yes, it absolutely is,' said Lucas. 'You don't believe it until you've been there for yourself. We could take a boat trip out to the lagoon, it's where you'll appreciate it best. I was thinking October if it would fit in with your plans?'

Something held me back from committing to the trip, but there was also a reluctance to disappoint Lucas; I did want to go, but not so soon.

'Would it be all right if we waited until the spring?'

Lucas hid his disappointment well. 'Of course, whatever you prefer.'

'So much has happened, a pause for breath would be good, and I'm only just getting to know Lytham and the surrounding area. I'll be in a better place to appreciate Venice properly if we wait a while.'

'We could go for the February carnival?' offered Lucas, alight with new enthusiasm. 'Emilie said the costumes and masks were magical, and there are parades on the canals. It might be too late to book the best hotels, but I'll get onto it and find us somewhere nice, an apartment perhaps.'

'It sounds wonderful,' I told him gratefully.

Of course, the real reason I didn't want to go anywhere was my developing relationship with Simon, but it was very early days.

FIFTEEN

As September and the new school year began, my maths pupils, including the two new ones, were coming after school and at weekends, leaving much of each day free. I was continuing my exploration of Emilie's cookery books when Polly rang to tell me about the trip to New York.

'It was all wonderful, the food was incredible, but the property prices were crazy! Even with two of us working, I don't see how we could have anything close to the quality of life we have now, let alone room for Harriet's collections. Our hopes of going to live there are very much on hold.'

'I'm sorry, that must be a massive disappointment?'

'It was Harriet's dream rather than mine, but if she still wants to live in the USA, we can make it work – just somewhere less expensive than the big city.'

'And how are the wedding plans?' I asked.

'Cancelled unless Harriet's mother can be persuaded to abandon her grandiose ideas. It isn't what we want. My parents don't care, so why should she? And how about you – finding your way through the maze?'

'Yes, I think maybe I am.'

'I'm so glad, Mattie. Hopefully, you are finding a way to be at peace with your gift and on the up from here on in.'

'I'd like to believe that's true. Turns out it's just the beginning of a whole other journey.'

After hearing about my visit to Evelina, and what she'd told me, Polly snorted. 'I know you've never believed in your strength, but maybe you'll start now. You daft cow, how on earth would a weak person have coped with the things that have happened in your life? You've always been strong.'

'What about when I was depressed, overwhelmed and in hospital, drugged up to the eyeballs?'

'Not weakness, Mattie, never think that. Harriet says you've survived incredibly well.'

Which felt like another foothold on solid ground; learning to trust the strength I'd inherited from my birth mother.

Even in mid-September, there were already leaves blowing around the streets as the days turned cooler. "Cardigan weather" my mamma used to call it. Then Lucas came to visit with a big smile on his face, which hadn't been visible very often in recent weeks.

'Fantastic news, Tom's coming back to live with me for a while.'

'You've missed him, I can tell; the two of you are very close.' I had to smile at his excitement.

'Tom's dad was military too; they lived all over the world, and, like a lot of army kids, Tom went to boarding school. His parents chose a local one, so I could keep an eye on him, and we spent most weekends and a lot of school holidays together. When his mum and dad divorced, and later his father died, I was the one who picked up the pieces, so he's very dear to me. The son I never had, if that isn't too corny.'

'Will he be staying long?'

'Well, that's the best part. He's decided what he wants to do next and signed up at the last minute to do a course in Preston – a postgraduate master's in psychotherapy. He's going to live with me and commute, at least in the short-term.'

'*Such a fine young man,*' commented Emilie. '*Turned out very well, thanks to Lucas.*'

I didn't relay this remark; three-way conversations became wearing.

By the end of the morning, I'd fielded calls about two more potential pupils, and spoken to Sienna's mum, who was full of praise for the way I'd succeeded in getting her difficult daughter to understand the mysteries of linear equations. My little tutoring business might just possibly be headed for success.

No one knew about Simon yet, because I wanted to take things slowly and see how it went. We'd progressed to holding hands in the coffee shop after our early morning run, so the village grapevine would be onto us before long. It was hardly a surprise that Evelina had seen from my aura that there was someone I cared for. Let's be truthful, I was utterly crazy about him, head over heels in love, and ready to cast caution to the winds if he wanted me to. Maybe being unmedicated put me back in touch with all the feelings that had always been dampened down. But then again, my newly discovered sense of strength and confidence meant I didn't see any reason to hold back. I wasn't 100% sure of his feelings for me, but the signs were all good.

During our coffee shop conversations, we'd exchanged life stories. When I described the years of my "depression" he'd been deeply sympathetic.

'I've been through that,' he told me. 'Not in the same way, of course, but I once did a six-month contract in Sweden, during the winter months, and working from home was so miserable I stopped going out and wasn't feeding myself right. It took a colleague at one of my few face-to-face meetings to notice I'd lost loads of weight and ask if I was OK. He was so kind I began to cry, something I hadn't done since I was a little kid.'

'Telling boys to be manly and strong, always in control of their feelings, might be the worst thing society does to them,' I said, squeezing his hand. 'I had any number of young men in tutorial groups who struggled with the whole university experience but didn't feel able to admit it.'

'Yes, exactly,' said Simon. 'There was a strong sense of shame at not coping, so I never told anyone. I got help eventually, but way later than I should have done, and the experience left me with the understanding that it's OK to be vulnerable.'

'Which, in my book, makes you a grown-up,' I said.

'I've never met anyone like you before,' Simon told me, stroking my cheek. 'You're so natural, easy to talk to, and not slathered in make-up, which I hate.'

Now that was funny. 'Only because I never got the hang of it, or the dressing up and high-heels thing.'

'A beautiful woman like you doesn't need make-up.' He smiled, but then drew back as if concerned he might have said too much. Another thing I'd appreciated about him – he hadn't rushed me into anything – but now, perversely, I almost wished he would.

*

One of my new pupils had failed GCSE maths a few months earlier, and we were working intensively to coach her through to the resit in November. Sitting together at the table in the orangery, I could hear raised voices from next door throughout the whole two hours. It suggested marital relations had soured, although they went quiet soon after Scarlett left.

Meeting Simon the next morning by the windmill as usual, the sea was charcoal grey and the clouds a threatening shade of purple, resembling a livid bruise with hints of green. We'd barely set off when the sky went darker still and sudden driving rain bounced off the walkway, drenching us both.

'Time to make a run for it,' said Simon, picking up Mary, who was whining and hiding close to his legs; she hated rain.

We sprinted for the coffee shop but were so wet on arrival, we had to sit on the plastic benches at the back. Simon fetched blue paper towels to mop ourselves (and Mary) up, but our wet clothes steamed in the heat, which made us both laugh.

'We deserve chocolate brownies with our coffee,' said Simon, squelching off in damp trainers to make the purchase but when the brownies arrived, they were disappointing.

'Bit dry,' was Simon's verdict, 'been on display in the counter too long.'

'My home-made ones are much better, even if I shouldn't say that. I've got the recipe cracked now.'

His face lit up. 'You make chocolate brownies? Mattie, you are a dream come true.'

As he looked at me with sparkling eyes, all sorts of things were going on in my body; I could only manage a sheepish grin. 'You should have seen my cooking before I set to teaching myself from a book. The brownies are a recent addition to my repertoire, and they're really good. I made them to soften up my friend, George.'

'Boyfriend?' he asked, suddenly serious.

'No, there's nobody. And you?'

'Not anymore,' said Simon. 'I was away too much… story of my life.' Shades of regret and sadness played across his features, so I held his hand again.

'Mattie,' he said slowly, 'if I were to ply you with food and wine at a very nice local restaurant, would it persuade you to make some brownies for me?'

'It might,' I told him.

That's how we came to have our first "date" which didn't

involve running, and Mary came too because the place was used to Simon bringing her along.

'It's one reason why I come here; because they make her welcome,' he said. 'Plus, it's a change from the hotel dining room.'

When I arrived in the pale-blue dress which had been the best choice from my limited wardrobe options, his eyes lit up with all the appreciation I could hope for.

'You look fantastic in that colour,' he said, with such warmth that my heart sang.

He cleaned up pretty well himself – we'd only ever seen each other in sports gear until then. I was just enjoying the dessert – locally made sticky toffee pudding – when, across the room, I saw Ruth arrive, accompanied by an older man. She managed a nervous smile and raised a hand in acknowledgement but didn't come over.

Over coffee and brandy, Simon asked, 'If I said there's a rumour going about that my contract might be extended, would it be good news?'

'Yes, very,' I said simply, disinclined to play games and pretend I wasn't keenly interested.

He reached for my hand. 'It's by no means a done deal, but hopefully they aren't sending me away again just yet. Mattie, I mean it when I say you're special, and I didn't want to rush you, but there might not be enough time to take it slow.'

'I'm not gonna lie, I think you're special too,' I told him.

That was a huge, hulking elephant of an understatement; I'd fallen for him almost from day one and could hardly believe my luck that he seemed to feel the same. I was sufficiently aroused by his proximity that my skin prickled every time he touched me. Honestly, I'd have liked to jump him there and then but managed to restrain myself.

'Could you be available tomorrow afternoon?' I asked.

'Jordan's mum has postponed his session, so I might be free to make chocolate brownies if you fancy some?'

Simon held my gaze, his face serious. 'Mattie, are you absolutely sure?'

We both understood the unspoken question, about taking our relationship to the next level. But I was off the brain-dampening medication, excited and happy, ready to break out of the quiet, safe existence I'd lived for many years.

'Damn right I'm sure,' I said, hypnotised by his beautiful blue eyes and the curve of his mouth. At this point, Mary got bored of sitting under the table and leapt into my lap, attempting to lick my face. We both burst out laughing, and the moment passed, but something had been agreed between us. From across the room, Ruth was watching, but I pretended not to notice.

I made the brownies almost as soon as I got home. Although they didn't usually last long, by chance I'd discovered that they were even better a day or two after baking. They kind of got more fudgy, and if Simon was going to be blown away by my chocolatey wiles, they'd have to be my very best efforts.

'*Somebody's putting a spring in your step,*' commented Emilie as I put the brownies out to cool at midnight.

'Yes,' I said briefly, almost afraid to jinx things by saying too much. Then a horrid thought occurred to me. 'Emilie, if I bring him home will you, er... be there?' The idea of trying to seduce Simon with my mother watching was disturbing, to say the least.

She gave a husky laugh. '*Don't worry, I know when to make myself scarce, and voyeurism was never my thing.*'

That was a relief, but what had Harriet told me about setting firm boundaries with my sitting tenant, or any other presences I might encounter? I'd have to have another look at the books she'd lent me.

Rain continued to lash my windows overnight and hadn't stopped the following morning. Simon texted to call off our usual run and said he'd see me later. I was gazing out at the sodden garden wondering how long the awful weather would keep up when Ruth paused in her diligent vacuuming to say, 'It's a high tide, brings this weather in. It'll blow through. Be fine later.'

This was the most I'd heard Ruth say in some time; she'd been nervous around me ever since her exposure. Perhaps her concern had to do with being "on probation", but, having got the key back from Nigel, I was happy enough to leave things as they were.

It was even more out of character when she said, 'Nice food at the Vinery, innit? That was my dad I was with. He owed me a birthday treat from way back.'

Suspecting this was an attempt to pump me for information about Simon, I clammed up and went upstairs to consider the contents of my wardrobe. While engaged in the process of selecting a seduction outfit, especially in the underwear department, I heard Ruth leave to go next door to Lucas's, where, according to her, the oven needed a good seeing to.

Fizzing with excitement, I had to talk to someone. When Mamma rang me in the late morning, I shared that I'd met someone lovely, but we were only on our second actual date. Then I changed the subject because I'd decided not to mention anything about Emilie's presence in my house or being psychic. After the trauma of telling Lucas, I wasn't ready to do that, and certainly not over the phone.

*

As forecast by Ruth, the rain had stopped by the time Simon arrived, driving a dark-green sports car I hadn't seen before.

He'd left Mary with a colleague, and looked so good in jeans and a striped Breton top that my stomach stirred with what can only be described as unadulterated lust. It had been too long since anyone had made me feel that way.

Like every other visitor I'd had, Simon was wide-eyed at Emilie's eclectic interior and insisted on a tour of the house. His response was interested but a bit short of enthusiastic, and it was clear that he preferred the study with its modern bookcases and desk, because he smiled for the first time when we got up there.

'You don't share Emilie's taste in interiors, do you?' I asked.

He pulled me close, saying, 'The house is amazing and has to have been the work of a lifetime, but it's all too busy and cluttered for me. I prefer a simple, modern look, not so much to dust. God, I must sound lazy.' He tightened his arms around me. 'Maybe I'm just used to hotel interiors – I haven't had what you'd call a proper home for years.'

I led the way to the front guest room, where I'd asked Ruth to make the bed up fresh, and pretended to be looking out at the street below. He came to my side and turned my body to face him. Then he kissed me – properly – in a way we hadn't before, and as if a switch had been pressed, we were both on fire. One of the few things I remember after that was wondering if Emilie was watching, before reaching a point where I ceased to care, lost in the urgency of now.

Damn, he was good; the first partner I'd ever had who prioritised my needs. After the first heat of passion, when it was all over too quickly for both of us, he took his time, searching with exquisite slowness for what would please me, always asking, "Do you like this? How about this? Oh yes, you do…"

Much later, I lay in his arms, stroking an impressive set of muscles. Not something I'd previously associated with accountants.

'Oh,' I said, 'you never had your chocolate brownies.'

'Did you really make some for me? Mattie, you are my perfect woman.'

'You haven't tried them yet,' I teased. 'They were supposed to be tantalising delights to lure you into my bed.'

'As if I needed brownies for that.' He stroked my hair, studying me intently as if he wanted to learn every detail of my face. 'You are more than enough, Mattie, I can't believe I've found you. Is it too soon to say that whenever I'm with you, it feels like I've come home? I've been looking for you for the longest time.'

This was very satisfactory and I encouraged him to expand on the subject.

Later, we had a takeaway from the Orient Queen, and the brownies provided pudding.

'These are fantastic,' he pronounced, closing his eyes in bliss as he savoured the taste. 'The best I've ever had. It's been such a wonderful day; I may have to ask you to marry me.'

'You're only saying that to get more brownies,' I protested.

*

Inevitably, the sports car became a regular fixture outside my house, whenever Simon's work commitments allowed. Of course, Mary was also a frequent visitor, and in the same way as Mutt she could be ill at ease in certain rooms, the kitchen in particular. One day, chopping herbs with Emilie's rocker blade, a gadget I'd grown to appreciate, my now-unmedicated brain came up with the reason for the dogs' behaviour.

'Emilie, it's your presence they're reacting to,' I said aloud.

'*Have you only just worked that out?*' was her reply. '*I sometimes go away because, although I'm fond of dogs, they don't seem to like me now.*'

'I don't think it's dislike; they don't growl or raise their hackles, but they're aware of you being here.'

'*I have the same effect on them Simon has on me.*'

That was unexpected, a drench of cold water. 'You don't like him?'

'*You're putting words into my mouth. But there's something not quite…*'

This was overstepping the boundaries big time, and, according to the books I'd read, strong action was necessary.

'Emilie, your opinion of my boyfriend is not required. Is that clear?'

There was a long pause, and I thought she'd gone, but then she said, '*I can see he makes you happy.*'

'Then leave it, right?'

This time there was silence.

Simon and I had joyfully embarked on a new phase of our relationship, and when he said wonderful things to and about me I went all fizzy with the sheer joy of loving and being loved. Yes, we'd only known each other a few weeks but we were both adults in our thirties; why take it slow if there was no need? He never mentioned leaving the hotel but didn't spend much time there either.

Lucas had to have noticed the car being outside a lot, often overnight, and seen Simon coming and going. For obvious reasons, I hadn't seen much of either Lucas or Tom in recent weeks, something I kept meaning to put right. Whenever I suggested inviting them to dinner, Simon said he wanted me all to himself and, in the heady rush of new love, I was happy to go along with that. Then, one morning, Lucas "happened" to be doing a bit of light pruning in his front garden as we arrived back from our run, so I took the opportunity to introduce them. Lucas was warm and friendly, smiling his approval, which mattered to me.

'You think a lot of your neighbour?' asked Simon when we got inside.

'He's a special friend, a link with my real mother.' Simon had heard the whole story about the twins, and the arrangement between them which had shaped my life. I'd followed Harriet's example in not disclosing the psychic part. That could wait.

'So, you aren't Italian, your father was Asian?' was all he'd said. 'I don't care who you are, I love my brown-skinned girl.' He then proceeded to demonstrate just how much. Who knew sex could be so fabulous when you weren't medicated into numbness?

George continued to visit regularly, but I never told Simon she was a psychiatric nurse and made sure he was never around when she came. After all, if I was sure my problem wasn't mental illness, there was no need to tell him the full history of all the unnecessary treatment I'd had. It wasn't shame which held me back from telling him, but the woman Simon loved was the new Mattie, not the old one, someone ready to embrace life with both hands. I didn't want the past cluttering up a wonderful present.

I should have anticipated that George would know about Simon even though I hadn't told her, and they'd never met.

'Local grapevine,' she said. 'The word is he's drop-dead gorgeous and spending a lot of time here.'

'Which is a good thing,' I said, with new confidence. 'It shows I'm recovered enough to form a successful adult relationship; the first in a long time.'

'You certainly seem happy, and your eyes are shining.'

'Shall we put it this way,' I suggested. 'The physical side of things is spectacular.'

'I'm glad to hear it,' said George drily. 'But it's a concern for me that you might have rushed into this before you're ready. So, is he moving in?'

'Not at the moment,' I said, glaring. 'It's early days yet.' In addition, I was all too aware of his contract being due to end at Christmas; there'd been no more talk about it being extended.

George nodded her approval. 'Take it slow, there's plenty of time.'

Except there wasn't. In October, Simon came home from a meeting in Leeds with a preoccupied look on his face. It was obvious something had happened but despite his normal openness and honesty, he seemed reluctant to tell me.

Then in the evening, we drank more gin than usual – he was usually careful on working days. OK, let's be truthful, it was quite a lot of gin.

'It's obvious there's something on your mind,' I told him. 'You've been preoccupied and distracted as if you're somewhere else.'

'Oh, my darling, it isn't you,' he said urgently, taking my hands in his while Mary sat snuggled between us, sensitive to the growing tension. 'My heart is always here, wherever I go, but that's just it.'

'A new contract.' It was obvious, and I'd seen this coming but chosen to ignore it.

'The good news is that it would be for three years, possibly even longer. It would allow me to have a settled home, maybe buy a house, everything I've been wanting for a long time.'

'And the bad news? Where's the job?' My heart was pounding, a sense of dread creeping over me, turning my skin cold.

His eyes met mine, full of pain and anguish. 'California.'

SIXTEEN

I gaped at him, suddenly sober. The bombshell about a California posting rudely pulled the rug from under my romantic dreams of a life together in Lytham. These had been bubbling up in unguarded moments, but I'd barely begun to indulge the idea of him moving in, let alone raised the idea with Simon. He liked the town, and me, but would he be open to staying? After all, lots of people worked remotely online, didn't they? But we hadn't talked about any of this, and, without warning, it was already too late.

The turmoil I was experiencing must have been plastered all over my face. 'You hate the idea, I get it,' he said miserably.

Everything in me wanted to plead for us, beg him not to go, to turn down the job and stay, but for the first time in our wild and wonderful affair, something held me back. Maybe it was the memory of Sven, who'd gone home to Sweden without inviting me to join him. Simon and I had been living in the moment, delighting in each other, while the rockets and fireworks of new love lit up our skies. At no point had we discussed a long-term future, only our joy in finding each other here and now.

Poor Simon was utterly miserable. 'They offer me my dream job in a beautiful part of the world, and all I can think about is you,' he said, over and over.

'And I don't want to hold you back from something you've wanted for so long.'

How could I ask him not to leave when he hadn't actually suggested I should go with him; maybe that wasn't on his agenda. It seemed to be a choice between his going or staying. Even chocolate brownies couldn't make this better, though I'd made some.

The next few days were hideous for both of us; he told me more about the job and it was perfect for him, the fulfilment of a dream. But I had dreams too, and most of them involved him staying in the house I'd grown to love. Could I leave everything to go with him – and did he even want me to? Because he hadn't said the words out loud. I daren't ask the question in case the answer wasn't what I wanted to hear.

On Wednesday morning, Simon was due to get the train to London for a series of meetings to discuss his new contract. He'd be away at least two nights, possibly more.

With the taxi waiting in the street, on the doorstep he held me very close. 'I'm leaving Mary here to make sure you don't forget me.' His voice was choked with emotion.

'I couldn't possibly forget; we're both going to miss you so much,' I told him. I'm not someone who cries much but it was close. The prospect of being without him sat heavily, a tightness in my chest, making it hard to breathe. How quickly this beautiful man had become my whole existence.

When the taxi honked at him, he picked up his leather travel bag and set off down the path, before turning back to look at me. The bag lay abandoned on the path as he rushed back to hold both my hands in his and say the words I'd been waiting to hear.

'I love you, and I've been such a fool. Run away with me, we can do this, and I can't live without you. Sell up here and come to California. It would be a dream life in the sunshine and between us, we'd have enough to afford somewhere special.' Then his face twisted. 'Sorry, my darling, I shouldn't put you under pressure – I've been trying so hard not to. Forget what I just said.'

'But I love you too, and I'll think about everything while you're gone,' I promised. 'We'll find a way forward together.'

I stood on the doorstep of my treasured home, watching the taxi until it was out of sight, while the man I loved desperately left me behind. I'd got up early to make us a cooked breakfast so Simon wouldn't have to face railway food, but now it sat uneasily in my churning stomach. Mary was whining behind the door, and I wanted to do the same thing, already lost without him.

After a while, she and I went next door, where I could rely on Lucas's wisdom and perspective. Mary and Mutt had hit it off from their first encounter, and they now greeted each other with such joy we had to put them in the garden to run off their exuberance. Lucas made coffee and gave fatherly advice his best shot, which wasn't quite what I'd hoped.

'Mattie, I can't tell you what to do, it wouldn't be right, and you can only follow your heart.'

'But?' I asked. 'I get the feeling there's something you aren't saying.'

He sighed, watching the dogs as they romped around outside. 'Look, Simon seems like a nice bloke, but you haven't known each other long. Isn't it a little premature to be making such big, life-changing decisions?'

'How long did it take you to fall in love with Emilie?' An unfair question, but I was on the defensive.

'Less than a day,' he admitted. 'I knew right away, and my feelings never changed, even when…'

'Then your objection doesn't stand up to scrutiny, does it?'

Lucas was earnest, eyes searching my face. 'But how much do you know about him? Can you trust this man with your heart and your whole life?'

'He's thirty-six, a forensic accountant who's lived all over the world. The family name is Ransome, and he grew up in Worcestershire. His mother died of breast cancer, and he sees very little of his father – they don't get on. What more do you need, his birth certificate?'

'Mattie, please, if you're going to talk about selling up here and moving to another country, I only want to be sure you aren't making a mistake.'

'I'm sorry,' I said, reaching out to hug him. 'I know you care about me, and I'm deeply grateful for that. But you had years with the love of your life, so can you blame me for wanting the same? I've never experienced such strong feelings with anyone, until Simon.'

'Have you talked to your mother?'

I managed a wry smile. 'Which one?' Not the time to admit that Emilie hadn't taken to Simon; she'd said his aura was sometimes a funny colour, whatever that meant, and I wasn't planning to ask. For me, the evidence of his touch, taste and smell, not to mention the wonderful words he said to me, were enough. Mamma Sofie was deep in the process of setting up home with her new love, so I couldn't talk to her, but found myself hoping they'd come to California to visit. If I went.

Back at home with a clingy Mary, I was no nearer to making a final decision. Only one thing was clear: it came down to choosing between head and heart. Practical common sense reminded me I'd only recently become settled in a home of my own, with financial security, while my heart wanted to throw caution out of the window, give everything up for love and make a new life in the sunshine. It made me think of my twin mothers: Sofie, inclined to safe well-thought-out decisions, and Emilie, someone who lived life on her own terms and wouldn't have recognised caution if she'd fallen over it.

That first day without Simon was awful, I missed him on both an emotional and physical level. He phoned me from the London hotel, but all his loving words couldn't make up for the deep ache of his absence. Mary helped, giving me something outside myself to focus on.

The next day, I was doing my best to get a grip when, coming back from a windy and lonely morning run, it was a surprise to see the van from Lucas's favourite florist outside my house. I immediately assumed that the glorious bouquet the driver placed into my arms must be from Simon, but the card read:

> *A gesture of friendship.*
> *Regards,*
> *Nigel and Davina*

She must have been looking out for the van because Davina then appeared on the pavement, beautifully groomed and polished, as always. Not a strand of her blonde hair moved in the breeze.

'Oh good,' she said, 'it's come. I hope you like it because I so wanted to make things right and for us to be friends again.' She stood at a distance, visibly nervous around Mary, who was straining at her collar, supremely confident of a welcome from all humans. 'Sorry, I don't care for dogs. Silly of me, I know.'

'The flowers are lovely; you shouldn't have.'

'I'm glad you like them because we wanted to make it clear there are no hard feelings about your decision not to sell the house, though of course if you should ever change your mind, our offer still stands.'

I couldn't come up with a response because my hands were full juggling the bouquet and Mary, who now wanted to go inside and rest after her exertions. I thanked Davina again and she gave an airy wave before disappearing back inside. While Mary collapsed on the kitchen sofa, I arranged the flowers in a vase but couldn't help thinking about a quick and easy sale if California won out in the tug-of-love stakes.

*

George came at 4.00pm on Friday as usual, made a big fuss of Mary and admired the flowers I'd put on the kitchen island.

'From the new man?' she asked.

'Simon is away right now; they're from the neighbours.'

George looked up from the file she was studying. 'I didn't think you were on good terms with them?'

'Read the card,' I told her. 'It's a kind gesture, although I don't entirely trust their motives. They still want me to sell them the house but I believe all that... unpleasantness was part of a campaign to persuade me to leave.'

'*You could be right,*' said Emilie.

'*Yeah, something doesn't add up,*' Hal put in.

George's eyes were on me, and her intent, professional look was back. 'Come on, Mattie, even you must admit this all sounds a bit paranoid.'

'You think I don't know that? But it's what my instincts are telling me,' I said.

Her face told me she didn't agree, and fury boiled up in me like a head of steam – another thing being unmedicated no longer kept under control – and I was already tense and fretful over Simon. Emilie's voice urged, '*Mattie, stay calm,*' and I tried, but George was watching me.

'You're angry with me for mentioning that,' she observed.

'It's the immediate assumption that anything out of the ordinary has to be going on in my head, rather than being external harassment!' I exploded. 'Why must it be something wrong with *me* if I have a perfectly reasonable suspicion that my neighbours are trying to drive me away?' Mary was uneasy at my raised voice and went to hide under the dining table.

'You're right, of course, except I'm not assuming anything, merely making an observation about what I hear,' said George, keeping her voice calm. 'How are things with the boyfriend?'

'Bloody marvellous, if you must know, except he's away and I miss him.' I'd made some more brownies, but she wasn't getting one after her mention of paranoia.

'And is that what's upsetting you, or is it the neighbours?'

'Both,' I said. 'And I'm not upset.'

In that instant, I came to a decision: I would go to California, as far away as possible from my supposed mental health history, and put the whole nightmare behind me. Tomorrow if necessary, whatever it took for us to be happy.

'Mattie, something is going on here; are you off your meds?' asked George.

'*Oh, be careful*,' urged Emilie.

I was about to deny it but then lost patience with the whole charade. 'Yes, I bloody well am, and for the very good reason that I don't need drugs because I'm not mentally ill. I'm psychic, like my granny, and have been since adolescence.'

George's eyebrows went up, but all she said was, 'Tell me about it.'

I gave her the whole story about the voices being in old buildings, describing the clamour in parts of York which had at times driven me to despair, and ending with the realisation that the voice now in the house was my mother. I left out the part about her brother Hal.

George listened without interruption. 'The way you tell it certainly sounds very logical and plausible,' she said when I came to a halt. 'Is Emilie here now?'

'*Of course I am, and so is her brother. Hal would love to talk to her, but he can't.*'

I could hear his distant voice, saying, '*It wasn't your fault, Gee…*'

'Yes, she's here,' I said, grateful George was at least taking me seriously.

'And Emilie explained all this to you?'

'Gradually,' I said. 'Everything began to make sense afterwards, so I chose to wean myself off the pills, and there haven't been any ill effects at all, except for experiencing everything more intensely. It might interest you to know that it's a wonderful feeling.' Thinking about Simon brought a glow of happiness, a warmth inside and out. There were other things I missed about him too. 'Look at the person I am now, George,' I told her. 'This is the real me, the one who's always been waiting to emerge.'

'There's no denying what you're telling me makes a kind of sense,' said George, 'but you'll understand that, as a professional, I have to take a cautious approach.'

'Of course,' I told her. 'But you can't know what a huge relief it is to know I'm not ill and never have been. Even just a few weeks of living my life without the drugs has been like walking out of a fog into daylight. I don't need to be a psychiatric patient anymore because there isn't anything wrong with me and never was. I just have an unusual gift which is going to take some getting used to.'

'I can see how happy you are, what with Simon and everything,' said George, 'but I know you'll also appreciate that I can't discharge you from my care without due diligence. You're seeing Dr Parks on Monday, so the timing is fortuitous, but you might have to explain all this again, for her benefit. If you're still planning on attending.'

'*Her aura's gone a very odd colour; best go along with it, Mattie.*'

George's calm reaction had been better than I could have hoped. 'I've always intended to keep the appointment,' I said, 'and Lucas will look after Mary for me. I do understand there are procedures you have to follow. It might even be a good idea to complete the discharge process, since Simon and I may be leaving the country soon. We're going to live in California.'

George paused and gave me a long look. 'That all sounds incredibly exciting,' she said. 'But are you sure about rushing into this so soon? A brand-new relationship and life on another continent are a lot to take on.'

'To hell with it,' I told her. 'For once, I'm going to follow my heart and see where life takes me.'

*

I duly attended my appointment at the Wellspring Unit in Blackpool, a modern building that looked like an office block, on the same site as the main hospital. George was right on two counts: Dr Parks was warm and friendly, in contrast to my former psychiatrist, who had been consistently morose, and I did have to go through the whole story all over again. My outfit for the appointment had been chosen with care: I wanted the psychiatrist to see a professional woman who should be taken seriously. For the first time in weeks, the black-and-white lecturer uniform had come out of the wardrobe. I'd also added opaque tights because the wind off the October sea was bitingly cold.

When I arrived, there was another person present – Dr Chowdari – whose mixed-race descent was obvious because we had similar colouring, even down to the curly hair.

Dr Parks smiled a welcome. 'Hello, Mattie. Would you mind my colleague sitting in, as no one from the department except George has met you before?' When I nodded assent, she continued, 'I'm aware of what's been happening since you moved here, but I'd like to hear it in your own words.'

I'd gone along determined to explain myself clearly, even down to rehearsing what I wanted to say. Even so, it took ages to unravel the story for them, and I could hear myself gabbling in my haste to get all the salient details in.

When I eventually ground to a halt, Dr Parks smiled again. 'Thank you for telling us all this, Mattie, and what you've said is in line with the report George made from your last meeting. Perhaps I can summarise to be sure we've understood you correctly?'

When I nodded, she continued, 'OK then, in recent months you've come to believe that the voices you've been hearing since adolescence are not auditory hallucinations as part of your ongoing depression, but the spirits of people who have passed over. As a result, you have reached what seems to you the logical conclusion that you are not now, and never have been, mentally ill, and, in fact, possess psychic abilities.'

'Yes,' I said, grateful to be so clearly understood. 'I know it's an unusual gift, but I'm very far from alone in my experiences. There is a whole body of evidence on the internet and in some books I've been lent. With my academic background, you can imagine how careful I've been about using only reliable sources, not some of the more weird and wonderful ones out there.'

Dr Parks gave a sympathetic smile. 'Parts of the web should come with a health warning, shouldn't they? And there is of course no consensus on whether spiritualists or mediums are charlatans making fraudulent claims, or in possession of abilities most of us don't understand.'

'That's exactly it,' I said, 'and I wouldn't want to call myself either of those things. I only hear voices and nothing more. Even knowing and understanding what's happening it can still be hard to cope with, and I've had to work hard to retain some control of what I hear.'

'Then this must have been a difficult time for you, coming on top of the revelations about your family history,' said Dr Parks. 'George was further concerned when you reported harassment and persecution from your next-door neighbour?'

'They've denied it, even sent me flowers, but there's been both motive and opportunity,' I said. 'I've kept what evidence I could, but the bottom line is they're desperate to buy my house and trying to drive me out.'

'Which must have been a distressing experience. Yet I understand that you're now planning to sell up and move to California with someone you've only recently met?'

I flushed, beginning to realise how this must sound. 'Yes, it's been something of a whirlwind romance, which is a new experience for me, but it feels right to leave the baggage of my past life behind and start all over again with Simon. It'll be good for me, I'm sure of it, and that's why it's time for me to be discharged from your care.'

Dr Parks leaned back and exchanged looks with her colleague, who took out his phone and began typing into it. That seemed a bit rude unless he was just making notes.

'I'm very interested in what you've told me.' The doctor's expression was unreadable. 'George reported extreme anxiety for your well-being and, having heard this story, I share her concerns.'

This brought me up short, devastated to hear her say that, and my skin prickled with cold. *Dammit, I thought they'd been listening and taking me seriously.* I should have stayed calm but was so angry at the way I'd been manipulated, despite my careful, rehearsed presentation of the facts.

Jumping to my feet, I said, 'OK, now I get it; you think I'm paranoid? George suggested the same thing, but the truth is that I'm thinking with more clarity than I have in years. You've no idea how good it feels.'

Behind the desk, Dr Parks put her hands flat on the polished surface. 'Mattea, I want you to listen to what I'm saying. Will you at least admit there is possibility that everything you are experiencing, including "falling in love", could be the result of coming off your medications and being on a "high"? You may not be in the best place to be making serious long-term decisions about your future.'

At a nod from the psychiatrist, Dr Chowdari stood up.

'We'd like you to come into hospital for a while,' said Dr Parks. 'There are justifiable concerns about your mental state, and for your own protection...'

'No!' I protested. 'You've got it all wrong, and I've explained everything fully. You can see for yourself I'm not crazy.'

Dr Parks pursed her lips. 'That is not a term we use, and nor should you, but we do believe you are extremely vulnerable right now.'

Shock and disbelief sent my skin from cold to hot. 'You haven't listened to anything I've said! In your terms, if I hear voices it means I'm ill, and if I say I'm psychic that also counts as delusional. Either way, I'm fucked.'

'Try not to be angry, Mattea, it isn't helpful and we do have your best interests at heart, even if you don't believe that right now.'

'I'm not coming into hospital; I don't need to be here.'

The psychiatrist was implacable. 'Look,' she said, 'we can do this the hard way or the easy way. I hope you will calm down and agree to be admitted as a voluntary patient.'

I turned around in a panic to discover Dr Chowdari was physically blocking the door, standing in front of it.

'You're threatening to section me?'

'It's your choice, Mattea. We can and will detain you under the Mental Health Act if necessary.'

'What about a Community Treatment Order?' I clutched at this last hope.

'With the very real risk that you will abscond and fly to the States?'

Damn right I would; they'd got me there.

After all the years of misdiagnosis, never being heard or understood, mountains of pills and living a half-numb life, I panicked the way an animal in a trap responds. An entirely appropriate reaction because I *was* caught, and, worst of all, by my own words.

I lost my temper completely, kicking and screaming in protest and two more nurses arrived, probably called by Dr Chowdari. All my rage was wasted energy, made no difference and they still didn't listen. When I fought against the restraint techniques, from their point of view, it was all further evidence that I was dangerously out of control and in need of protection. When threatened with sedation, I surrendered to the inevitable and agreed to be admitted as a voluntary patient.

Simon would be back in a few days, maybe earlier if he told his boss it was an emergency. I could count on his help, and Lucas's too. It was all a misunderstanding, and they'd soon get me out, wouldn't they?

SEVENTEEN

The Wellspring Unit in Blackpool was all right, as such places go, modern with single en-suite bedrooms decorated with framed pictures (securely screwed to the walls) and floral curtains. The bed was standard hospital issue, and neither the artwork on the walls nor the faux wooden headboard made the room look anything other than institutional. The windows didn't open more than a little and I already knew that the main doors into the unit were kept locked, as I'd had to be buzzed in for my appointment.

After the initial formalities, a nurse called Jacqui took me to my room, by which time I was sunk into a silent, despairing submission.

'I've got towels for you here, and a nightshirt to sleep in for now; not new but it's freshly washed,' she said. 'I know you must feel awful that this is happening, but we'll take good care of you; there's no need to be afraid.'

I roused myself enough to say, 'It's all a misunderstanding; the doctor didn't believe what I was telling her. My boyfriend is away, but he'll come as soon as he can, and everything will get sorted out.'

This sounded improbable even as I spoke the words because Simon had no idea I was psychic, but I did know he loved me and once he understood the whole story, would be there for me.

Jacqui was gentle and sympathetic, speaking the way you might to a child recovering from a major tantrum, which, in many ways, was an all too accurate description of the last hour. Sedation was unnecessary because I'd exhausted myself fighting back. I lay on the bed and offered no further resistance.

'Let's get you settled first and take it one day at a time. There's a three-pack of knickers in this top drawer – don't worry, they're new. They'll keep you going until someone can bring your things from home.'

She was apologetic about it but proceeded to search my small handbag for sharp implements, drugs, or alcohol. I hadn't brought any, but she took away my keys.

I'd been planning to use my phone to call the cavalry as soon as she'd gone, but then realised I didn't have a charger with me. The phone wasn't young, and the battery didn't function as well as it once did.

'Don't worry about it,' said Jacqui cheerfully, when I explained. 'There's a drawerful in the office that people have left behind, so we're bound to have one to fit. I'll leave you for now but come and find me if you have any questions. Someone will pop in every thirty minutes or so, to make sure you're OK.'

I knew from experience that this was standard practice with a new patient – observation to ensure I wasn't trying to break out, trash the place or harm myself. The despair I was feeling must have been written all over my face because Jacqui tried to be reassuring.

'I can see you're upset, Mattea, it's bound to feel strange being here at first, but you'll soon get used to us. We suggest no visitors for the first few days, while you settle in. We're here to help if you want to talk. Oh yes, and dinner is at 5.00pm.'

That was another thing I remembered about hospitals, meals at strange hours and dreadful instant coffee via the mini kitchen I'd been shown on the quick tour of the unit. Even though I was hoping for the briefest of stays, it might be an idea to write a list of stuff I needed from home.

Once alone, the first number I called was Simon's, but it went straight to answerphone; he must be in a meeting. I left a slightly garbled message trying to explain everything – not easy when he didn't know my psychiatric history (or even my psychic one) – but the gist of it was a desperate plea to be rescued.

Then I called Lucas. When he heard my panicky explanation of what had happened, he said, 'Oh, God, Mattie, how awful for you – I know how you feel about hospitals. But, my dear, was it wise to be truthful with the psychiatrist? In her terms, claiming to speak to the dead makes you delusional.'

He was right; there was no need to hammer the point home. 'I wanted to explain, hoped she might get it. George seemed to, although it's clear now that she was only pretending to understand. But you believed me.'

'Of course, because you were able to tell me things you couldn't have known. Look, what's done is done. I could use my key to get your things from home, tell me what you need. I'll pick up Mary too, of course. Does Simon know where you are?'

'He must be busy; I had to leave a message.'

'Tell me what I should bring; even if they won't allow me in, I can drop off a bag for you tomorrow.'

After that, a series of texts went to my maths pupils letting them know I'd be out of action for a few days, maybe a week. Once this was sorted out, I tried Simon again, but, when there was no response, left another message, trying to be more coherent this time.

'Simon, it's me again. Where are you? Like I told you, they've put me in a psychiatric unit in Blackpool. I said some things which made them think I was off my head and stupidly told them I'd stopped taking the medication. The doctor thinks our plan to go to California is evidence of me losing the plot, and she might not even believe you're real. Please, my darling, come as soon as you can and get me out of here.'

That left my battery almost flat. Then another nurse knocked on my door, introduced himself as Mark, and said dinner would be ready in a few minutes.

'I'm not hungry,' I snapped back, unable to raise enough energy to be calm and polite. It was shooting myself in the foot because I understood all too well the importance of being cooperative; I'd be discharged sooner that way.

'Maybe you could fancy a sandwich?' he suggested, ignoring my rudeness. 'Any particular flavour? There's egg or cheese.'

I agreed to cheese just to get rid of him. Lying on the bed, my chest felt tight as if I couldn't breathe, but this was only panic and fear. A part of me wanted to let everything out in a storm of grief, but, after my hysterical outburst, the gates on my emotions seemed to have slammed shut, holding all the desperate feelings inside. More than ever, I longed for Simon. The situation made me feel isolated and afraid, so I needed him desperately.

*

Thanks to Jacqui, I managed to charge my phone overnight but hadn't heard from Simon, which scared the hell out of me. He had to have listened to my messages by now, so I tried again but it went straight to answerphone. Almost sobbing, I recorded yet another voicemail.

'Simon, please call me as soon as you get this. I'm in big trouble and I need you. Why aren't you answering?'

Lying on the bed, worrying about why he hadn't yet been in touch, my imagination soon had him dead under a bus or lying broken in some London intensive care unit. It was necessary to breathe deeply and remind myself that his phone could just as easily have been lost or stolen.

Another knock on the door and it was Jacqui again. She came and sat on the bed.

'Mattea, you haven't had any breakfast. Did you sleep all right?'

'Of course, after those knock-out tablets.' I'd accepted these rather than lie awake fretting.

'Dr Parks has prescribed some anti-psychotic medication for you.'

I groaned. All of my worst nightmares were happening at once. 'Look, that stuff is awful; it makes me feel foggy and disconnected. Please don't make me take it.'

'No one is going to force you to do anything, but this is something new, and patients report minimal side-effects. We hope you'll at least give it a try. Oh, and a Mr Fallon has rung asking to see you. I understand he's your uncle, but I told him we don't normally allow visitors for the first few days.'

Clever Lucas. 'Yes, we're extremely close, he's like a father to me, and I want to see him very much.'

Jacqui's expression was dubious. 'We'd prefer you to settle in first.'

Sitting up, I said, 'Here's the deal. I'll take the medication if you let Uncle Lucas in. It would make me feel so much better to see him.'

When he was escorted to my room the same afternoon, I all but collapsed into his arms, overwhelmed by the love and concern in his face. Wisely, "Uncle" Lucas didn't say anything about what an idiot I'd been to try and tell my doctor the truth – I'd had more than enough time to see that for myself.

'It's going to be all right, Mattie, and, before you ask, Mary is fine. I'd prefer to report how much she misses you, but the little minx has attached herself devotedly to my nephew and spent last night snuggled up on his bed. Tom sends his love and says to tell you "*nil desperandum*". They won't let me stay long today but I'll come every afternoon if possible, and you can call me if you need to talk. Come on, love, don't cry. You're a bright girl and a brave one; you've done this before, so start putting that excellent brain to work on convincing the doctors they should let you go.'

When he'd been marched away by Jacqui after only ten minutes, I recovered enough to look through the bag he'd brought – which had already been searched for contraband and sharp implements. As well as the clothes I'd asked for, the blessed man had included a flask of proper coffee, which went down well. He'd also sent me a jar of halfway decent instant and included a couple of bars of the special dark chocolate with chilli from the deli. The staff had confiscated the glass jar in case I used it to harm myself and put the coffee granules in a plastic bag.

Trying Simon's phone again, there was still no answer. Where was he? I sent a text message to say how much I loved and missed him, and to please get in touch. I tried not to think any more about him dying in a ditch somewhere and set my brain into calculation mode instead. Jacqui had been right about the medication; so far, the tablets I'd been given weren't making me foggy at all. Additionally fortified by sugar and caffeine, I lay down to work out a plan of campaign. It took some time, distracted as I was by anxiety about Simon, whom I bombarded with more texts.

The following day, I had a plan to put into action – nothing very original as I'd used the same tactics in York – and became a cooperative patient. This included going to the dining room for a breakfast of cardboard cereal and cold toast with that margarine which repeats on you all day, before asking Mark if George could come to see me.

He frowned. 'It's not usual, we take over your care from the community staff while you're in hospital.'

'Please,' I said urgently. 'Something's worrying me about my boyfriend, and George knows all about it. Please ask her to come; we've built up such a good relationship.'

*

It took another three days of being pleasant, cooperative and persistent in my request, while trying not to climb the walls wondering why Simon hadn't called. Rather than view any daytime TV, I'd read a couple of turgid paperback thrillers and was about ready to climb the walls when the sight of George in the doorway saw step one of the plan accomplished.

'Mattie, I know you must be angry with me.' She stayed well out of reach in case I was ready to wreak a horrible vengeance upon her.

I held up my hands in the universal gesture of peace. 'Hello, George. As you see, I'm unarmed, and no, I'm not out for your blood. But when I realised what was happening, and the doctor threatened to section me, I did feel betrayed, and very angry, but not now. You were only doing your job.' Telling her that it had been one of the absolute worst moments of my life would be counterproductive to what I had in mind.

'I'm so sorry,' she said. 'But can you understand how worried I was by the things you were telling me? My main concern was to protect you from yourself.'

'I know, these last days I've had time to appreciate how it must have sounded to both you and Dr Parks.'

George was visibly relieved, enough to step into the room and sit on the salmon-pink plastic armchair.

'I went by the office first; they've got you on the new drug? I've heard good things about it.'

'Never mind all that,' I told her. 'You're here because there's something important we need to discuss, after which you might want to re-evaluate your position.' I took a deep breath; there was a chance I would be making things worse, much worse.

'You had a brother, Henry. He died.'

All the warmth and friendliness went out of George's face, and her mouth set in a hard line.

'Mattie, this is overstepping the boundaries; I don't discuss my personal life with patients.'

'Please hear me out.' This was dangerous territory, but I had to take the risk. 'I wanted you to know that you haven't lost him because he's always with you; I hear his voice, and Aunt Emilie told me who he was.'

George got to her feet, anger darkening her face. 'You're going too far. I appreciate you're not yourself right now, but...'

There was nothing left to do but go for it. 'His name was Henry, but you always called him Hal. He was ten years younger than you, what they used to describe as a "late baby". He called you "Gee" because, when he was little, he couldn't manage Georgina.'

She went very still, and I tried to remember everything the books had said about "tuning in" when I'd been more interested in the chapters about shutting voices out. I couldn't hear Emilie in the hospital, but I remembered her saying George's brother was always with her, and I'd heard him occasionally when she visited.

'*I'm here, Gee. I love you, don't blame yourself.*' His voice was faint but audible.

'He wants you to know the accident wasn't your fault, and you shouldn't blame yourself.'

'That's enough!' George was furious now. 'This isn't some kind of game, Mattie, and I get that you're angry, but that's no reason to try and hurt me this way.' She was reaching for the door handle when Hal spoke again.

'*Tell her Toots is with me.*'

When I did, George stared at me in disbelief. 'How could you possibly…' She held my gaze, wanting, needing, to believe me. I understood, with real pain, why Harriet had said she didn't do "readings". The responsibility for other people's grief was too much to bear.

With Hal prompting me, I said, 'Toots was his kitten. He loved her so much, but there was something wrong with her kidneys and she only lived for twelve months. He was heartbroken, but Toots is with him now.'

George sat down again, hope beginning to dawn across her face.

'Hal knows you blame yourself for the accident, it's why he stayed, and he can't go until you believe it wasn't your fault.'

There was a long pause, in which I forgot to breathe. It could all so easily go tits up.

'It was six years ago,' George said after a time, her voice wobbling a little. 'Mum and Dad had gone away for the weekend to a wedding, so I was staying at theirs to look after Hal. Mum was worried about him holding parties, but he was never that kind of kid.'

'You were making a cake, and he was being a pest, so you told him to go outside and ride his bike,' I said.

She nodded. 'And some bloody idiot came too fast through the estate, using the street as a rat run, and hit my little brother head-on. He never stood a chance…'

'You did CPR.' I relayed what Hal was telling me. 'The neighbours called an ambulance. No one could have tried harder to save him, but the post-mortem showed that his heart muscle was torn, resuscitation was never possible. George, it wasn't your fault, simply a random accident. He's telling me that if he hadn't had his earphones in, he might have heard the car and got out of the way.'

'I always blamed myself. He was the person I loved most in the world.'

'He loves you too but needs you to let go of the guilt and grief. Hal doesn't want his death to overshadow your entire life.'

'*Lay it down, Gee. Go out there and find love again.*'

When I relayed this, George cracked, hands curling into tight fists and tears starting in her eyes. 'I was engaged when the accident happened, we'd been together three years and were planning our wedding. When Hal was killed, it drove us apart because my fiancé couldn't understand, wanted me to pull myself together and get on with life.'

Holding her hand while she cried, I shed a few tears too, some of which were from sheer relief.

'Thank you,' was all she said.

A member of staff came in and found us sitting side by side on the bed.

'Everything all right here?'

George managed a smile. 'It's all good,' she said. When the nurse had gone, she turned to me, her face stricken.

'Oh, God, Mattie, what have I done to you? I told Dr Parks you were on a high and probably suffering from the onset of severe paranoia.'

'You did what you thought was right. But now will you please help me figure out a way to get the hell out of here?'

*

The next day I woke up feeling more optimistic, particularly when my phone rang. I leapt across the room to get it, sure it would be Simon at last, after five days of total silence, but it was Lucas.

'Mattie? I don't want to worry you, but there's a recovery vehicle outside your house and they're taking Simon's car away. Have you heard from him yet?'

'Not a word,' I said sadly. This simple truth sat inside me like a stone. In my heart, I knew then it was all over, but still clung to a slender thread of hope.

'Tom's out there talking to the men loading the truck; maybe he'll find out what's going on? I'll be in to see you later.'

At visiting time, it was Tom who knocked on my door, carrying a bag with fresh clothes and a batch of his uncle's home-made fudge.

'Lucas is fine, but he had a bit of a dizzy turn at lunchtime, so I persuaded him to let me come instead. He sends his love, and we made you this.'

The sight and smell of the fudge triggered something in me; tears began to roll down my face and I was powerless to stop them.

'Simon's not coming back, is he?' My voice came out toneless with these words I didn't want to say aloud.

Tom filled up the room with his large frame, and the bed sagged when he sat beside me.

'Mattie, I don't know. The repossession guys said it was a rental car, and when I slipped them a few quid, they told me it had been hired in the name of Benjamin Whitton. It's not clear what's going on, but we'll get to the bottom of it, I promise.'

He couldn't stay more than the allotted half hour, after which a nurse came to usher him out. Tom's kindness was more than I could bear; if he'd been brisk and business-like, it might have been possible to hold it together, but his genuine sympathy and gentleness had unstitched the seams of all my grief and worry. I couldn't eat the fudge either; even the smell upset me, but the staff and other patients enjoyed it.

Something inside my heart and mind had broken, and I couldn't understand what had happened with Simon to make him cut off from me so abruptly. Going over and over it in my mind, the one thing which had changed was that my messages had told him about my mental health history. The inescapable conclusion was that this lay at the root of his rejection. My panicky voice messages must have sounded as if I was bouncing off the walls.

When my period came, it was hard to know whether to be sad or relieved; in the heat of passion, we hadn't always been careful. A part of me would have loved to have Simon's child, but only if we were together. It might be for the best nothing had happened, but it left me with the familiar ache in my belly alongside the pain of losing him.

The nurses were very kind, and always prepared to listen, but nothing could alter the fact that I was utterly heartbroken, and my dreams of a new life in California lay in ruins. It took days of lying on my bed and crying, but when the staff suggested taking tranquilisers, it pulled me out of the dark place I'd gone to hide. It was a massive effort, but I got myself together enough to behave like a compliant patient again, and then apparently Dr Parks wanted to see me.

'Come in, Mattea. The staff tell me you've been distressed and tearful in the past few days, and kept to your room much of the time?'

'I'm not being deliberately antisocial, but my boyfriend... Well, I'm beginning to think he's dumped me.'

'So I've been informed. I'm sorry this is happening to you, but we often find partners and families don't cope well with the realities of mental illness.'

'I've been wondering if that might be it,' I said. 'Simon didn't know about my history, but I was going to tell him when the time was right. As you know, we'd planned to go away together and start again in California. I guess it's not going to happen now.'

'No wonder you've been upset.' Dr Parks was kind, which almost set off the tears again. 'But, Mattea, your current fragile state of mind makes it all the more important you should come out of your room and engage in social contact with the other patients. Being alone and ruminating on your problems can make things seem worse. You need to be with people who can understand your experiences. Nobody will push you, but you might take part in some of the group activities, for distraction if nothing else.'

I nodded, willing to give it a go since it was marginally better than doing nothing and brooding over my lost love. Art class would be OK, even the knitting group; I'd always intended to learn. But if they tried to make me play bloody bingo, my cooperation would be withdrawn.

'And how are you getting on with the new medication?'

'In terms of side effects, it's better than anything I've ever taken before,' I said truthfully. 'Some of the other drugs could make it very difficult to function at work.'

'You're a maths tutor, I believe?'

'My field is data science and analytics, and I was a lecturer at the University of York,' I said firmly. It was vanity, of course, but I wanted this doctor to know she was dealing with an educated, intelligent woman. If she wouldn't grant my psychic abilities any credibility, I could at least impress her with my qualifications.

'How interesting,' she said, leafing through my file. 'But you've recently been tutoring local children in maths?'

'Since I moved here a few months ago, yes.'

'There's been a considerable amount of change for you to deal with lately. George expressed concern it might all be too much, and perhaps the trigger for this episode. You do seem much calmer than you were. Are you hearing any more voices? No ghosts haunting you?'

'Not in the past few days, no,' I told her with perfect truth.

Dr Parks nodded. 'It's a little early to come to any such conclusions, but it might be down to the new medication; we've had excellent results with this drug.'

'Then I hope it will be the same for me,' I said, trying not to show the excitement that had begun to bubble inside me. She'd planted the seed of an idea in my head which just might provide a way out.

EIGHTEEN

When George came again a couple of days later, I was slowly beginning to accept that Simon wasn't coming back. It was also an opportunity to share the idea which had come to me during my interview with Dr Parks.

'I've got a plan, but I need your help. We're going to get me out of here.'

Her face went blank. 'You're a voluntary patient, Mattie, which means you can leave any time you like.' The look I gave her must have indicated extreme cynicism. 'OK don't give me the evil eye, you'd probably be looking at being sectioned if you tried to discharge yourself right now. They do think you're improving because there's been no mention of ghosts or spirits since you got here.'

'Ah, well that's all part of the plan. I'm on this new medication, which is known to have terrific results, so I'm going to be one of the patients who does well on the drug. A miracle will occur before their very eyes, as I make an astonishing recovery from my delusional state of mind.'

George flushed, shame in her eyes. 'You were never delusional; we didn't believe the truth because hearing dead people doesn't fit with the current model of consensual reality.

I'm so sorry.' She hesitated, then asked, 'Mattie, is Hal here now?'

'Always,' I told her, but his presence was distant, and the voice hard to hear. I focused all my energy on tuning into him.

'*Tell her I love her; she'll be all right now.*'

When I relayed this, tears brimmed in George's eyes, but she said, 'He's right. These last days it's as if a huge burden of guilt has been lifted off me. I'm beginning to believe I can start my life over. Will see him again, one day?'

I relayed his answer, '*Of course, but I can leave now because you're going to be fine.*'

George nodded. 'I hated to think of him being stuck here because of my reluctance to move on. Tell him goodbye and thank you.'

As I've since discovered, the psychic thing is often more of a burden than a gift, but it can occasionally be a special privilege, the way it was with George and Hal.

Later, when George had had time to recover, I said, 'Look, I need to know what evidence Dr Parks and the other staff would be looking for in terms of my demonstrable recovery on this new drug. I hate to be so deceptive when everyone involved has been more than kind, but the truth isn't going to get me anywhere.'

George acknowledged this with a nod. 'On this drug, people can become calm and rational in a matter of days. Patients talk about it in terms of returning to their real selves again.'

'OK, I can do calm and rational. Not sure about recovering from being sad though.'

'Don't worry, everyone understands the pain of a broken relationship, and grief is an entirely normal reaction to losing someone special, but now you have to demonstrate your ability to get over him. It would help if you talked about realising that your plans to move to California were only ever a wild fantasy.' George didn't know how close she was there.

'Fair enough, I can do that.'

'Look, Mattie, I shouldn't visit any more after today. It's unusual for community staff to be part of inpatient care. Dr Parks has already asked me if I'm in danger of losing my professional distance with you, and I might well be. After what you've done for me, I count you as a friend, but I could lose my job or even my nursing registration. So now the rest is up to you, but if the plan works, I'll be seeing you soon.'

*

With the best intentions to do the calm and rational thing, there were still days when my despair over Simon was of deep concern to the staff and had them fussing in a way I wanted to resist. Mark, as my designated nurse, always encouraged me to talk, which did help. I showed him the pictures of Simon on my phone.

'Wow, I can see why you fell for him,' said Mark appreciatively. 'What a hunk. Pity he's not gay.'

'He was wonderful,' I said. 'We agreed on so much and shared the same attitudes to life. I even loved his dog.' Even as I spoke, the words "too good to be true" began to run through my head.

Telling the story of our romance to Mark made me realise that it had all been something of a fairy tale. Simon the handsome prince who'd appeared out of nowhere and swept me off my feet. In reality, I knew almost nothing about him beyond what he'd chosen to tell me. Now I was left wondering whether anything he'd said could be trusted, and who the hell was this Benjamin Whitton who'd hired the sports car? I clung to the hope that there was a sensible explanation; perhaps it was

Simon's boss, or something as simple as that? A small corner of my heart was hoping there would be a logical explanation for his silence, but one day I tried his phone yet again and got a recorded voice saying, 'This number is no longer in service.' That was a low point. Very low.

Lucas had phoned Mamma Sofie to let her know where I was, and she drove across the country within a few days.

'Oh, *piccolo*,' she said the moment she saw me, 'you're thin again.'

'The food in here isn't great,' I said, 'but, to be honest, I've been so unhappy it's put me off eating anyway. Lucas brings me snacks and cookies, which is all I seem to fancy – comfort food, I suppose.'

She gazed around my small room. 'You've been in worse places, but I know how much you hate being cooped up. I suppose they've changed your medication again?'

I nodded. 'Yes, and the side effects are nothing like as bad. It's OK here, really, and everyone is kind, but I just want to go home.'

'Lucas told me about this Simon person. He dumped you out of the blue?'

She had to hear the whole story (leaving out the psychic parts), and, even to my ears, the plan to sell up and move to California sounded more than a little over-the-top bonkers.

'You were in love, and it made everything seem like magic,' said Mamma. 'Oh, my poor darling.'

'I trusted him too easily, another silly girl falling for a handsome face without seeing he had no depth. I'm only grateful to have found out before I went to the States with him.'

Mamma took my hands in hers. 'Darling, you have always been intellectually gifted, but perhaps not so wise in the ways of the world, or love. I was always afraid you would get hurt, like after Sven.'

I shrugged. 'All my life I've taken people at face value; assumed they are the way they seem to be. Well, now I've learnt the hard way, again, and won't be making the same mistake in future.'

'My darling, most of us make the painful discovery that not everyone can be trusted before we're out of our teens,' said Mamma, stroking my hair. 'But you always had your head in a book, never part of the same world as most of your peers.'

'Being clever was a place to take refuge,' I told her. 'And because I was seen as "flawed", if not downright crazy, it always felt like I had to prove myself, so it was onto the next exam, another qualification. In the end, I ran out of places to hide.'

'But you've been making a good life for yourself in Lytham,' said Mamma. 'This experience with Simon doesn't change any of that, and it's all waiting for you when you're ready. I'm here for another day, but then I have to get back. We're going for a fast completion on the house; it's been standing empty for two years. There'll be building work to do, so we won't be straight for months, but I hope to bring Rachael to meet you soon.' With a pang, I saw her happiness and envied the two of them their future together.

'Come for Christmas,' I said on impulse. 'It'll be easier for you both if your house is a building site. I'd love to have you.'

Mamma's face lit up. 'Oh, darling, it would be marvellous, the kitchen won't be in until late January at the earliest, it's coming from Germany. But seriously, will you be up to having us? The nurse I spoke to did say you were doing very well.'

It was encouraging to hear this, despite all the heartbroken moping about I'd done.

'It seems I've inherited a dog,' I said, thinking how much I missed Mary. 'Would Rachael be all right with her?'

Mamma grinned. 'Rachael adores dogs and is already talking about a puppy once the house is finished. She's always lived in flats where pets weren't allowed.'

The anticipation of Christmas gave me something to look forward to, and in the meantime, the plan appeared to be working. I was taking the medication and saying how good I was feeling at regular intervals, not to mention displaying at every opportunity evidence of a complete recovery. It took a lot of effort on my part but I even played bloody bingo. That's dedication for you.

*

It was well into November before Dr Parks was convinced enough to let me go, but the small unit was under considerable pressure for bed space, and it must have made sense to discharge someone who was more heartbroken than depressed or delusional.

'This drug has been a real success story for you,' she told me with a smile. 'No more troublesome voices?'

'Absolutely none,' I assured her with a clear conscience. The only voice I'd ever heard on the unit had been Hal's, but he wasn't a presence because George had stayed away, as agreed. I suspected he wouldn't be with her the next time we met.

Dr Parks was smiling encouragement, and it made sense to complete the picture of a fully recovered patient when they'd all been so kind, but I couldn't lie to any of them.

'It's obvious to me now why all the stuff about my dead mother talking to me would have worried everyone; I'm quite embarrassed even thinking about it now.' This was the absolute truth, but only because I'd been a complete idiot to imagine health professionals would ever believe what I said.

'And you aren't still planning to sell up and move to California?' she asked.

I shook my head sadly. 'No, it was my boyfriend who wanted to go, and he seems to be firmly out of the picture anyway. Maybe it's just as well, I can see now it was only ever a wild dream.'

'Grandiose schemes are part of the delusional state, but from everything you've told me about your circumstances, you're happy in Lytham, and have supportive family and neighbours. With Georgina's ongoing help, I think you'll do well, so I'm happy to discharge you.'

This was wonderful news, but I resisted the urge to do a happy dance. Lucas came to transport me home, bringing Mary with him in the car. After the overly warm temperatures inside the hospital, it was a shock to discover how much colder it was outside; the season had moved from autumn into full winter while I was an inpatient. As soon as I climbed into the passenger seat, Mary launched herself joyfully at me, licking my face and making it clear how delighted she was to see her favourite human again. The little dog healed some more cracks in my fragile heart; her small body in my arms a warm reassurance that somehow it would be all right.

'Don't think I'm unaware of your shameless transfer of allegiance to Tom,' I told her in a mock stern voice. 'But you're stuck with me now; at least, I hope you are.' I glanced across at Lucas, who was smiling with affection for us both. Mary licked my face again and whined as if I'd been gone for months rather than weeks.

'First thing to do is check whether she's microchipped,' I said. 'And if she isn't, then I'm claiming her as the one good thing Simon left behind.'

'Let's hope that's true,' said Lucas. 'I'm taking you straight to my place for lunch. Tom's making soup, which should be welcome on this chilly day.'

As we headed home, the shops were brightly lit, sparkling with Christmas decorations; all contributing to a sense of unreality, as if I'd been away for years like a female version of Rip Van Winkle.

'You do look much better,' Lucas told me, patting my hand as we waited at traffic lights. 'I was terribly worried for a while.'

'But I was never ill, not mentally, anyhow.'

'You went from being a sparkling, happy girl to a white-faced shell of yourself with tragic, haunted eyes,' he told me. 'I wanted to tear Simon limb from limb, and, if we ever find him, I just might.'

'Are you looking?'

'Tom is, he's put some of his ex-army friends onto it; a lot of them transfer into the civilian police force, so he has contacts. We think Simon lied to you, but Tom will tell you everything we know so far.'

I was in no hurry to hear it, knowing it would destroy any last vestiges of hope. Simon was gone, and I had to face up to that. As we sat in the Blackpool traffic with Mary burrowed into my neck, I said, 'Let's not talk about him; I'm trying to practise gratitude instead. One of the nurses told me about it; she keeps a journal of daily reasons to be happy. So much has changed for me, Lucas; the weight of my diagnosis has dogged me for all these years, constraining everything. Now I'm free of it, I can become my own person, discover who I might have been if I hadn't always been told that my voices were a mental illness.'

'It makes perfect sense,' said Lucas, waiting for the lights to change. 'You've lived your life in fear of another episode, and now you needn't anymore. I can see why it might be something of a rebirth. You aren't still thinking of moving away?'

'No, that was only ever because of Simon; it was his dream, not mine.'

Lucas beamed. 'Mattie, I'm so glad, we'd all miss you terribly. What are your feelings about him now?'

'It hurts like hell,' I said. 'But less every day. I've been through all the stages of shock, loss, anger, wondering if it might have been the depression thing that drove him away. Dr Parks told me lots of people can't deal with it; there's still so much stigma around anything like that.'

'There might be more to it than that,' he told me. 'But let's get you home first.'

The fish chowder Tom had waiting for us was unbelievably delicious, with a hint of saffron, glorious after grim hospital food. His brown hair had grown from its former military shortness and the tan faded, but he was happy and full of enthusiasm about the psychotherapy course in Preston.

'Lucas isn't the only one who can cook,' he said when I complimented the soup. 'Us army types have to be extremely self-sufficient.'

'And here was me, thinking it was all eating reconstituted rations out of mess tins under a bivouac.'

'Did that too, of course, which made me appreciate good food all the more,' he replied, grinning.

'Do you miss military life?' I asked, hoping it wasn't an intrusive question. Lucas's head came up, suggesting he'd wondered the same thing.

'Not the army itself, no. I was more than ready to put it behind me after what happened. What I miss is people: my team, and particular mates; friendships forged under extreme circumstances are an ultra-close bond. I'm still in touch with many of them who came through it all.'

After we'd seen off the cheese and sourdough bread, Lucas and Tom exchanged sideways looks which made me say, 'You'd better tell me what you've found out. I'm strong enough to hear it now.'

Tom's expression was relieved and doubtful, both at once. 'It's not good news, Mattie.'

'I wasn't expecting it to be. I'd rather know, so just tell me.'

He took a deep breath. 'OK then, I'm afraid there's no such person as Simon Ransome. At least, there is, but he's seven years old and lives in Scotland.'

I didn't seem to feel any surprise at this. 'You were right, Lucas, he wasn't who he said he was.' It was confirmation of everything I'd feared, but as the days and weeks of silence had gone by, it had been the only conclusion I could draw.

'There's more,' Lucas said. His sympathetic eyes told me it was even worse.

'Ruth put us onto it,' said Tom. 'Do you remember being at a restaurant in Lytham with Simon, and she was there with her dad?'

'Vaguely, yes, but we didn't speak, only waved across the room.'

'Ruth came to us because she was worried. It was blindingly obvious you'd fallen for Simon big time, and she was concerned over something her dad said about him.'

'Go on,' I said, wondering what was coming.

'She was embarrassed to tell us this part, but her dad isn't long out of prison,' said Tom. 'He knew how grateful Ruth was that both you and Lucas gave her a second chance, so when he recognised Simon, he told her about it. Ruth thought we should know.'

'He can tell us who Simon is?'

'Not exactly,' said Tom. 'Her dad was in two different prisons during his sentence but was sure he'd seen Simon in one of them; he is quite distinctive-looking.'

Nurse Mark had summed him up: drop-dead gorgeous would cover it. I could see how his face would be memorable.

'Ruth's dad couldn't remember which jail or his name, but he definitely identified Simon. It seems he has a good memory for faces.'

'Which gives us a place to start looking,' said Lucas. 'I told Tom you've got pictures of him on your phone.'

'If you could send me some, I could get my mate in the force to help,' said Tom. 'Maybe you've got something with his fingerprints or DNA, like a toothbrush.'

Did I even want to know, and would it even matter when it was all over anyway? In the end, I concluded that it was important to know why he'd gone, and whether he'd ever loved me. No point in leaving loose ends.

'Are you all right, Mattie?' Lucas's concern was so kind. 'This must be upsetting for you.'

'It is a little, although it only confirms my suspicions,' I told them. 'Thank you so much for lunch; now, I'd better get Mary home, but before I go, Mamma Sofie and her partner are coming for Christmas, and I wondered if you two might join us. I've never cooked a turkey before, but Mamma has, so there's no risk of burnt offerings.'

They both turned happy faces towards me. 'It could have been a bit dull with us two bachelors and Mutt,' said Lucas. 'But I'll bring the Christmas pudding; I make my own and this year's has been maturing for weeks already.'

Walking through my front door, it was with a new appreciation of my beautiful home, in that same way you somehow see it afresh when you come back from holiday. Ruth had kept the place spotless, and Mary bounced around happily enough before rushing off to check nothing had changed in the frosty garden.

'*Mattie, are you all right?*' asked Emilie almost as soon as I was through the door. '*Lucas told me where you were when he came over to supervise Ruth.*'

'I'm doing OK now; they let me out of hospital because I'm officially no danger to myself or the general public,' I told her.

'*I was bloody furious with George, but Hal explained. By the way, he's gone now, because his sister's going to be fine.*'

'We both are. Each of us can heal, start over and make something new of our lives. I'm finally free to become the person I always should have been,' I said, liking the sound of that.

'*You've still got Simon's dog,*' said Emilie, as Mary barked to come back inside. '*Didn't I tell you his aura wasn't right? Won't Mary be a reminder of an unhappy experience?*'

'Far from it,' I told her. 'She's the only genuine love to come out of this, and we're keeping each other.' Mary snuggled contentedly on my lap and licked my hand. 'But I do want to find out what the bloody man was up to, and there's any number of questions I'd like answers for.'

NINETEEN

I'd been emotionally bruised when Sven left me, but this was something else altogether. It was a bitter experience to realise that I'd been a gullible fool and Simon had been a total fake; the words I'd so treasured probably all lies. I'd never been quite so badly hurt before or felt such a damn fool to be taken in by someone who seemed perfect – too perfect, in fact.

I wanted to stand in the street and howl like an injured animal, but my tears were shed in private to let the feelings out (advice from the Wellspring Unit). I also gave preferring Lytham in winter over dreams of California my very best shot. Emilie helped; I'd begun to be aware when she was with me, even if she didn't speak.

Having Christmas to plan for was the best therapy, and seeing the local shops decked out with trees and sparkly lights lifted my spirits in anticipation. At first, I saw Simon everywhere I went: in the back of a stranger's head, in a corner where we used to sit, out running. My heart would leap involuntarily, but of course it was never him, and I slowly learnt to stop looking.

Christmas trees had begun to appear in the windows of neighbouring houses just a couple of weeks after Halloween was over, and, when out on my regular runs, I mentally awarded points for the most impressive. One bay window had a whole Santa's grotto on display, whereas Nigel and Davina's tree was black with gold decorations and scored low – too contrived and artificial for me. Not that I was being overly judgemental or anything.

Most of my gifts were sourced locally, especially from the tiny bookshop on Clifton Street where I'd become a regular. Ordering a fresh, free-range turkey from the posh supermarket, I nearly passed out at the price! Telling myself that my guests deserved the very best, I set to studying the chapters of Emilie's cookbooks relating to Christmas. The plan was to keep it all simple and cheat wherever possible. Anyway, I had a shrewd idea Mamma Sofie would take over the kitchen as soon as she arrived, and I had every intention of encouraging her to do so.

Most, if not all, of my former pupils returned to their tuition sessions. I even had a compliment from Sienna (at least, I think that's what it was).

'I'm proper glad you're back,' she said. 'That other bloke my mum found was a total knobhead and didn't explain things right.' I hugged her because it was nice to feel appreciated, even if I did have to persuade her to do some actual work rather than play with the dog.

Mary could have been a painful reminder of Simon, but, oddly enough, she wasn't, just her sweet self. I took her to the vet at the earliest opportunity, on a mission to establish ownership. Annie looked far too young to be a qualified anything, let alone a veterinary surgeon as her brass plate proclaimed – or perhaps that was only me feeling old and cynical.

'Oh you are a super girl,' she said as Mary practically leapt into her arms in an attempt to corroborate this assessment.

'She was left with me by someone who then abandoned both of us. We're helping each other recover and I've adopted her.'

'She's a healthy little thing,' Annie said, her gloved hands moving over Mary's belly. 'Still just a puppy and probably around six months old, going by her teeth. But no sign of a microchip.'

'Then she's mine,' I said without a moment's hesitation. 'I'd have fought for her anyway, citing desertion, but will you microchip her now, please, and what should we do about preventing an outbreak of puppies?'

'We'll book that in today, in case she's small for her age and a little bit older. You don't want her coming into heat unexpectedly.'

Mary also got her vaccinations since we had no idea if these had already been done. On the day of the surgery in mid-December, I paced the floor like any anxious parent, waiting for the call to say she was OK. My girl was soon back home, wearing a little bodysuit which stopped her from bothering the stitches. Having an operation didn't stop her thinking that 6.00am was a good time to wake me up, and although I was not necessarily in agreement, it did mean I got my regular run when the streets were dark and quiet. For the time being, Mary had to stay behind in her dog crate, as recommended by the vet, but she hated it if I was gone more than half an hour. This meant I'd developed a different route and found a shortcut home behind some shops where deliveries were made.

Some of the back streets on my circuit had no streetlights and turning into the dark alley, it was unexpected to experience a prescient sense of threat. If I'd been a dog, my hackles would have gone up and I might have growled. Coming to a halt halfway down the street, where the shops had their delivery entrances, I was confused by my instincts, searching for the source of my prickling skin and deep unease.

A dark-coloured car with no headlights showing appeared almost silently at the head of the back street, but I was only mildly curious as it nosed forward. Someone looking for a free parking space, perhaps – Lytham had a traffic problem but not usually this early in the morning. Without warning, the lights blazed up on full beam and the engine roared as the car accelerated towards me. Even if I hadn't been temporarily blinded, there was nowhere to go, the alley was only a little wider than the car, and there was a matter of seconds in which to register with sickening certainty that it was going to hit me.

*

A week later, I woke up in the high dependency unit of the hospital, with no memory of what had happened.

'Mattie, can you hear me?'

My head was hurting and nothing felt right. 'Where am I?'

A face swam into focus closer to the bed. 'This is Blackpool Victoria Hospital and you've been in an accident.'

'I don't… remember,' I replied, and then I think I fell asleep again.

Later, when I was reliably awake, the doctor tried to explain it all to me, but in those early stages of my return to consciousness, I drifted in and out and kept forgetting most of what was said. The nurses kept having to remind me what had happened and where I was.

It might have been the next day when I could sit up without the room whirling around me, and the doctor asked, 'Do you remember anything about the accident?'

I didn't. It was only later when flashes of memory about the car coming towards me began to return, often in dreams.

I moved my head slowly to indicate no. It hurt.

'Going by your injuries, we think you may have been run down by a vehicle, but there were no witnesses so early in the morning, and I'm told the street behind the shops isn't well lit. A store owner coming in early to open up discovered you bleeding and unconscious at the roadside and called an ambulance.'

So much for wearing a personal alarm, I thought. It was still there but I hadn't even had time to press the button. Maybe the doctors had done it.

'Our immediate concern has been the head injury you sustained, there was a small bleed on the brain, and we've kept you under sedation, but your latest scan shows that to be resolving now. You also had a displaced fracture of the left tib and fib – the bones in your lower leg – which have been pinned in surgery. In addition, there were multiple abrasions and contusions, and although your face was somewhat bruised and battered, that's improving now. Please don't worry, it's all likely to heal and there shouldn't be any permanent facial scarring.'

'Bloody hell,' I managed, shocked to have got out of one hospital only to end up in another. At that point, I could remember everything up to and including the evening before the accident, but nothing afterwards.

'How do you know what happened?'

'Working backwards from the physical evidence, the police believe everything suggests you were hit by a car. I'd agree with that, which explains the leg injury, and then you were probably thrown up onto the windscreen, which would account for the rest. The paramedics said you were at the side of the alley, which must have been where you fell off the car bonnet.'

'Doesn't sound good,' I managed to say. My mouth was unbearably dry.

'Scout's honour, you've been relatively lucky, and you will heal. We'll have you home before Christmas,' he said, with a cheerfulness which seemed inappropriate.

I didn't *feel* lucky; my body hurt all over, and the pain in my head was so excruciating I couldn't think straight.

The doctor patted my hand. 'I can see you're struggling to take it all in. The nurse will bring you some pain medication in a moment and, if everything goes well, we'll move you onto the orthopaedic ward tomorrow.'

When Lucas and Tom came to visit me there, I was still feeling dazed and confused, but otherwise more or less in touch with reality. The strong painkillers made me dopey, but deeply grateful not to be feeling a thing.

'Oh wow, you look so much better,' said Tom as soon as he arrived. I'd seen my face in a mirror by then, so was doubtful this could be an accurate assessment.

'Darling girl, we've been half out of our minds with worry.' Lucas sat down and took my hand. 'It's so good to see you awake.' They both looked a touch haggard, as if they'd been neglecting themselves worrying about me. Tom's beard had grown longer, and it suited him.

Not up to doing much talking, I listened as they related the story of how the police had come to my house, looking for a next of kin. Polly had always told me off for not using a password on my phone, but this lazy neglect had worked in my favour as it provided sufficient information to identify me. I'd put Lucas under ICE (in case of emergency) because what point would there have been in calling Mamma, who lived two hours' drive away? Lucas had seen the police arrive from his window and dropped everything to rush across and find out what was happening.

'As soon as their car drew up, I figured it had to be bad news,' he said, 'so I thought you might need support. But I never imagined... Oh, God, Mattie, it's been terrible.'

'Seeing you on the ventilator,' added Tom, 'white as a sheet under all the purple bruising. You gave us quite a scare, especially when the doctors were talking about possible surgery to relieve pressure on the brain.'

'Thank God it wasn't necessary in the end,' said Lucas. 'They told us it goes that way sometimes, and it's why they kept you under sedation, because as the bruising and swelling went down, the bleed was able to dissolve.'

Tom grinned and winked at me. 'My upright uncle lied shamelessly and told the officers he was your nearest relative, providing what information he could. Later, the hospital gave him your personal effects and phone, so we could ring people who needed to know; Sofie, for starters.'

'Mary?' I asked. I could do single words if not whole sentences.

'She's safe with us, and pretty much recovered from her surgery,' said Tom. 'The stitches are out, and the wound has healed. She's progressed to gentle pottering around the garden, and then we'll be trying short walks: therapy for both of us.'

'Your mamma came to visit, but you were still under sedation. She made me promise to ring her every day with a bulletin on your recovery,' said Lucas. 'We've got Christmas all sorted – Sofie and Rachael are coming over to stay as planned and will be there to take care of you when you get home. We're all going to pitch in and make the festivities happen; you needn't do anything except lie on the sofa while you get better.'

'Don't remember…' Wow, two whole words.

'Don't even try, sweetheart,' said Lucas. 'Let the police deal with it. They'll want to talk to you, but you may not be able to help.'

An understatement if ever I'd heard one, although the officer who came to see me wasn't surprised. He said they were treating what had happened as "non-accidental" after what the doctors had told them. Tyre marks in the alley suggested deliberate rapid acceleration towards me. After he'd gone, I lay there wondering why someone would deliberately drive a car at a passing maths tutor. No answers occurred to me, and I had to let it go.

My memory slowly returned, but I could never fully recall the moment of impact. There was only a mental image of the lights blazing up, and a brief time afterwards when I lay broken at the edge of the empty alley, half-conscious but knowing I was badly hurt. One part of my brain was thinking I should have listened to Evelina's warnings about dark clouds. Odd details registered, such as the grittiness of the road surface beneath my cheek, and not being able to move, before a merciful blackness enveloped me in a welcome embrace.

It's amazing how fast the (relatively) young body can heal, and I was home four days before Christmas with few visible signs of what had happened, beyond some faint green bruising, the healing cut on my head and a cast on the broken leg.

My house had been transformed into a Christmas grotto; Mamma and her doctor partner, Rachael, dug out Emilie's decorations and Lucas explained where things usually went. Thanks to these efforts, a festive interior welcomed me home with a huge tree and a kitchen full of good smells. Mamma wanted to make up a bed for me on the big parlour sofa, but I was able to demonstrate my ability to get up and down the stairs to my room, as long as I only had to do it twice a day, morning and evening, and with someone watching. Crutches make your hands hurt like hell at first, and the physio had also instructed me in the art of tackling stairs on my bottom but I resisted this as it seemed undignified. Yeah, I know, pride goes before a fall, or, in this case, after one.

Rachael and I got on well from the start; she was lovely, not much taller than Mamma but even plumper, with fluffy grey hair. She was every child's idea of a granny, with round gold spectacles and a smiley face – all she needed was some knitting and a plate of cookies. I soon discovered that under this benevolent exterior lay a formidable intelligence.

'I'm a paediatrician,' she told me. 'Mainly on the research side these days rather than on the wards. I'm more or less retired anyway, but I keep my hand in, consulting on projects, speaking at conferences and so on. Fortunately for you, kids are always breaking their arms and legs so I can remember just about enough basic medical care to make sure you're OK.'

'It's so kind of you and Mamma to come and help me,' I said.

'Don't give it a thought,' she said with a grin, 'you're doing us a massive favour. Our new house is going to be gorgeous when it's finished but, right now, we're camping out in a nightmare of builders, brick dust and boxes. It was a blessed relief to leave.'

Sofie still didn't know about my psychic abilities, as I was following Harriet's advice to keep it to myself for now. It wasn't my intention to hide anything exactly, but I didn't know if she'd be hurt or horrified to know that Emilie was present in the house and talked to me. It seemed better to leave those things unsaid, although, with my permission, Lucas had told Tom.

Rachael and Mamma were so in love; it was evident in the way they looked at each other, and the sheer delight they took in being together. They had what I thought I'd found with Simon, but now I understood that he'd never been the wonderful man I'd fallen for. I did miss the glorious sex, but then, with my leg in a cast and doped up on painkillers, it wouldn't have been on the agenda at any price.

Mary kept me company as I got settled on the kitchen sofa, enjoying all the busyness going on around me. I could have helped more, not least for the physical therapy value, but nobody would let me. Lying there like a princess, I was given bits and pieces to taste test, which Mary insisted I share by pushing her nose in my face.

'Your mamma is a genius with flaky pastry,' said Rachael. 'It's one of the many things which made me fall in love with her. Hmm, this sausage meat might need a bit more onion, and maybe some garlic?'

'Back-handed compliments,' said Mamma indignantly, but her eyes told a different story. 'Give my poor daughter some medicinal brandy.'

'Oh, but should I, with the painkillers?' I asked.

'Of course you should,' said Rachael. 'The ones you're taking now aren't exactly heavy duty, so a brandy will do you more good than harm. At worst, you'll nod off.'

Emilie had been hovering close ever since my return home. *'It's so wonderful to see the kitchen full of people again and especially to have my sister here. Darling, I've been so frightened for you, but Sofie and Rachael have talked a lot about what happened, and your time in hospital, so I could eavesdrop and understand what was happening. At times like these, I do wish I could leave the bloody house.'*

When Mamma and Rachael went off upstairs to do some secret present wrapping, I was half asleep in front of some festive nonsense on TV but sat up straight when Emilie's voice suddenly said, *'I think you're in danger; I can feel something malevolent, and it makes me uneasy. My darling girl, take care.'*

By this time, I was a lot more inclined to take such warnings with appropriate seriousness, remembering Evelina's words about the black cloud, and the sense of threat I'd experienced in the alley.

'Not much choice about being careful right now,' I told her. 'What with the cast and the crutches.'

'Please, darling, I'm serious. What happened to you wasn't an accident.'

'That's what the police believe, and the surgeon who fixed me. They said the car had to have been going very fast, but you wouldn't normally drive through a back alley at speed, and the tyre marks provided conclusive evidence of how it accelerated,' I said. On my lap, Mary whined, still a little edgy when Emilie was around, but growing accustomed to her presence.

'*So it had to be deliberate.*'

'But who would want to harm me? What could they hope to gain?'

Emilie's tone was sombre. '*That's what you need to find out.*'

*

On Christmas Eve, a crisp clear day, Rachael and Mamma took Mary out for a long walk in the afternoon, and Tom came from next door to sit with me. He looked good in a light-blue cable-knit sweater which accentuated his red beard.

'There's no need for a babysitter,' I protested. 'I could have managed by myself.'

'Well, if you want the truth, I only came to see Mary, and she's not even here,' he said.

'She'll be back, I promise, though Rachael promised her a long run on the shore.' His broad face was more homely than handsome, but he had the nicest smile and was such easy company. I tried to shift position on the sofa, and a twinge of pain must have shown on my face because Tom became concerned.

'Is the leg hurting?' he asked.

'It's not agony, but it aches miserably,' I admitted. 'Rachael says all the muscles and ligaments will have suffered from the trauma.'

'Don't forget, I know how this works,' he said ruefully.

I blushed, remembering too late the many operations he'd needed, and the final unsatisfactory result. 'Tom, I'm so sorry to have forgotten. Wrapped up in my own problems,' I said with an embarrassed smile.

'It's fine, but I do understand what leg injuries can be

like. What you need is some distraction and perhaps alcohol. I brought pear brandy, in honour of it being Christmas Eve.'

'Won't Lucas be missing you?'

'He's deep in a new seed catalogue with Mutt snoring on his lap. I hope he remembers to put the oven on later.'

Rachael and Mamma returned, faces pink from the cold outside, and found the two of us equally pink (pear brandy) and engaged in a fiercely competitive game of Scrabble.

'Madam, I'm afraid your daughter is an outrageous cheat,' Tom told Mamma.

'Is it my fault you don't understand mathematical terms?'

'If they're so obscure they aren't even in the dictionary, how do I know you aren't making stuff up?'

'Hey, that's rich coming from someone who uses legal terms.'

'Peace, children,' added Mamma, smiling. 'Did you leave us any of that brandy? It's Arctic out there and we need thawing through.'

Tom was visibly reluctant to go back home, but in the end said he'd have to go wake up Lucas and put their dinner in the oven. I hauled myself up on the crutches and walked him to the door, hoping to impress them all with my progress. I regretted my vanity later when the gruesome aches in my leg set up again.

*

On Christmas morning, Mamma and Rachael came down wreathed in smiles and both flashing sparkly engagement rings.

'We chose them a few weeks ago when I proposed,' said Rachael, 'but thought it would be a nice idea to wait until today to make the announcement.'

The pair of them talked wedding plans until Mamma

nudged her fiancée and rapidly changed the subject. It *had* been making me feel a little wistful, but I didn't begrudge their happiness for a microsecond and told them so.

A few hours later, the wonderful aroma of golden-brown turkey filled the kitchen, along with fresh cranberry sauce and, later, Lucas's fruity (and alcoholic!) Christmas pudding. The joint efforts of Mamma and Rachael meant our festive lunch was gorgeous, all of a much better standard than I could ever have managed, even with help. Lucas and Tom, in their Christmas jumpers, were the best possible company, and we laughed a lot, especially over Mary in her new green dog coat with red pom-poms. We all opened our presents after the food, and then Lucas demanded we play charades, which was difficult from my position on the big parlour sofa, so Tom and I agreed to team up. There were loud protests about this being an unfair advantage, but we got away with it, even if Lucas won.

It all seemed to go by so quickly, but I was enjoying the comfortable, cosy days after Christmas. Then Mamma took a call from their builder to say he was able to make an early start on the kitchen, requiring them to choose taps and worktops.

'We've tried looking online,' said Rachael after twenty-four hours of intense research. 'But it's just not the same as seeing the actual fittings.'

Mamma looked worried. 'We've decided to go home before New Year rather than stay on as planned, but only because Lucas promised that he and Tom will care for you like precious china.'

'Hey, I'm fine,' I said, only telling a teensy white lie. 'And the physio would say it's time I started to do more for myself.' I even managed to wave them goodbye with real regret, standing on hated but necessary crutches at the front door.

Lucas and Tom then spent more time at my house than in their own. Getting up and down stairs at the beginning and end of each day was still an ungainly performance, but I was making good progress, and mobile enough to get to Emilie's "throne room" under the stairs without any assistance or too much wincing. I'd also been able to cut the painkillers to night-time only.

The three of us (plus two best-buddy dogs) planned a quiet New Year's Eve with no staying up till midnight – I turned into a pumpkin by about 10.00pm and needed my bed. Lucas promised to cook us a special dinner and was reportedly already at work in his own kitchen when Tom came over to help me get up in the morning.

I was already dressed in what had become a temporary uniform of a tracksuit with the side seam of one leg split to accommodate the cast, but still needed help to get downstairs. Rather than supervise my careful descent, Tom solved the problem by simply picking me up, and when I protested, threatened to throw me over his shoulder in a fireman's lift. Like a damsel being rescued from distress, he proceeded to carry me downstairs as if I weighed nothing. As a feminist, I couldn't possibly say that it was kind of enjoyable.

Once I was safely established on the kitchen sofa, Tom made us coffee and picked up a manila envelope he'd left ready. 'I've got some more information, but didn't want to spoil Lucas's plans for this evening by telling you tonight. However, I figured maybe you'd rather begin a New Year knowing the facts.' His eyes searched my face, so I nodded, bracing myself for bad news, which is exactly what I got.

He sat on the floor beside me, eyes full of concern. 'We began by looking for a Benjamin Whitton, the name on the car-hire documents. That search produced nothing until we tried Simon Whitton, and then bingo.'

'That's his real name?'

'Yes, but he's used several other fake IDs over the years

and served two jail terms on various charges of financial fraud. Ruth's father was right about seeing him in prison; they were both in HMP Durham at one time. Simon does have the accountancy qualifications he claimed but, for the most part, has used his expertise to get involved in money laundering and other dubious schemes.'

He stopped at the sight of my stricken expression. Knowing my great love had probably been a fake was one thing; having it proved to me hurt like hell.

'Go on,' I told him. 'Might as well tell me the rest.'

'I'm so sorry, Mattie, he lied to you about pretty much everything and was almost certainly after your money.'

'*Told you his aura was a funny colour*,' said Emilie.

'Perhaps word had got out locally that I'd inherited money, but that has to be small change compared to money laundering. And why leave without warning when I ended up in the psychiatric unit? It doesn't make sense. If he was looking for a victim, I'd never been more vulnerable.'

'I can't answer those questions,' said Tom. 'Sometimes it's hard to know what motivates someone like him.' His face was full of sadness and sympathy. 'At least you know now.'

A horrible thought occurred to me. 'Could it have been Simon who drove the car at me?'

Tom shook his head. 'Unlikely. We know he was in London from his phone records. I… er… had someone check. Since he then cut off everything including the mobile number you had for him, it just wouldn't make sense for him to come back north.'

I'd been targeted by a conman, and then someone *else* had tried to kill me, but the one thing I didn't understand was why. Overwhelmed by the perfidy of my erstwhile boyfriend, I wearily leaned my head onto Tom's shoulder, and his arms went around me in a comforting hug.

TWENTY

The three of us celebrated New Year's Eve at my house in suitable style – Lucas fed us royally with duck breasts with redcurrants and black pudding. Yes, I do know that sounds dubious, it did to me, but the result was fantastic, an unexpected collision of sweet and savoury flavours. For dessert there was a lemon mousse, delicate and subtle after the richness of the duck. Having sought Emilie's advice, I'd ordered some excellent champagne from the local independent wine shop, which Tom collected for me.

Sitting at the table, over the remnants of our meal, the two of them squabbled amiably over the relative merits of different cars Tom was considering buying. Watching but only half listening – due to a food coma, not to mention a surfeit of good wine – I realised just how much these two had come to mean to me. They were my family in all but name and, in Lucas's case, with a strong connection to Emilie. She was there too, of course, offering her usual acerbic commentary.

At 10.00pm, with great difficulty, I straightened my bad leg by holding onto the table. 'Happy New Year to us all, since it must be past the midnight hour somewhere. A toast to better times coming in the New Year.'

'They will be, I'm sure of it,' said Lucas, standing to raise his glass. 'You two have been everything to this old man in the past months; I love you both.' He was flushed and positively misty-eyed, so it could have been the drink talking.

'The "old man" part is bullshit,' I told him with a stern look, sitting down again with real gratitude. 'You're sixty-six not ninety-six, the same age as Mamma Sofie, and neither of you is exactly over the hill. I hope you will both be part of my life for decades to come.'

'I second those sentiments,' put in Tom. 'And to next year being even better.'

'*Amen to that*,' added Emilie.

Given my tendency to turn into a pumpkin early, especially when alcohol was added into the equation, Tom and Lucas left around 10.30pm, having seen me safely up to bed. I lay there with Mary snuggled cosily on my chest, full of gratitude at how much my life had changed and improved since moving to Lytham – even considering the negative aspects of a campaign of harassment, a conman lover, followed by a busted leg. At least many questions had now been answered. My new and growing feeling of self-confidence gave me a sense of peace as I drifted off – even Mary's gentle snoring couldn't keep me awake. I slept through all the spectacular fireworks reported by Tom the next morning; good job he'd taken pictures on his phone.

*

The early days of January were unexpectedly mild and dry, so Tom insisted we should begin to go for walks up and down the road. The physio had told me to increase my exercise activity gradually but gently, and Tom had taken it upon himself as a sacred duty to get me moving again. The bulbs Lucas had planted in my miniscule front garden were already showing vivid green shoots, providing a metaphor for the emergence of a whole new me. No longer the depressed and downhearted person I'd been for so long, my self-belief had grown to a point where it now seemed possible to build the life I wanted.

When I wanted to turn back because my leg ached fiercely, Tom insisted I go a bit further.

'No pain, no gain,' he told me with a grin. 'We'll continue the remaining steps to the finishing post at the end of the street.'

'You're such a bully,' I complained, but held tightly onto his arm for support, while the other was occupied with the NHS-issue crutch that Tom and Lucas had decorated for New Year.

'Slave driver,' I told him. 'And exactly where is this imaginary finishing post?'

'It's right here, though some fool has defaced it with the words "Give Way".'

'Can we call it Give Up instead?' I said, leaning against the red-brick wall.

'You'll thank me later,' he said. 'Gentle, regular exercise is the best thing you can do; we'll have you running on the seafront again by Easter.'

'But you won't be joining me?'

A shadow crossed his face. 'Not according to the consultant; he says the knee will always be stiff, because of the localised tissue damage. Some of the muscle was lost; blast injuries are like that, they have to put you back together from whatever bits are left. I'll use an exercise bike to try and keep it supple but will probably need a knee-joint replacement within a few years. The result won't be great, because the tendons and ligaments are damaged, but it would get rid of the pain if nothing else.'

'And here's me moaning when I will at least heal in time; I'm so sorry.'

'Don't be. At least I got out of there alive when some of my mates didn't.'

Turning around to head back home, we were almost there, outside Nigel and Davina's, when I had to stop. Something in my leg didn't feel right and I was afraid I'd done too much, so stood there to rest my aching muscles while balanced on my crutch and Tom's arm.

'We've only got two good legs between us.' He laughed, just as Davina appeared on her doorstep, beautifully dressed as usual in leather trousers and an expensive-looking fluffy white sweater. It was the ugly, hate-filled expression on her face that took me by surprise.

'Why aren't you dead? You ought to be!' she shouted, her shrill voice full of venom.

Tom frowned and instinctively put a protective arm around me.

'Why would I be?' I asked, feeling suddenly cold. Where had this come from?

An odd expression briefly crossed her face before she was careful to rearrange it. 'I heard about the terrible accident you had. It must have been close; you could have died. Pity, really.'

I looked up into Tom's face, which was as puzzled as my own, when Nigel appeared beside Davina. 'That's enough, darling, come away now.' He was physically trying to pull her back inside, but as he did so she spat over his shoulder, 'You think you're so clever, don't you? Stuck-up bitch.'

'Davs, please,' begged Nigel. 'Sorry, Mattea, she's not been herself lately.' He managed to get her into the hall and close the door, leaving Tom and I baffled by what had just happened.

'Hell's teeth, what brought that on?' he said.

'No idea,' I said, staring at their front door. 'I thought they'd accepted my decision not to sell, and she's even been quite friendly and suggested lunch. But of course, what with two stays in hospital, I've barely seen her to talk to.'

It was disturbing because Davina was still nursing anger and resentment that I wouldn't change my mind about the house. Apart from feeling briefly sorry for them both, I didn't give the doorstep episode much further thought. After coming so close to selling up and going off with Simon, it was more certain than ever that this was my forever home, a sanctuary I hoped never to leave. My goal was to get fit enough to walk the distance to his office without mobility aids, then Mr Haltwhistle could show me the dotted line and I'd sign on it without a backward glance.

*

January is always a bit flat after the festivities, and life in Lodge Road was more or less back to business as usual. The new term of Tom's uni course began, and I gradually became more and more independent, looking forward to the day when the cast came off. The hospital had said after that, physiotherapy would be needed to get me back to anything resembling normal, but I was prepared to do whatever it took.

George continued her regular visits and reported back that the patient was doing extremely well, which I genuinely was, even if bored by the limitations the injury imposed on me. Not wishing to compromise her professional integrity, I never mentioned not taking the medication but had tailed off the dose before I stopped ordering the prescription every month. Most of my maths pupils were still with me, despite some muttering from a few parents about my absences, and there might be more clients following the mock-exam results. My main problem was not sleeping; the flashbacks were getting worse rather than better, but I was reluctant to ask for medication.

One weekend, Lucas and Tom invited me for lunch. I could just about manage to walk next door without assistance at this point, with Mary's lead looped around my wrist. It doesn't sound ambitious, but she was pulling eagerly ahead in anticipation of the superior dog biscuits Mutt favoured, and I almost lost my balance more than once.

Opening the door, Lucas studied me and asked, 'Mattie, are you sleeping?'

'I'm fine, honestly,' I said. Neither he nor Tom looked convinced.

They kept giving me sideways glances so, as we ate stilton and broccoli soup, there was nothing for it but to confess. It was important to behave like a grown-up, and that's what they do: admit to a problem and ask for help.

'I've been having flashbacks about the accident, most often in dreams, which disturb my sleep. All I can ever remember is the vivid image of a car without headlights, turning with agonising slowness into the alley, before the lights blaze as it accelerates towards me. I wake up in a lather of sweat, seconds before it hits, with my heart beating fast and gasping for breath. Then it takes ages to get back to sleep.'

'That's awful, Mattie. No wonder you look tired.' Lucas meant to be kind, but I didn't need to be reminded that I looked like someone who'd pulled too many late nights fuelled by booze. The mirror (and Emilie) told me that often enough, but I was living the life of a nun and my alcohol consumption had dropped back to almost zero.

'It's a form of PTSD, as I know all too well,' said Tom. 'A reaction of the brain to extreme stress.'

'But I don't remember what happened, except that in my dreams the car is a BMW. Is my subconscious inventing this level of detail, or is it a genuine memory returning?'

'Nobody can answer that,' he said. 'And God knows there are plenty of upmarket cars around here. I have the same problem with what I recall of our truck blowing up; I never know which of the fragmentary images my mind replays are real, lived experience, or the parts my mates told me about later. I've ended up with a composite picture which takes in both.'

Lucas always encouraged me to let Tom talk about his experience, but I didn't want to press too hard on a sensitive spot. 'Was it one of those home-made bombs you hear about?'

'An IED, yes. I was in the truck cab with the driver, and my lads were in the back. It was the rear wheel that hit the mine; the poor sods never stood a chance. The blast threw me clear of the burning truck, and I not only got a huge piece of shrapnel in my knee but landed heavily on it as well, making everything worse. The people from the vehicle in front picked me up and took me to the base hospital, and some days later I was airlifted home. End of military career.'

'But the beginning of something new?'

'I hope so. It would mean a lot to give something back after all the help I've had to get through the dark times.'

'You're helping me,' I pointed out with a grin.

*

It seemed like forever before the cast came off, but then it became all too clear how much I needed to do the physio exercises, which I tackled with appropriate diligence. This was less to do with heroic determination and more that physical exercise helped with sleeping. As my walking improved, I once again promised myself a driving licence, as the limited and unexciting life I'd once chosen now seemed way too quiet and dull. I was desperate to get out there and *live* my unmedicated days, eager to grab everything on offer with both hands. As therapy against boredom, Tom persuaded me to have another go at knitting, although nobody would ever want to wear the wonky scarf growing under my fingers. It was soothing in a way, but I felt like somebody's granny. Bad attitude, as Tom reminded me.

One slow afternoon, trapped inside by driving rain, I was delighted when George made a quick unofficial visit to return a book I'd lent her. My CPN had become a recent convert to Emilie's novels, but she didn't stay long and had only been gone a couple of minutes when Davina burst into my house. I mostly left the front door unlocked when at home. Emilie only had time to shout an inchoate warning, and Mary was snoring on my bed upstairs, or else she might have barked.

I was leaning against the kitchen island, leafing idly through a cookery book, when suddenly Davina was there, her normally immaculate hair hanging in dripping strands. She pointed a black handgun at me, eyes wild with manic energy.

'Well, isn't this nice? Got you now,' she said, savagely triumphant. 'I'll do a proper job this time and you're going to die.'

'*Oh, God, Mattie, she means it.*' Emilie's voice was full of panic.

Time seemed to slow down. Books sometimes talk about someone being frozen to the spot, unable to move. I'd never experienced the sensation before, but it was very real. My brain was firing on adrenalin, telling me to run or duck behind the island, but my body absolutely would not obey me.

I managed to say with artificial calm, 'Davina, if this is about you getting the house, it won't do any good. The terms of Emilie's will mean if anything happens to me, the whole estate goes to charity.' A big black lie of course, but an inspired effort under the surreal circumstances.

I'd have to describe Davina as taking this badly, with me watching her expressions change in a weird kind of slow motion. Mary dashed downstairs to defend me and appeared in the kitchen barking and growling, trying to nip my assailant's ankles. The little dog got kicked viciously in the ribs for her bravery and whined as she made her way to crouch at my feet.

Davina didn't care what I told her. 'Fuck you,' she said, her voice rising to a shrill crescendo. 'If you think not getting the house will make a difference, you snooty bitch, forget it. After all the time and money I've invested in trying to get rid of you, did you seriously think I would let it go to waste?'

'I don't understand,' I said, in genuine bafflement, before light dawned. 'The letters, that package… we blamed Nigel, but it was you. Davina, why?'

'Thought you were supposed to be clever?' she sneered, waving the gun around in a scarily unstable fashion. 'I even sent my baby brother to get you out of this house, but the fool legged it when he found out what a nutter you are.'

Understanding what she meant came slowly, but when it did it was like being hit by a car all over again. 'Simon… is your brother?' I managed, with a sick recognition that it had to be the truth, the final piece of the jigsaw which at last made sense of everything.

'*I bloody knew his aura wasn't right. Mattie, take care… This woman's lost all control and her aura is wild; she's off her head.*'

Davina gave me a glittering smile; it wasn't a pretty sight.

'I wasted all that money setting him up here, paid for the hotel and the car, and he fucking blew it. Had you eating out of his hand, though, didn't he?'

There was no answer to that.

Over her shoulder, I saw Tom and George quietly appear behind her in the kitchen doorway, but I daren't even look at them properly for fear Davina would realise they were there.

'And it was all for fucking nothing, so I'm going to kill you now and make a proper job of it.' She pointed the gun at my chest, and the hate in her expression convinced me she meant every word. Mary growled again and my legs wobbled. All my frozen brain could think about was what the impact of a bullet would feel like.

'Davina, that wouldn't be a wise course of action,' said Tom in a calm voice, slowly advancing a couple of steps towards her. 'You'd go to prison for a very long time.'

Davina whirled her head to face him, still keeping the gun pointed at me. George had disappeared.

'I don't care,' Davina sneered. 'If I can't have the house, I will at least have the satisfaction of blowing her fucking head off.'

Tom moved so fast that I barely understood what happened next until it was all explained to me later. He stepped up to her side, put one hand on the barrel of the gun and *pushed* it away. I heard it go off, and the next minute Davina was on the floor, with one arm twisted behind her, and Tom's knee in the small of her back.

'It's OK, Mattie,' said Tom, reaching up to place the gun on the worktop, holding it by the barrel. 'Put this somewhere safe, out of reach, but don't touch the handle. Prints.'

I reached for the rolling pin to push the horrible thing to the other side of the island, breathless at the speed of events.

Davina squirmed on the floor. 'You're hurting me!' she protested.

'Stop wriggling then,' Tom told her. 'Mattie, it's all right, you were never in any danger. Davina obviously believes otherwise, but it's just a starting pistol.'

'Then why is there a bullet hole in the kitchen wall?' asked George, reappearing in the doorway with two police officers behind her.

As he allowed the police to take over, Tom got to his feet and stared first at George and then at me, horror dawning on his face. 'Bloody hell, don't tell me it's been modified? I'm supposed to be a professional – should have guessed – Mattie, are you OK?'

I nodded mutely, having picked Mary up with one arm, but still clutching the island for support, unable to believe what had just happened. My kitchen filled up with people as more police came in, firearms officers by their body armour, not to mention guns.

Nigel appeared behind them. 'Oh, my poor girl…' he said brokenly, as Davina was handcuffed, hauled to her feet and marched away. He followed the grim procession, telling his wife urgently, 'My darling, whatever you do, don't say anything; just keep quiet and I'll make it all right, I promise.'

Tom had just settled Mary and me on the big kitchen sofa because shock had turned my legs to jelly and I couldn't stand up any longer. Mary whined when her side was touched, meaning I was more worried about her than myself. Lucas came in through the garden door, alerted by the arrival of police cars in the street, so we briefly filled him in on Davina's attempt to shoot me. His face was a picture.

An hour went by as endless questions from the police followed, and we all gave statements, including George. They extracted a promise that we'd go to the police station the following day to sign them and add anything else we might remember. When my house became a crime scene, we decamped next door where – fortified by strong coffee and takeaway fish and chips – we pieced everything together. To my relief, Mary seemed to be OK, playing with Mutt as if nothing had happened, but I'd still get the vet to check her out.

'The only reason for my coming back was because I'd forgotten to ask you for another of those books,' said George. 'Thank God I did, because the front door was standing wide open, and Davina was screaming about killing you. When I saw the gun she was waving about, I went back outside and called the police. Tom appeared as I was waiting for them, and once I told him what was happening, he said there was no time because they might take too long to arrive. And, well, you know the rest.'

Tom looked pale and shaken, as if events were catching up with him. 'I was only coming to see if you could spare some dog biscuits until our shopping arrives tomorrow.'

'But what did you *do*?' I turned to the hero of the hour. 'One minute Davina was threatening to blow my head off, and the next she was on the floor.'

Tom's face flushed above the red beard. 'It was nothing, really, a simple disarm technique taught in basic training. Anyway, I didn't think you were in real danger because the gun wasn't real. I recognised it immediately as a starting pistol.'

'One with an illegal modification, according to the police,' said Lucas. 'Mattie's got a hole in her wall to prove it.'

'Better than one in her head.' George was as traumatised as the rest of us. 'I've had training in patient restraint techniques but wouldn't have dared to use them on someone who was armed. Tom was so brave; he simply took the gun out of Davina's hand.'

My saviour ran a hand through his thick brown hair and tried to make light of what he'd done. 'It's easy if you know how, and once you've got hold of the barrel, the situation is pretty much under control. I'm just so incredibly relieved Mattie is safe, and with Davina under arrest we can be sure of that because now we finally know who was behind it all.'

'Poor woman,' I said, somehow filled with sadness. 'It's not her fault. I think she's mentally ill.'

'It's generous of you to see it that way, but you could have been killed.' Lucas hugged my shoulders very tight as he sat on the sofa next to me.

'Anyway, it's just rude to attack somebody in their own kitchen when they're not expecting it,' observed George drily, which, for some reason, set us all off laughing and into mild hysteria. Funny how you need to do that after the high adrenaline of real danger. Tom says it's a normal stress reaction.

TWENTY-ONE

OK, I'd wanted my life to be different and more exciting, but it was still a helluva way to begin a new year. The past twelve months had been something of a rollercoaster, with the crowning glories of getting mown down by a car, and a crazy person trying to shoot me. Poor Davina. I did at least understand enough about mental illness to worry if she'd be OK. It would be a long road back from the dark places her mind had gone.

The physiotherapist was a *tyrant*, but she made me stick at the exercises and my leg gradually improved and I was blithely imagining being able to put everything behind me. That was wishful thinking on my part, as it became obvious that I'd been so focused on my physical recovery, I hadn't even begun to process all the changes in my life.

Setting aside the traumatic recent events, I still didn't know how to navigate my way from being one kind of person – supposedly depressed and unstable – to becoming the one I should always have been without this misinformation. Turns out change of that kind isn't something that can just happen overnight but an ongoing process of adjustment. As January became February, I found myself without road maps, signposts or anyone whose experience might help me. I was a thirty-two-year-old woman who had never fully known or understood myself, or my family history. The only solid reference point was the new knowledge that I was *not* ill. It was a place to begin, to build on, but only a step on the journey, rather than an arrival. The obvious conclusion was that some kind of counselling might help. I had, by any standards, been through a lot.

Tom was the only person I knew who might be able to offer some insights – he had personal experience of extreme trauma and PTSD, and his recent psychotherapy training was a bonus. So, after one of our regular walks with Mary, I suggested we go for coffee. Since the Simon episode, I'd never visited my favourite place, but memories of those times weren't going to keep me away from the best Americano in town anymore.

We got settled in a pair of leather armchairs, with Mary tucked under the table, while I explained where my mind was going and what I needed help with. Tom's broad face had a deep, thoughtful expression, making me worry that I'd crossed some kind of boundary in asking his advice.

'Look,' he said, 'it's a brave decision to confront your problems head-on, but I've barely begun my training and anyway, it wouldn't be proper for me to work with you. What's needed is someone who hasn't been part of the events and brings an outsider's clarity and perspective.'

'And who won't go into a spin at the mention of ghosts and psychic abilities.'

'That too,' he acknowledged. 'I could talk to some people at the university and ask for recommendations. But in the meantime, what I can do is make some suggestions for you to be thinking about, ahead of finding a therapist.'

'Go for it,' I said.

He leaned forward, almost knocking his coffee over. 'OK, so the first is a classic, but it works. Make a list – the traditional way with pen and paper, or on your phone, it doesn't matter. What you'd be trying to do is come up with an honest assessment of where you are now; what is true and what isn't.'

'Such as I'm no more mentally vulnerable than the next person, and I've proved myself to be much stronger than I ever imagined?'

'Exactly. You have to work on getting rid of the stuff which isn't true and focusing on what is. You've been taught over decades to believe "I can't do that" or "I shouldn't do this", and it's time to challenge the truth of the things people have said or that you tell yourself. Only when you've completed that process can you be free to look and plan ahead.'

'Is that what you did? After…'

'Yes, something very similar,' he said, with a faraway look which said he was momentarily back in the desert with his unit. 'For me, it involved slowly accepting the reality of the damage to my leg being permanent, and also that I had to stop blaming myself because I couldn't have saved the people who died in the explosion. Once I'd got my head around those basic facts, it was a start and a way to move forward.'

I nodded. 'So that's step one? What happens next?'

'Then you can begin to set goals for yourself, as short- or long-term as you want, whatever works for you.'

'Like building up my maths coaching?'

'Exactly,' he said, 'or starting a fitness programme to build up your muscles again.'

'Working on both my mental and physical health?'

He grinned. 'Definitely.'

'Thanks, Tom. You and Lucas have been so kind to me, not to mention saving my life. You're such a good friend.' I squeezed his large hand and he reacted to the touch by pulling away. Maybe I was crossing some kind of professional boundary? I didn't know how to read his signals, but something wasn't right.

'Those clouds outside look threatening. Maybe we should get back?' he said, draining his coffee and standing up.

The atmosphere had changed; was he uncomfortable with being thanked? He wasn't the kind of man who'd accept hero status easily, but that's what he'd been.

'Maybe I'll stay in town for a while,' I said, trying not to let the confusion I was feeling show. 'All my tracksuit pants had to have the side seams slashed to accommodate the cast, and now I don't have a thing to wear. All the stuff Mamma bought me was summer-weight.'

He smiled, but it didn't quite reach his eyes. 'Shall I take Mary home then? Her tolerance for clothes shopping is sure to be low.'

'Mine too; I'm going to take the grab-it-and-go approach,' I said.

*

Once the physio had signed me off, I embarked on a graded fitness regime at the gym, but it took longer for Tom to eventually find me a CBT therapist. Frances Collins, in St Annes, came with excellent recommendations, didn't freak out at the mention of psychic abilities, and the best part was I could get there on the bus. I popped in on Evelina a few times while I was there, to catch up with the old lady. The money realised from the sale of the long-forgotten shares had lifted so many of her anxieties and she beamed when I said she looked ten years younger, which was true.

'The dark cloud has gone from your aura,' she told me. 'I'm sorry to hear about Simon letting you down like that, what a rat. But there is someone, I can see that.'

'Well, no,' I said. 'I'm swearing off romance until I've got my head back on straight.'

Evelina shook her head. 'Have it your way, but the colours don't lie.'

After a few bus trips to see my therapist, I resolved again to add learning to drive to my list of goals. I'd also formed the beginnings of a social circle with some parents of successful pupils, who were grateful for the help I'd been able to give. The drinks and dinner party circuit wasn't an entirely comfortable place for me, but I made myself go out and meet new people. It was all part of a determined effort to become someone who relished new experiences, in contrast to my previous policy of always staying home or choosing the safety of the known and familiar.

The weeks marched past, and daffodils were nodding in the sea breeze off Lytham Green when, one day, Emilie came to me. She hadn't been around as much since Christmas, or maybe I'd been too busy and preoccupied to notice.

'*Mattie,*' she said. '*I've come to tell you it's almost time for me to go. I'm not meant to be here anymore.*'

After Hal had been able to leave George, I'd wondered if this day might come but never allowed myself to fully acknowledge it. He'd gone once he knew George would be able to heal, so it shouldn't have been a surprise when Emilie said, '*I stayed because I was worried that your illness would make life hard for you, which is why I left you the money. I wanted to make things easier, give you choices.*'

'Please,' I said, overwhelmed with sadness and the beginnings of panic. 'Don't go yet, I still need you.'

'*No, you don't, my darling. You're going to be fine. Your aura is so different from when you arrived here. Your Mamma is back in your life, Lucas is always there for you as a father figure, and you're growing stronger every day; my job is done. Besides…*'

'Besides what?' I demanded.

There was a husky chuckle. '*Now you've met the love of your*

263

life, I think you'll be OK. The two of you will be equal partners, the way Lucas and I were best friends as much as lovers.'

'Bloody hell, where has this come from?' I protested. 'I've chatted to a few single people at dinner parties, and some of the teachers at the local grammar school, but nobody has so much as asked me out. You're as bad as Evelina. After Simon, I'm absolutely not looking for love so what on earth are you telling me?'

'You'll figure it out, and I'll stick around until you do.'

'You can't drop that kind of bombshell and then leave me dangling…' I protested, but she was already gone, leaving me baffled and desperate to know more. I'd just have to wait for a random handsome prince to show up and sweep me off my feet.

*

Although I lived most of the time in the kitchen area of the house, with the dining table the centre of most activities, I'd grown to love Emilie's front parlour. My evenings were spent in there, reading or listening to music, and I wanted to personalise it a little. Tom volunteered to help me sort out which of her books I wanted to keep, and we boxed up the rest. The result was some empty shelf space for me to colonise with the local history books I'd begun to acquire. If I joined the group which met regularly in the library, George could put all this positive activity in her report.

We also sent to the charity shop some of the weirder items Emilie had collected: a stuffed monkey with a baleful gleam in his eye and a faded parcel tag around his neck which said "not for sale". Taxidermy is just not my thing, it grosses me out, and I wasn't fond of his grumpy expression, so he went into a box, alongside a small teddy bear which produced realistic farting noises. Tom and I argued over the teddy and one or two of the signs he wanted me to keep, but I was adamant.

'While I do love all this, there has to be space for something of me in here,' I told him. 'Otherwise, it's no more than a museum of eclectic items with no connection to me. Emilie doesn't mind because I asked her, and she said, "*Do what you like; it's your house now.*"'

'But are you really sure you don't want to keep this?' enquired Tom innocently, holding up a small dark painting of a cross-looking bloke with an improbably green parrot perched on his heavy oak chair.

'Tragic as it may seem, no,' I said, taking it out of his hand for the final box. 'This has been a good morning's work so how about I buy you lunch at the Italian? Their gnocchi is to die for, and my first pupil isn't coming until 4.00pm.'

'I'd love to,' he said with a smile, picking up the box of books as if it weighed nothing.

'Shall we ask Lucas to join us?'

His face changed. 'If you like. Whatever.'

In the end, just the two of us went, Lucas having plans to be busy in the garden. Tom and I ate gnocchi with pancetta and saffron cream sauce, and because he asked, I told him about the therapy and how much it was helping.

'It sounds such a cliché, but I'm beginning to discover myself as a whole new person, a real one.'

'Me and Lucas quite liked the old one too,' he said, grinning around a glass of red wine.

'Frances says the goal of therapy is integration, allowing the old and the new me to become one whole person, without… what's the expression?'

'Cognitive dissonance?' suggested Tom.

'Exactly. The end goal being that I'm no longer conflicted between the past and the present, which allows me to move on into the future. Sorry, you must know all this stuff.'

'Two terms of study don't make me an expert in anything,'

said Tom ruefully, 'but I recognise what you're saying from my personal journey. It's not easy, though, is it?'

'No, it bloody isn't,' I said, grateful he understood so much. 'Some sessions are tough, but I can see it's worth the effort to confront everything and deal with it.'

'You know, Mattie, the things that have happened to you in the time since the move here might have broken someone else, but, to your enormous credit, they didn't. Lucas is so proud of the way you've come through it all,' Tom told me.

'He's a darling. I love him like a father. And now I have a brother too,' I said happily.

Tom went still, his face unreadable. 'Are you talking about me?'

'Of course, you don't mind being my honorary big brother, do you? I always wanted one rather than a sister.'

He signalled for the bill. 'Look at the time,' he said. 'We'd better get home before your new pupil comes.'

We argued over who would pay for lunch, and I made him agree that it should be me, as a fair exchange for his morning's labour on the bookcases. Walking home, the atmosphere crackled with a tension I couldn't identify. Had I embarrassed him again, insisting on paying for lunch? Some men found that kind of thing emasculating, but I'd figured he was more grown-up than that. Whatever, his mood had changed abruptly and I daren't ask questions for fear of making things worse.

Turning the corner into Lodge Road, an ambulance stood outside Lucas's open front door. Tom proceeded to demonstrate an unexpected turn of speed given his mangled knee, with me following as close behind as possible, while a terrifyingly grey-faced and sweating Lucas was stretchered out of the house and loaded into the ambulance.

'Heart...' he managed to say.

'This is an emergency, and we have to take him right now,' the paramedic said. 'Only one of you can come.'

'Go with Lucas,' I told Tom immediately. 'He needs you. I'll sort things out here.'

Tom needed no further persuasion to climb into the back before the ambulance blue-lighted away, leaving me standing blindly on the pavement, terrified of losing Lucas, who'd become so important to me. Taking refuge in practicalities, I made sure his house was locked and scooped up an anxious Mutt before heading back to mine in agonies of fear.

On my doorstep stood Art Gilchrist, my new pupil, aged ten. For a moment I thought about sending him away because my worries over Lucas were all-consuming. Then I saw his anxious little face with its scattering of freckles and remembered that he'd been sent to me because he was so stratospherically gifted his primary-level teachers couldn't keep up with him. Having had the same experience myself, I knew all too well that it wasn't an easy place to be.

'Hello, Art, are you OK with dogs? Come on in,' I said, 'and tell me all about the special syllabus you've been working on.'

The session provided a welcome distraction in the end, while Mutt and Mary entertained each other outside. When Art had gone home with a more optimistic smile on his face, I paced about the kitchen, willing my phone to ring with news. It was too soon for there to be any, but that didn't stop me desperately hoping the supposed heart attack might have been a false alarm. Sometimes it was just indigestion, I knew that, but Lucas's grey, sweating face and blue lips had made me deeply afraid.

My phone still had its Christmas ringtone that I'd never got around to changing, and when it chimed, the display told me it was Mamma. I explained what was happening but all she could say was, 'Oh, God. I hope he makes it; poor dear Lucas, that's awful!'

I already knew that and really wanted her to tell me that he'd be fine. Once she'd scared me silly with stories of people who had dropped dead without warning, I managed to end the call on the excuse that Tom might be trying to ring from the hospital. Slumped on the kitchen sofa, Mary and Mutt both picked up on my anxious state of mind and insisted on staying close; another helpful diversion from terrifying images of Lucas dying in Tom's arms.

The cheese-and-tomato sandwich put together as my evening meal sat uneaten on the kitchen island. My churning stomach didn't feel like a safe place to put food. Then Emilie's voice said, '*Don't worry, my darling, Lucas will be fine.*'

'How can you possibly know what's happening, when you aren't even able to leave the house?' I was irritable, perversely rejecting the easy platitudes and reassurances I'd wanted from Mamma.

'*You're right, I don't have a clue what's going on at the hospital, but I do know it's not his time,*' said Emilie. '*Lucas and I will be together again one day, but not for a while yet. He'll get to grow old even though I didn't.*'

'Emilie, are you sure?' I asked. 'You wouldn't bullshit me?'

'*Of course not, darling. You know that. He will recover.*'

So the dogs and I watched a baffling thriller pretty much filmed in the dark, followed by a documentary about Egypt, all without really seeing either. Emilie had reassured me to some degree, but my mind kept going back to Lucas, so when Tom finally rang at 10.00pm, I leapt on the phone, almost flattening Mary in the process.

'Mattie, it's all right, he's going to be OK. It was a heart attack but a mild one, a warning of sorts. He's going up to coronary care once they're sure that he's stable, then they'll probably do an angioplasty, if the blood clot hasn't cleared…'

'Thank God,' I said, having sent up powerful prayers to a

deity I wasn't sure existed but hoped might be available in my hour of need.

'They say he's been lucky,' Tom told me. 'He called the ambulance himself and was able to let them in, so he received rapid treatment in the form of clot-busting drugs, which they said makes all the difference. There should be no cardiac damage, and they're telling him to treat it as a message to mend his ways. The doctor also congratulated him on having stopped smoking.'

'Poor Lucas, I know he likes a crafty ciggie now and again. How did he take that?'

'With remarkable calm. Said he knew it was time to stop, and he was down to maybe five a day anyway. I plan to become the pain-in-the-arse smoking police once he gets home.'

'I've been sick with worry. Oh, Tom, what if we'd lost him?'

'Tell me about it. I went to hell and back in that first hour, waiting in the relatives' room while they got him stabilised. He was such a bad colour on the journey, and even with oxygen his breathing…'

'It must have made a big difference to have you there with him. But what if he'd lost consciousness without calling the ambulance, or we hadn't come home when we did?'

'Don't, it doesn't bear thinking about. I should get back now, but I'll be home once he's settled on the ward.'

Wrapping my untouched sandwich in cling film, I took it next door and left it visible in Lucas's kitchen. If Tom wasn't hungry when he got home, it wouldn't matter if it went uneaten, but I wanted, needed, to do something, anything that might help. I was still awake around midnight, snuggled in bed with both dogs, when a quick text from Tom came in to say all was looking good, and he would soon be on his way home.

He appeared at my door the next day around noon, looking worn and tired but optimistic.

'I rang the ward first thing to see how he was,' I told him. 'But all they would say was that he's comfortable.'

'I'm registered as next of kin so spoke to them too, when I woke up. Got to bed pretty late and then lay awake too hyper to sleep,' said Tom. 'Apparently, he's sleeping much of the time, which is common after a cardiac incident. Look, I'm sorry to ask, but there's a lecture by a visiting professor this afternoon, and he's so brilliant I can't miss it, so are you available to visit Lucas? They say only one person at a time and to keep it brief, ten minutes or so.'

'Consider it done,' I told him. 'I'll book a taxi and arrange for it to wait for me.'

*

The coronary care unit was hard to find in the maze of hospital corridors, but Lucas was awake, if sleepy, and a much better colour than when he'd been loaded into the ambulance. I sat by the bed as the monitor bleeped with comforting steadiness.

'I love you so much, Lucas, please get well.' My eyes brimmed with tears.

He moved the oxygen mask away from his face, which alarmed me, but he was insistent, wanting to say something.

'Have to tell you…' he said.

'Whatever it is will keep, you should rest now.'

'No, need to say this, just in case. Tom. Be careful with him.'

'I don't understand. Tom's fine, he's gone to a lecture in Preston.'

'No, listen, please. Not right to encourage his hopes if you don't have feelings for him. Wouldn't want him to get hurt.' Lucas seemed exhausted after this speech, and closed his eyes, while I was left wondering what he meant.

'Are you saying Tom is in love with me?'

Lucas nodded. 'Bonkers crazy about you; can see it,' he managed. 'Be gentle with him.'

He appeared to have gone to sleep again, so I put his oxygen mask back in place and tiptoed away before a nurse could get cross with me for upsetting the patient. During the taxi ride home, I sat silent in the back seat, my brain trying to process what Lucas had said.

Tom had never shown the slightest sign of being attracted to me, even though we were mates, to use his own expression. Emilie had insisted that I'd met the love of my life, but she couldn't have meant Tom; my feelings for him weren't like that. I loved him, of course I did, but only as a brother or friend.

When I said all this to Emilie back at home, she snorted. *'For a clever girl, you can be remarkably dense at times.'* She'd told me that before, and it didn't get any easier to hear.

'But he hasn't said anything,' I protested. 'Never given any indication…'

'He wouldn't, would he? Tom probably thinks you're still upset over Simon.'

It was my turn to laugh. 'As if. My only regret is being enough of an idiot to fall for his lies.'

'Well, maybe Tom's trying to give you time to recover, being all honourable about it? His aura goes some interesting colours when he's around you, and nobody else has that effect on him.'

Honourable was a good word for the steady, utterly reliable Tom. It would be typical of him to hold back and assume I wasn't yet ready for a relationship.

'I've been… blind.' The words came out slowly as everything fell into place.

'You certainly have,' said Emilie. *'When I said you'd met the love of your life, who the hell did you think I meant? And he's not the only one whose aura reveals his feelings; yours looks different*

when you're with him. All warm, fuzzy and contented, kind of safe.'

I didn't get much sleep that night, what with there being a lot to think about. The next day, on the bus to St Annes for my counselling session, I felt jaded and stale, not to mention confused.

When I told her my story, Frances was pragmatic.

'Look, being told someone has feelings for you doesn't place you under any obligation to return them. But here's the question: if you genuinely don't feel the same and only see him as a brother, then why has this information thrown you into such turmoil?'

'Because it isn't the way it was with Simon,' I protested. 'Then, the physical attraction was so strong it was overwhelming. Just being together made me see fireworks and want to drag him into bed on the spot.'

'But the kind of heady excitement you're describing is no more than infatuation, which rarely lasts because it can't. Such an experience can be part of the early rush of a new relationship, but far more often, love begins with being friends and grows from there. At least, the lasting kind does.'

'But friends is all we are.'

'Really? So you're prepared to explain that to Tom, as Lucas asked, and put an end to his hopes that it can ever be more?'

Her words hit me with all the force of a punch.

'No...' I said slowly. 'I can't imagine life without him.' The cogs in my brain were doing that moving into place thing again. The maths was very simple.

Frances asked some more searching questions and helped me understand what should have been obvious. All the way home, on the top deck of the bus, I kept thinking how Emilie's description of me as "remarkably dense" was embarrassingly accurate. But this kind of revelation called for careful thought, not to mention preparation.

The next evening, Tom knocked on the door on his way home from visiting the hospital and reported that Lucas was continuing to improve but feeling exhausted. Par for the course, the cardiac staff had said.

I was wearing my best blue dress and had made some chocolate brownies, since the occasion called for a big effort. I'd even included Tom's favourite pecan nuts as an added bonus. He munched them with gratifying appreciation, while Mutt and Mary fixed their eyes on him, begrudging every mouthful.

'These are just fabulous and I was so hungry; there's hardly been time to eat,' he said.

I shooed the dogs out into the garden and sat beside him on the pink sofa, taking the brownie plate out of his hands. 'Speaking of not realising, I need to ask you something.'

'Fire away,' he said, 'but don't expect to get much sense out of me, because I'm way too tired for joined-up thinking.'

'Not necessarily required,' I told him. 'But please, Tom, would you just… kiss me?'

Slowly, dawning hope spread across his sweet face, and the way his eyes lit up told me everything I needed to know.

'Mattie, are you sure?'

'Shut up, stop thinking, and go for it.'

And he did, with entirely satisfactory results. I don't know what our auras were doing, as Emilie was the soul of tact and absented herself, but they must have been spectacular. Fireworks and everything.

TWENTY-TWO

Lucas was released from hospital a few days later and, together, we went to collect him, holding hands and wearing conspiratorial grins. It must have been obvious to the meanest intelligence that we were dizzy with love. From his perch on the bed, Lucas looked first at Tom then me, with joy and incredulity on his face.

'I've been hoping this would happen for such a long time,' he told us. 'I was beginning to think you'd never get it together. Oh goodness, Emilie would have been so pleased.'

'She is,' I said. 'Quite vocal about it, in fact.' I showed him the antique silver sapphire ring we'd chosen from a shop in town.

'You're engaged too? Well, you two don't let the grass grow, do you?' He was so thrilled and hugged us both close.

'Nothing to wait for,' said Tom. 'I'm going to marry this wonderful girl sharpish before she can change her mind.'

'It's not as if we've only just met,' I added, squeezing Tom's hand.

Lucas nodded. 'Except that you took your time figuring it out.'

'Got there in the end,' said Tom, with the joyous smile of a man who'd just won the lottery. 'Slow and steady wins the race, and anyway, neither of us can actually run so we're both tortoises. I'm so happy I might be blathering. Tell me to shut up.'

I kissed him instead.

Back at Lucas's, where Tom had left lunch ready, Nigel was on his doorstep, talking to a man in a business suit. He raised a hand in the briefest acknowledgement of our arrival before the two of them disappeared inside.

When we'd finished our meal, and Lucas had been persuaded to follow hospital instructions and have an afternoon nap, taking Mutt and Mary with him. Tom went to answer a knock on the door and came back with Nigel, who looked acutely uncomfortable, squirming even.

'I may be the last person you want to see…' he began, 'but I had to thank you for not pressing charges against Davina. You'll never know how much I, well, we, appreciate it.' Nigel had bags under his eyes and written on his drawn face was evidence of a painful journey.

'None of what happened was your fault,' I said, standing up to face him. 'And how would putting poor Davina in jail do any good when she's mentally ill. She needs help, not punishment. Anyway, how is she getting on?'

'She's in Manchester, a private hospital, and I'm renting a studio flat to be near her. Please try to understand; Davina isn't a monster, I hope you can believe that. She became so obsessed with getting her hands on your house, it got to the point of her not seeing things clearly. They say she'll recover with the right treatment, time and patience. I do love her, you know; nothing can ever change how I feel.'

'That's always been obvious. She's lucky to have you,' I said.

The look he gave me was pathetically grateful. 'When she's discharged from hospital, I'm planning to get her away from the house, both houses. We can begin again somewhere else, preferably in a location a long way from her family. Pressure from them played a major part in sending her off the rails. So, what I came to tell you is, I'm selling up here. That was the estate agent you just saw; he'll see to everything.'

'A wise decision. Where will you go?' asked Tom.

'Davina has always loved the sun, so I'm thinking maybe somewhere warm, an expat community where lots of people speak English. Lots of property in Europe available right now since Brexit, and you're still welcome if you plan to stay. When she's better, I can run my business online from pretty much anywhere, as long as she's happy.'

'And her brother?' I hoped that mentioning Simon didn't hurt Tom, but needed to draw a line under the whole episode.

'Gone to ground; disappeared off the face of the earth. Just as well, he's rotten to the core, that one,' said Nigel. 'I hope he doesn't turn up again until we're gone.'

'Thank you for coming. I hope everything works out for you and Davina,' I told him.

'It's generous of you, Mattea. We've both got a lot to thank you for. Um, is the leg all right?'

'Healing well; getting better with exercise every day.'

Nigel managed a smile but weariness was evident in every line of his body. 'Well, that's what I came to say. The agent believes the house should sell fast, and perhaps whoever buys it will be better neighbours than we were.'

Then he was gone, and as we watched his car disappear up the street, Tom hugged me, saying, 'Poor bugger. He may be a dodgy businessman, but he's not all bad, and absolutely adores his wife.'

'I sincerely hope you'll do the same,' I told him.

He grinned, tightening his embrace. 'Allow me to demonstrate…'

*

It was a summer of weddings: Mamma and Rachael, Polly and Harriet; but ours was the first. We married "in haste" without a care in the world, on the earliest available date Lytham Hall was available. I wanted it to be small, simple and meaningful; not being a big meringue or huge wedding reception kind of girl.

I'd hoped George might be a bridesmaid, but she said no because we still had a professional relationship, even if we were doing our absolute best to bring it to a conclusion.

'Later, I can be godmother, if you want?' she said with a grin.

White is a bit stark against my skin, so Lucas took me to a big department store in Manchester, where he knew Emilie used to shop. I wanted something classy and the simple column dress in heavy cream satin with a tiny train was perfect. The wonderful local florist made a wreath of flowers to crown my curly hair, and I carried a matching posy. Wearing Emilie's pearl necklace, the woman I saw in the mirror was radiant, lit up with a special glow I'd never experienced before.

Mary was bridesmaid instead, with a bow around her neck, and spent the day being spoilt rotten by our select company of guests, before snoozing with Mutt, who acted as best man. My mamma was fabulous in pale blue topped by an extravagant hat, the proudest mother of the bride you've ever seen, and Tom looked delicious in a dark suit. What is it about men in formal dress or uniform?

Walking down the aisle on Lucas's arm was a deliriously happy moment, and Tom told me I was beautiful at satisfyingly regular intervals throughout the rest of the day.

After a lot of late-night discussions, and mainly to please Lucas, we both took the surname Fallon. Lombardi had never been my true name anyhow, so I was more than comfortable with the change, and Mamma approved. Tom said his late father wouldn't have minded one bit, and since his mother had remarried twice since, she could hardly complain. Anyway, she was in Mexico and couldn't attend.

The honeymoon had to be delayed until Tom's university course ended for the summer, so, after a wonderful wedding day, we went home in the small hours of the morning to Emilie's house – no, *our* house.

Tom was letting Mary out for a final pee in the garden, and I was upstairs reluctantly taking off my beautiful dress when I heard my mother for the very last time.

'*I'm so glad I got to see you as a bride. Be happy, my darling. I won't stay because you don't need me now.*'

'Thank you,' I told her. 'For everything you gave me: my life, my happy childhood with Mamma, this house. I'll never forget you.'

'*Ciao, bella,*' she said softly, and then was gone.

*

Sometimes I seem to hear her husky chuckle as our three-year-old twins roar around the house at top speed, but it's probably wishful thinking. The girls are a constant delight, even if we don't get much sleep, and Lucas is the proudest "grandpa" there ever was. He adores them, is famously a supplier of illicit treats, takes them out on exciting adventures looking for bears or fairies in the woods, and has a very special place in their lives. They are undoubtedly everything he lives for, and because of our family, his heart is physically and emotionally whole again.

Life is good, but now and again, in the rare quiet moments, I do miss my "sitting tenant".

THANK YOU

To the people who were my first readers and kind enough to provide feedback – my husband Jeff, always my best friend, and Marian Hartley.

To Meg Davies, proof-reader and friend extraordinaire.

To Milla Reed, fellow author and writing buddy who made time to give me an honest opinion.

To Jericho Writers whose courses, editors and mentors guided me all the way from my first stumbling beginnings to publishable work.

To the Book Sisters just for being there.

To all the friends and family who had my back throughout the long gestation process which is a novel and allowed me to bore them endlessly with talk about books and publishing. Special mention has to go to Beverley and Mike on this front for service beyond the call of duty.

ABOUT THE AUTHOR

When a rare form of arthritis ended her career and left her using a wheelchair, Rosie Radcliffe set out to fulfil her lifelong dream of becoming a writer. Her novels are set on the Lancashire coast, where she lives in a rural village with her long-suffering husband. A retired priest, Rosie writes about life's challenges with a light touch, weaving in her love of coffee shops, cake, food, and people-watching – just as in her own life. Her debut novel, *Frankie & Dot*, was published in 2024.

If you liked *Sitting Tenant* look out for *Frankie & Dot*, available now in paperback and ebook.

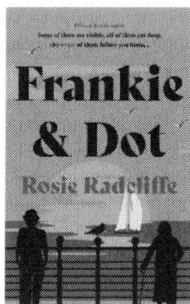